Baby Daddy Mystery

Shady Hoosier Detective Agency Series
Book 2

Daisy Pettles

First Print and ebook Editions: December 2018

Hot Pants Press, LLC
Underhill, VT 05489

ISBN: 978-0-9815678-4-6 (Print)
E-ISBN: 978-0-9815678-5-3 (Ebook)

Website: https://www.DaisyPettles.com

Email: daisy@daisypettles.com

Facebook: https://www.facebook.com/daisy.pettles.author

Twitter: @DaisyPettles

CHAPTER ONE

The windows of the detective agency rattled like God's wind chimes as Shap Reynolds thundered by on his combine of death. Shap had been driving up and down Main Street all morning, honking at the agency and screaming death threats at Harry Shades, my boss. Shap's normally pasty-white face was watermelon red, and his blue eyes, normally as quiet as a summer sky, were shaking in his head. He had more spittle and sweat running down his face than a boxer dog gone mad.

I'd been trying all morning to ignore Shap. I had my head down, my whole body hunched over my computer keyboard. I wasn't getting a lick of work done because of the road racket and Shap's shouting. Clearly, the old coot felt he'd been wronged, and he wasn't going back to farming until somebody paid him some mind.

Veenie, though, was sitting next to me, sympathizing with the brokenhearted fart. She peered up over her thick glasses. "Harry been diddling Shap's wife, Dottie, again?"

"That'd be my guess."

"Why you reckon he keeps hitting on that? You ask me, she looks like the type of gal he'd be best renting by the hour."

"She was Miss Starlite Bowling," I reminded Veenie.

"Back in the seventies."

"The heart wants what the heart wants."

Veenie thumped the return on her keyboard. "Looks to me like a heap of other organs might have gotten involved."

Lavinia Goens—Veenie—is my best pal. She's seventy-one years old with a chipmunk face and a white wisp of Kewpie doll hair. Her blue eyes twinkle like stars behind her Coke bottle glasses. People think she's a little doll—until she opens her pie hole. Most days she itches for excitement with so much energy she practically bounces around the office.

My name is Ruby Jane Waskom—RJ to most—and at the age of sixty-seven, I itch for a weekly paycheck. Veenie and I had been best pals since we worked side by side on the auto button line at the Bold Mold Plastics Factory. This was way back, before the EPA decided that pouring plastic waste into the White River was a doo-doo of an idea.

The Harry Shades Detective Agency, where we work now, had received a passel of threatening phone calls from Shap earlier that morning. In his defense, Shap had good reason to bark at us. That reason was not me. It was not Veenie. It was our boss, Harry Shades, private eye and champion man skank. It was spring in Knobby Waters, Indiana, and Harry, like most of God's creatures, had been busy rattling the sheets.

The last time Shap caught Harry dicky dunkin' his wife, he'd sprayed our office with a 20-gauge. Veenie wanted to leave the scatter holes visible. This being a detective agency and all, she thought it added "atmosphere." I thought it'd scare the poop out of our clients, most of whom were not all that eager to be on the receiving end of a buckshot shower.

Harry's affair with Dottie Reynolds was seasonal—a perennial, I reckon you'd call it. Shap tried to mow Harry down with his combine last spring. You'd think Harry would have learned his lesson, but oh no, like Dewey, Ma Horton's prize rooster, he was back on the strut. Not wanting to be reaped and threshed by Shap, Harry, who lived upstairs above the office, shimmied out the alley window early this morning. He tore out of town. If history repeated itself, he'd be gone about a week, two tops. Harry liked Dottie, and he loved sex, but he wasn't about to die for either of them.

"Harry here?" Veenie asked. She'd come in late—stopped to watch the Widow Guthrie shooting noisy, lust-puffed woodpeckers off the lip of her grain elevator—and had missed the circus of phone calls.

"Skedaddled. Said the place was ours."

"On a bender?" Veenie loved saying "bender." She loved to pretend that we lived on the set of *Dragnet* instead of tucked between cornfields in the soggy bottomlands of Indiana.

"On the lamb," I said. "Boy, I wish just once Harry would hang around and take his medicine like a man. Maybe we could get some work done. It's mighty hard concentrating with dingdongs like Shap taking potshots at us."

Veenie peered up over her glasses. "Harry hiding out until the affair blows over?"

"Or Shap runs out of shotgun shells."

Harry Shades wasn't a bad man, just not the brightest. He was on the right side of sixty and still wore the same size pants as in high school, same style too: wide-waist, rayon dress pants from Sears. He was a bowling prodigy, able to pick up pocket change and loose women with regularity at the Tuesday night Starlite Bowling for Dollars Extravaganza. He had all his hair, which was the color of pewter, and he wore three piece suits. He was a catch, provided you weren't all that fussy about what landed on the end of your line. Only the good Lord knew why he only "dated" married women. Liked the drama, I reckoned.

Veenie printed documents and slid them into a "case closed" folder. The Mellencamp case was done. We'd caught Mr. Newt Mellencamp cheating on his wife, Betty, with Conchita, the countywide Mary Kay Cosmetics saleslady. Now everyone knew what a slimeball Newt was. He'd have to cough up alimony, maybe even an apology. Veenie and I both considered that a good week's work.

Harry, the boss, was always on us to work faster and pull in more clients. He considered us junior detectives in training, senior slaves near as we could decipher. Harry bought his PI license from one of those Internet colleges. He had a badge and a diploma. When he got uppity—that would be a buttload of the time, folks—Veenie liked to remind him that his diploma, a teeny-weeny laminated thing that fit in his wallet, looked exactly like something Barbie might carry to a job interview in her purse.

Hanky-panky was the bread-and-butter of the Shady Hoosier Detective Agency—what the locals called the Shades Detective Agency because of the boss's spotty reputation with the ladies. Most days our work was pretty humdrum. Veenie and I hunted down deadbeat dads and cheating spouses. Harry waved his gun around and shook down the offenders for loose change. There was usually more than enough work to keep us in bologna and cheese. Heck, on a good week, we might even afford a Dairy Queen run.

One thing Pawpaw County had in spades was cheating-heart Romeos. Over at the old folks' home, recently splashed with a fresh coat of yellow paint and renamed Leisure Hills, it was a badge of honor to die while in the throes of romance. Squeal Daddy, the anonymous blogger who ran the *Hoosier Squealer* website, loved penning lurid gossip about "death boners." Romantic injuries were also a favored topic of conversation down at the VFW. The VFW was the social hub of Knobby Waters, should you be over sixty and in need of some reasonably sane conversation—and cheap well drinks on Wednesdays.

Sliding aside the Mellencamp case file, Veenie popped open a drawer on her desk. Her tiny liver-spotted hands dangled a brown paper bag under my nose. "Made us some tuna fish."

I squinted at her. "You look slimmer. Tuna fish diet?"

"Nah. Got me some new old lady undies. Newfangled. Had a run of seconds down at the Goodwill." Veenie showed me the top waistband of her underwear. It was beige and read "Spankies."

By seconds, I hoped she meant irregulars.

"They help slim me up," she said, patting her stomach. "But they ain't Moses. Can't perform miracles."

Veenie was wider than she was tall. Four feet, seven inches. One hundred fifty pounds. She liked to wear outfits she thought disguised her beach-ball physique—mostly capri stretch pants and ponchos. Ponchos had been easy enough to find in the early seventies but had fallen out of fashion in the greater Midwest in the last forty years. That did not deter Veenie. On a tight budget, she shopped for clothes in the Goodwill dumpster in the alley between the Roadkill Café and the post office. She liked to get the good stuff before it got pawed through by the public. If she found anything worth snatching, she left a two dollar cash donation. That day's Goodwill steal was a zebra-striped poncho and a pair of bumble-bee-yellow capris.

Fetching.

I fished in the paper bag and yanked out a sandwich. It was wrapped in waxed paper. Yellow squished out the edges. "Mustard?"

"Yours has mustard. Course it does." Veenie nibbled at her sandwich. She washed it down with a carton of chocolate milk. "How long you think Harry will be gone?"

I shrugged and chomped on my tuna. "A week?" I pulled a lettuce leaf out from between my back molars. It was red, the kind I liked. I had another go at it.

With Harry on the lamb, Veenie and I ran the detective agency pretty much as we pleased. I wrote our paychecks. Veenie tallied and replenished the petty cash. We kept busy making Knobby Waters a respectable place to live—or die, as the case might be. Our clients tended to be elderly or heavy drinkers, often both.

We agreed that while Harry was out of town, we'd embrace any soul who hocked up the five-hundred-dollar retainer. We were all ears once we had the five big ones.

Taking cases indiscriminately was a decision we began to regret right after lunch. The tuna was barely licked from our fingers, and Shap, convinced Harry had fled, had finally wheeled out of town, when Avonelle Apple huffed through our door.

Everybody knew Avonelle, the bank president. She'd lived in Pawpaw County her whole life, lording it over the citizens of Knobby Waters, and she was the only person in town with home-dyed hair the color of apricots. Veenie, along with most of Pawpaw County, had been spitting and spatting with Avonelle for the better part of fifty years.

Judging by the determined look on Avonelle's face as she stormed into the office, I could tell that one heck of a new battle was brewing.

CHAPTER TWO

Avonelle's apricot-colored hair was puffed up like cotton candy. Her eyebrows, penciled on in high arches, were a darker shade of apricot. She wore a nice knit suit in a pastel green with a large white Buster Brown silk tie, like the kind Nancy Reagan used to wear. She carried a black purse with a gold clasp with both hands, placing it dead center across her lady parts. Overall, she was shaped like a bowling pin and had a personality pretty much the same.

Avonelle pulled out a white monogrammed handkerchief and dusted off the seat I offered her. She sat down like a lady and crossed her ankles, then nervously uncrossed them. She wiggled in the chair. It was a tight fit with those bowling-pin hips. She sighed deeply, as if already put out with the Shades Detective Agency and whatever misfortune had forced her to darken our door.

Veenie, playing it safe, had vamoosed behind a file cabinet. I could hear her tiny ears flapping, trying to snatch every syllable of Avonelle's distress. Clearly Avonelle had a problem, and Veenie wasn't about to miss out on any ear-busting gossip.

A natural born judge, Avonelle appointed herself head of every town committee. That was how she and Veenie came to lock horns. Back in 1968, Avonelle had judged the cat contest at the Pawpaw County Fair. The way Veenie told it, Avonelle had cheated Veenie's calico cat, Mrs. Puff Pants, out of the grand champion ribbon. The award went to Mrs. Hall's tuxedo cat, Cary "Claws" Grant. In exchange, Mrs. Hall voted Avonelle in as

Grand Poobah of the Knobby Waters Ladies Home Improvement Society. That incident was the beginning of a fifty-year grudge.

"How might we help you?" I asked Avonelle as I plucked up a pen and a legal pad and smoothed down my halo of white hair. Avonelle seemed like a good bet as a client, so I did my darnedest to look professional. Everyone knew Avonelle had oodles of money. She'd inherited controlling stock in the First National Bank of Knobby Waters from her husband's daddy. Her husband, Will Apple, had been the town dentist. He was recently deceased. His twin sons inherited his practice. One of his cousins ran the denture lab in Salem. Another was an orthodontist in Seymour. If you had lived in southern Indiana any amount of time, an Apple had had his hands in your mouth, and in your pocketbook. Dentistry wasn't cheap.

Avonelle clutched her purse and gritted her teeth. "You take all cases?"

"Licensed, full-service." I pointed to Harry's high-priced paperwork on the wall.

"Confidential?"

"Don't disclose our clients, unless required by subpoena." I wasn't totally sure if subpoena was the right word, but I reckoned mention of anything legal would impress Avonelle. Highfalutin people just loved talking Latin. I hoped throwing out a foreign phrase or two would put Avonelle's mind at ease.

It did. She sucked in her gut and spilled the pork and beans. "It's about my husband, William."

"Isn't he deceased?"

"Year ago, this April."

"My condolences."

"Thank you. He lived a good life, but he left behind a few issues."

I could hear Veenie's little ears twitching. I knew she was hoping that William Apple had come back to haunt his wife.

Veenie loved a good ghost story. Her secret ambition in life was to be a ghost buster, and we'd just come off a hair-raising case chasing down ghosts and hillbilly hoodlums at the old Wyatt mansion.

Avonelle pressed a hand over her mouth. Her blue eyes shined like cold ice chips. "He's dead, yes. But I've received some correspondence ... and ... it seems he left behind a few unresolved issues—three of them to be precise."

Avonelle unsnapped her purse. She pulled an envelope from her purse and a letter from that envelope. She unfolded the letter carefully and slid it across my desk.

The letter, handwritten, on stationary that featured mice in bonnets dancing in a chorus line along the top, was from one Ms. Barbara Skaggs. It appeared Doc Apple had spawned an illegitimate bushel of little Apples. His self-proclaimed mistress, Barbara, who lived in Hound Holler, had contacted Avonelle for child support. She had enclosed a snapshot of the fruit of William's loins, two boys and one girl. They were standing in height order in front of a picket fence. The fence was in need of a paint job. If you looked closely to the right, you could see a dog hightailing it out of the photo, just as it was snapped. It looked to be a beagle. The kids squinted into the camera, their tiny hands fisted at their sides.

"You responded to Ms. Skaggs?"

Avonelle twisted her lips. Clearly, she found that idea distasteful. "I was hoping the agency might do so on my behalf. Discreetly. I had never heard of this young woman until this letter arrived. And well, hang it, of course I'd want proof that these children, any of them, belong to my husband. I tend to doubt the whole accusation since Mr. Apple was never ... well ... never very experienced in that area."

Avonelle stood. "You will need a retainer?"

"Five hundred will do her."

She took out an embroidered clutch wallet and retracted the exact amount in crisp one hundred dollar bills.

I handwrote a receipt. "Give us a week," I said, handing over the receipt.

Avonelle hesitated. "You will be discreet?"

I nodded.

Satisfied, she headed toward the door but hesitated as her hand touched the brass knob. She turned on her heel and said, her voice a little shaky, "You can tell Veenie she can come out from behind that file cabinet now." Without waiting for Veenie to show herself, Avonelle strutted out, head held high. She marched across the street toward the bank.

Veenie waited a few seconds before popping out from her hidey-hole. She strolled over and studied the photo of Barbara Skaggs's kids. "Not very experienced, eh? Well that don't look like the work of an amateur to me."

"Think those are his kids?"

Veenie slid off her glasses. She pushed the photo closer to her nose. "Hard to say, but this one," she pointed to the oldest, a towheaded boy who looked to be about ten years old, "has the Apple ears." The boy's ears flared out like teacup handles. "This one too," said Veenie of the youngest, a girl of maybe four. "A shame. Girls with big ears don't outgrow them. She'll have to wear a shag all her life. That's what I'd do."

I had to agree about the ears. Most families had a defining feature. William's twin dentist sons, Bert and Bromley, were born with ears so generous they reminded one of wings. Avonelle, always mindful of looks, pinned her son's ears under hats on school picture days when they were younger. Things took an ugly turn when she found out the other kids had nicknamed her sons Dumbo One and Dumbo Two. In high school, she drove the boys to Indianapolis one weekend for some sort of secret surgery that tacked back their ears.

Veenie tapped the photo. "You ever hear of this Barbara Skaggs?"

"Knew some Skaggs over in Washington County. Hard to tell. Might be related." People in Pawpaw County weren't all that energetic. Most mated in county. It was like Genesis out in corn country. Everybody begat everybody else. Made it harder to solve crimes because everybody's DNA was pretty much the same.

Veenie twitched her nose. "Wasn't there a Skaggs worked the acid ponds at the plastics factory with us?"

"Yep. Think his name was Lennie. But he died a few years back. Worked nights at Kelly's Paper Mill up in Brownstown. Got wasted long about 1989 on a Christmas bottle of Jim Beam. A one-ton roll of newsprint fell on him. He was nothing but a big grease spot in the end."

"If it's the Lennie Skaggs I'm thinking of, he didn't amount to much more than that when he was alive."

"Same Skaggs," I said.

I sat down at my desk, adjusted my glasses, and fired up the old computer. "Let's snoop on Barbara." I was born to power-drive a computer across the World Wide Web in search of facts. I would have made a humdinger of a Russian spy. It didn't take me but half an hour to gather a dossier on Ms. Barbara Skaggs. First off, Ms. Skaggs had never been married. Second, she seemed to live alone with the kids. All the bills—utilities, Internet, phone—were in her name. Last of all, she was employed as the head hostess at the Pancake Palace on Highway 50.

Veenie read the pages on Barbara Skaggs as the printer spat them out. "Working at the Pancake Palace. Dealing with trade off Highway 50. That would make her more worldly than most. Probably where she met Doc Apple."

Everybody ate at the Pancake Palace. Sunday morning after church if you were a Baptist. Wednesday nights after Bible study if you were a Lutheran. Just about any time if you were drunk or down in the dumps. Pancakes cheered everybody up.

"The Pancake Palace never closes," I said. "People go there all hours for comfort food and the biscuits and gravy."

I eyed the photo of the Skaggs kids. It appeared Barbara Skaggs's womb might have been on the same 24/7/365 schedule as the Pancake Palace. It wasn't inconceivable that Doc Apple had enjoyed more than biscuits and gravy in his late-night quests for consolation. I reckoned anyone married to Avonelle might have needed a good bit of consoling over the years.

"Got a photo of Barbara?" Veenie asked.

I hit the print button. A photo slipped out of the printer. We studied the photo together.

Barbara wore square gunmetal glasses and squinted into the camera. Her forehead was creased in three places. Her hair was dark and dyed, with a wild flip above each ear. Her throat was long and skinny. It might also be described as scaly. She was wearing plastic daisy earrings, clip-ons from the looks of them. In the photo, she was wearing a flowered blouse with a rounded lace collar and a cardigan. She looked nothing like a jezebel, more like a runaway Pentecost in need of a fashion intervention.

"Maybe she can cook?" suggested Veenie.

I shrugged. Not much of life in the country looked like it did on TV. People loved to be big fish in small ponds. Knobby Waters was so small it was more like a mud puddle with all the minnows fighting for the crown. There was a real shortage of beauty queens, and Doc Apple had been more Don Knotts than Burt Reynolds. Still, I had no trouble seeing Barbara Skaggs and Will Apple lip-locked in a wanton embrace.

I glanced at my Timex. It was after five on Friday. Quitting time. I bundled up the paperwork on Barbara and stuck it in a file folder. I stuck the folder under my armpit, turned out the lights, and locked up.

Veenie and I ambled down the sidewalk to the Roadkill Café to see what was on the specials board for supper. Fridays, we always treated ourselves to a meal out. Halfway there I stopped thinking about Doc Apple and his biscuits and gravy ta-ta girl and began to wonder if the café would have any of Ma Horton's coconut cream pie. I hoped so, because I was planning on eating two pieces. All that talk about wanton sex had made me extra hungry.

CHAPTER THREE

I t was Saturday morning, and we assumed Barbara Skaggs would be home, so we gassed up the 1960 Impala and hot-footed it toward Hound Holler. The holler was a twenty-minute drive up the knobs, then down a gravel road that dropped into a butt-like crevice between two knobby hills.

In Knobby Waters, there were two kinds of people: town people and holler people. Everyone knew which they were, which they aspired to be, and which they hoped to God never to become. Barbara Skaggs was not among the fortunate. She lived smack on Hound Holler Road. One look at her rented house and you knew she'd given up all hope, along with a good bit of her self-respect, about a decade ago.

The plan was to stake out Barbara's place, see if anything untoward might be going on that would lead her to engage in unscrupulous acts to earn a little egg money on the side. Barbara lived in To-Jo Scott's old farmhouse, which had been nice enough back in the day, meaning the Depression. These days, the house looked more like something out of Mother Goose. The roof was a mossy carpet. Foot-tall maple saplings sprouted from the gutters. The front porch, which was missing most of its spindle posts, sagged. A sway-backed barn struggled to remain erect in the backyard. A scarecrow made of moldy corn stalks, wearing a tattered, brown-felt hat and a large overall jacket with patches, stood watch over rows of corn stubble and what may have once been tomato vines.

I had a pair of binoculars resting on the bridge of my nose. My glasses were off, laid on the seat of the Impala between me and Veenie. A family-sized bag of pork rinds we'd picked up at the Go Go Gas rested on the seat between us. It was almost noon. We were on stakeout behind a tall stand of weeds in a tractor pulloff on the soft shoulder of Hound Holler Creek. We were just across from Barbara's place.

Barbara's oldest boy, the one with the pitcher ears, was playing with a rusty-yellow dump truck along a line of mud puddles in the front yard. He was chasing a rooster back and forth. The rooster, all wings, was squawking, occasionally trying to peck the dump truck to death. Every now and then, another boy, dressed only in ragged denim shorts, the nipples of his bare chest blue as raisins, would burst around the corner of the house trying to lasso a chicken. He was wearing a red cowboy hat and shooting a cap gun.

Veenie asked, "You gonna eat them pork rinds?"

"Nah. Have at 'em."

For the next ten minutes, while I watched the boys trying to lasso chickens, Veenie crunched pig skin. Stakeouts had never been portrayed like this back when I was watching *Magnum, PI.* I tried to shut my ears as Veenie crunched pig skins, washing them down with a quart of chocolate milk. She topped off the skins with a fistful of fruit-flavored Tums. Why that woman suffered from perpetual heartburn was no mystery to me.

It had rained all night. It was getting steamy in the Impala. I punched out the wing on the window to let more air circulate and motioned for Veenie to do the same.

Veenie had been fidgety all morning. She wore stretch capri pants. The white leather seats on the Impala were heating up, and her plump little calves were sticking to the leather. She licked the last of the pork rind salt from her fingertips and belched.

"Dr. Duhaney," that was Veenie's cardiologist, "wouldn't approve of you eating all that salt and fat," I said.

"Dr. Doohickey can go suck an egg."

Veenie made a show of fanning herself with a fluorescent sales circular for chicken parts from the Hoosier Feedbag. She was growing impatient. "Let's bust on in."

I drew the binoculars away from my eyes and slipped on my glasses. "You want to do the questioning?"

"Nah. I want to be the muscle."

We never carried firearms—left that to Harry, who ran the collections department—but Veenie's BB pistol was in the glove compartment. The toy pistol looked real. It was the expensive model, with a solid wood handle and brass trimming. It shot BB pellets. Men tended to wet themselves when they saw two nearsighted old ladies packing a piece. The criminals we dealt with were the world's biggest pantywaists. Most surrendered as soon as Veenie waved the pistol. They fell to their knees and blubbered like babies. Veenie enjoyed cuffing them. The Shades Agency used those newfangled, plastic twist tie cuffs. Bringing a perp down was a lot like bagging the kitchen trash: very satisfying to any woman who'd wasted her youth as a frustrated housewife.

Bored with waiting, we scrambled out of the Impala and walked across the muddy road to the farmhouse. The oldest boy stared us down. "You Holy Rollers?"

I tried to look sweet. "We're looking for your mama, Barbara Skaggs? She home?"

The boy hiked up his shorts and circled me, then Veenie. He brushed a flap of dirty blond hair out of his eyes. His ears were big enough to catch and hold rainwater. "You bill collectors?"

Veenie eyed the boy. "We look like bill collectors?"

The boy wiped his nose on the back of his hand. "Nah, you look like old ladies."

We were standing at the porch now. The boy asked Veenie, "That a real gun?"

"Sure." She pointed the pistol at his head.

The boy screamed, "Mama!" and ran into the house. The torn screen door banged after him.

A squinting woman wearing gunmetal glasses appeared in the doorway. A girl child with big ears appeared in the doorway and clung to the leg of her mother's baggy shorts. One blue eye peeked out, trying to get a good look at us without exposing herself.

"Don't want any," Barbara said.

I slid my big foot into the doorway. "Mrs. William Apple sent us."

Barbara opened the door wide and stepped back. She bent and picked up the little girl, lifting her up until she could ride on her hip. "Well, come on in, then. Been expecting someone."

Once we were inside, Barbara seemed more welcoming, and not at all unreasonable. She sat the girl child aside. "I want what's due the children. Child support, you know."

I nodded sympathetically. "You have proof? Mrs. Apple would need proof before money could change hands."

Barbara pressed her knuckles to her lips and mulled over the question. "What would I need?"

"DNA. Tests cost a hundred dollars each. You'd have to deposit that with us."

Barbara looked at her two younger children. They were tumbling over each other like dung beetles on the braided rug in front of the TV. The TV was on, but Barbara had clicked down the sound when we took our seats in the living room.

"Can't we just test one of them? Assume the others would be the same? I work at the Pancake Palace. Don't make a heap of money. I mean, if I had money to throw around, I wouldn't be writing to Mrs. Apple now, would I? But William up and died. He used to give me an allowance. And that was fine.

But now Billy Junior there," she pointed to the oldest boy, "needs braces. William's cousin was supposed to take care of that. Wasn't supposed to cost me a dime. Show the nice ladies, Billy."

Billy Junior pulled back his gums, revealing a gap between his two front teeth. It was identical to the gap Avonelle's boys had sported at about the same age before their cousin the orthodontist had intervened.

I considered the options. "Maybe we could test the oldest boy. Make a good faith gesture. You could save up. Do the others one at a time."

"You mean like layaway?" The creases eased in Barbara's forehead. "I don't mean her no harm." She bit her lip. She gathered the collar of her cardigan closer to her throat. "I knew William was married, but he seemed sweet. And he was lonely. Guess I was too."

I could tell Barbara wanted to talk about it, but I didn't want to hear the Jerry Springer version of the whole sordid affair. Every time people talked about sex, I got hungry. My butt couldn't afford the extra pounds.

Veenie came to my rescue. "I can run out. Get a spit kit from the Chevy."

"Won't take but a minute," I promised. "If Billy Junior would oblige us, we could be on our way. Takes a week to get the test results back. We could discuss confidential payment possibilities and arrangements with Avonelle in the meantime."

Barbara stood and smoothed the front of her shorts. She eyed Billy Junior, who was rolling around on the rug on his back with all fours in the air panting like a dying dog. "All he has to do is spit? No written tests?"

"Yep, just spit in a tube."

"Well, I reckon he can do that all right."

Veenie was out the door. But almost as soon as the screen door slammed, she was screeching at me. "Ruby Jane? Uh, can you come out here for a second? We got us a little, uh, problem."

I ambled toward the door and peered out onto the porch. A man was slumped in the metal porch glider. He was wearing the tattered brown hat and denim overcoat that the barn scarecrow had been wearing when we had first arrived. At first I thought someone had dragged the scarecrow onto the porch. But on closer inspection, I could see that it wasn't a scarecrow but one of Avonelle's sons—one of the Apple twins, Bert or Bromley. I couldn't tell which. They weren't identical twins, but they were close.

His mouth was open. He could have been snoring. But from the cool white of his face—it looked like a peeled egg— and the way his body slumped, not a tense muscle in him, I could tell he was toast. A speckled chicken was perched on the glider rest next to him, pecking at his lifeless hand.

I looked at Veenie.

She shrugged. "Don't look at me. He wasn't sitting there when we went in."

Barbara stepped out on the porch and stood next to Veenie. She looked a little green, like a thinly sliced zucchini. She hugged herself. "I don't know a darn thing about that," she said, sounding defensive.

CHAPTER FOUR

I was happy to see Sheriff Boots Gibson inching down into Hound Holler in the police cruiser, red cherry spinning. I didn't want to have to explain the dead Apple on the porch glider to the new junior officer, Devon Hattabaugh. Devon was a skinny kid, fresh out of community college. He wore a ponytail and aviator glasses. Off hours he sported a beret. He also sported muttonchop sideburns, which seemed all the rage with the Millennials. His teeth were impossibly white, and he talked a lot. He chattered like a rabid squirrel, which some old ladies found sweet and endearing. I was not among them.

Boots stood on the porch. He had his hat off. He was balding on top, and the hat left a red band around his head. "Looks dead," he said as he mopped the sweat off the top of his head with a red kerchief. "Looks mighty dead."

Boots looked a good deal like Santa Claus in jeans and scruffy cowboy boots. He wore a closely cropped white beard. He had been in my class in school and had once kissed me in the cloak room in second grade, on Valentine's Day. That same year he had sent me a valentine that featured a policeman with a billy club dragging a girl, imprisoned in a giant red heart, to the jailhouse. The card had read, "Be my prisoner of love." People claimed Boots was sweet on me still, said they could tell by the way the tips of his ears blushed when I was around. I had yet to be won over.

I nodded toward the body on the glider. "Didn't touch him. Didn't want to contaminate a possible crime scene."

Veenie spoke. "I poked him with a stick. He's dead alrighty. Also, that chicken has been pecking at his hand. If he were alive, he would have hollered by now."

Boots ran his fingers around the wide rim of his hat, which he held in his hands. "You gals out here on a case?"

"Yes," I confessed. "But we can't talk about that. Not without the client's permission."

"No sign of foul play. No bullet holes. No visible strangulation. You shoot him?" Boots inspected Veenie, who had a tight, two-handed grip on her air pistol.

"Course not. You know this here is just for looks. Shoots BBs. Veenie held up her pistol. She shook it until the BBs rattled.

"You shouldn't carry that thing. Looks too real."

Billy Junior popped up in the screen door. "That old lady tried to shoot me."

Veenie stuck out her dentures at Billy Junior. He ran away crying, back into the darkness of the house. She popped her dentures back in and turned to face Boots. "Don't know what got into that kid. Seeing a dead body spooked him, I reckon."

Boots eyed us. "You ladies didn't hear a shot? Any untoward noises?"

We murmured no.

Barbara offered that her second oldest child, Teddy, had been running around the house chasing chickens with his cap gun. She'd been inside with the windows shut watching her recorded daytime TV programs with Wilma, the baby, and Billy Junior. It would have been hard for her to hear anything but the TV.

Boots flipped open his tiny notebook. "Did you know the deceased?"

Barbara eyed me.

I eyed Veenie.

Veenie eyed us both.

"Not exactly," murmured Barbara. "I mean, I hostess out at the Pancake Palace. I might have met him once or twice. We get lots of customers. Traffic on 50 headed to the interstate in Seymour. Some headed out west through Bedford."

I answered, "Well, horse pucky, Boots, of course we knew him. Who doesn't know the Apple twins?"

"But you had no reason to want him dead? Any of you?"

Veenie rolled her eyes.

"Oh for Pete's sake, Boots," I squawked, "you watch too much *Matlock*. You know we aren't killers."

"It's my official job to ask the difficult questions, Ruby Jane." The tips of his ears flamed red.

The coroner's white van pulled into the yard. It pulled straight up onto the grass, past the mud puddles, scattering the chickens. The coroner, April Trueblood, slid out of the van. She was a petite woman with curly salt and pepper hair. She was wearing a short, stained white lab coat and a black sock cap. She strolled up to the porch and sat her black leather bag down on the top step.

"That the deceased?" she asked, opening her bag and snapping on a pair of blue plastic gloves. She slipped a pair of clear plastic glasses over her eyes and a set of paper booties over her tennis shoes before walking closer to the porch glider.

Boots sniffled. "That would be him. One of Doc Apple's boys. One of the twins."

"The dentist?" asked April. As Boots nodded yes April knelt down, removed the tattered scarecrow hat, and peered at him closely. "Bromley? Oh man, he was a good dentist. A little handsy with the ladies. Did the neatest crowns though. Hate to see him go. Man, you just can't find a good dentist these days. Might have to drive to Salem now just to get my teeth cleaned. Gosh darn it."

While all the brouhaha was happening, I got Billy Junior to hock up some DNA into a test tube.

Veenie was getting impatient. "I want to skedaddle home in time to make deer chili for supper and watch *Hee Haw.*

"*Hee Haw* has been in reruns for forty years," I said. "You won't miss anything."

"That's what you think. I don't remember much of the seventies. It's all new to me."

I didn't argue. I knew as far as Veenie was concerned, *Hee Haw* represented the height of network television. I wasn't sure that I disagreed with her.

We squeezed out around April and hightailed it back to the Impala. Boots trailed after us. "Don't you ladies leave town. Might be a murder. Might be needing to talk to you two soon. Depends on what the coroner finds."

I fired up the Impala and shot one hand okay and good-bye out the window to Boots.

We were halfway up the steep Holler Road, the Chevy fishtailing on the gravel, when Veenie said, "Bootsie boy just wants an excuse to call on you. He's still sweet on you."

"I didn't fancy him in the second grade. I don't fancy him now," I said. "I don't want a man. You know that." And I meant it. My husband, Charlie "Whiskers" Waskom, had died suddenly twenty years ago. His ticker gave out right in the middle of a farm insurance quote. I'd grieved him for a good two years. Then one day I woke up and suddenly felt pretty okay. Marriage, in hindsight, had been a heap of work. Most days I didn't have that much get-up-and-go left in me.

I did wonder who on earth had killed Doc Apple's son. And if it had anything to do with Barbara and her bushel of little Apples. Surely there was some connection. One thing I knew for sure: Avonelle was not going to be pleased about this. She'd hired us to quietly clear up a child support mystery, and now things had progressed to murder. There'd be no keeping these things a secret in a town as slack-jawed as Knobby Waters.

CHAPTER FIVE

The dead fellow on Barbara's porch glider was Bromley Apple, the less popular of the Apple dental twins. Bert was known for his down-to-earth manner. Bromley was most noted for not being able to keep his hammy hands off the waitresses down at the Roadkill Café. Another family trait, I reckoned.

"What am I to make of this?" Avonelle asked. Her bottom lip quivered.

It was Easter Sunday, after church, and Avonelle and I were sitting side by side on the swing on my front porch. We were discussing the case. I hadn't been to church, but Avonelle had. She was wearing a lovey white felt pillbox hat with a purple veil that she had pulled back and pinned up. The hat really topped off the purple knit suit with mauve piping she had worn to Easter Sunrise Services. Avonelle was, per usual, keeping a stiff upper lip, but I could tell she'd been crying. I reckoned she wouldn't let anyone see her in tears, certainly not an employee like me.

Veenie was in the kitchen frying up a bologna sandwich for breakfast. I could smell the bologna and the toast through the open screened windows. Since Avonelle was feeling poorly, I aimed to keep Veenie in the kitchen and deal with updating Avonelle myself, just for safety's sake, given their past spats. Whatever Avonelle and I discussed, I'd update Veenie later.

Avonelle blew her nose gently with a monogrammed handkerchief before taking a small sip of the lemon iced tea I'd fixed for her. She showed me the screen of her iPad. The

Hoosier Squealer gossip website was displayed. It featured a banner ad for half-off ground chuck at the IGA. It also spotlighted a story by Squeal Daddy on the dead fellow found in Hound Holler. No one was supposed to know the identity of the body, but apparently Squeal Daddy had his sources. He wrote a fairly good description of the body and the mysterious circumstances.

Foul Play in Hound Holler?

Sorry to report that one of Knobby Waters own esteemed native sons, Bromley Apple, left town to meet up with his eternal maker yesterday. He was found deceased on a porch glider at the home of one Ms. Barbara Skaggs. Ms. Skaggs has enjoyed being lead hostess out at the Pancake Palace since arriving in Knobby Waters ten years ago. She has cousins over in Washington County. Her boss, Hubert Persinger, describes her as "a sweet church-going lady who minds her own beeswax and gives sick little children extra scoops of ice cream. She wouldn't hurt a fly."

Barbara told the Squealer last night, "Honest to God, I have no idea how that man's body got on my porch."

The strange event happened in Hound Holler, a place renowned in bygone days for its colorful characters and late-night comings and goings. Barbara, who says she never met the dentist, at least not that she can recall, would like to thank Coroner April Trueblood for removing him so quickly and neatly.

The body was wearing a hat and jacket that had previously been the attire of a nearby scarecrow. Nobody knows how that happened either. Foul play may be afoot. Sheriff Boots Gibson, who investigated, offered no comment for the readers of the Squealer other than his customary, "Stop pestering me."

Mrs. Lavinia Goens, who was visiting Barbara, along with her lifelong friend Mrs. Ruby Jane Waskom, went on record saying it is indeed unusual for poorly dressed dead bodies to pop up on people's porches.

Stay tuned for updates. In the meantime, remember it's Easter Sunday, and the Hoosier Feedbag is selling past date hams for only two bucks a can. Hurry on down and get yours. Yum! Yum!

I wasn't happy to see Veenie quoted in the article. We weren't supposed to comment on open cases. I was relieved not to see in print the real reason we'd been visiting Barbara Skaggs. There was no mention of our being on an open case, or of William Apple and his illegitimate children, thank you Jesus.

Mrs. Apple sniffled, bringing me out of my reflections on the *Hoosier Squealer* article.

"How long for the DNA?" she asked.

"A week."

"It will tell us without a doubt ..."

"Yes. They'll compare William's DNA, which you gave us, with the DNA from Billy Junior's spittle."

I could tell Avonelle wasn't pleased that Barbara had named her oldest son Billy Junior, after her husband, William. I had to admire Avonelle for being dogged in her pursuit of the truth, even though it was bound to reflect badly on the Apple family name.

Avonelle slipped her handkerchief into her purse. "You met the woman. What's your professional opinion?"

"I imagine she's telling the truth."

"And Bromley? Why was he at her place?"

"Don't know. You want us to look into the entire affair?" I realized as soon as I said it that "affair," might not have been the most judicious word choice.

"Yes, I would. There must be a connection. I'd like to know what that connection is before the *Squealer* gets hold of this mess. I have the bank's reputation and my grandchildren to protect. Don't want the whole family ending up on that Inter Tuber thing." She took five crisp one hundred dollar bills out of her purse and laid them on the table. "Will this suffice?"

I nodded.

Avonelle rose to leave. "Also, if you don't mind, could you ask Veenie not to be talking to the press?"

"Done."

Veenie waited until Avonelle was down the sidewalk and out of earshot before coming out to sit on the porch swing with me. She'd thrown on a ratty blue chenille robe and was wearing her mule house slippers. "You reckon Bromley was down in Hound Holler nosing around about his bastard kin?"

"Nobody calls them bastards anymore, Veenie."

"I do."

"Biological children is the polite term, I think."

Veenie pouted. "Can we still call the men dickheads?"

"I think they're called baby daddies." Like Veenie, I too had problems with the new terminology. Baby daddy sounded like a term of endearment. Itchy-pants idiot seemed to more accurately reflect the situation, but I liked to stay modern, keep up with the times.

"Thought you had a date tonight," I said to Veenie.

"I do. Dickie Freeman is taking me to the drive-in in his new Ford F-150. You know how I love trucks. Big trucks get my groove thing going."

The east Highway 50 drive-in theater was open for business again. Some Millennials from Seymour had bought a caboodle of old country drive-ins. They hoped to bring back wholesome family fun. They'd installed bouncy castles and an outdoor mini laser tag field. They showed family classics. They served meat and soy hotdogs. Popcorn with real butter. Local microbrew. Anyone who grumbled about the snack selection was free to pack their own. Veenie had a pallet of Ding Dongs and Big Red soda pop from the Costco squirreled away in the basement. She was hunky dory with bring-your-own snacks.

I kicked my feet, propelling the porch swing back and forth. "What's playing at the drive-in?"

"It's Easter week. They're showing *The Ten Commandments* and *Ben Hur*. I hope like heck they play *Ben Hur* first. If they play *The Ten Commandments* first, it's bound to put a cramp in Dickie's make out style. He was raised Southern Baptist, you know. One look at that twenty-foot Moses, and his gopher is going back in the hole, if you catch my drift."

Unlike me, Veenie had a sex life with someone other than herself.

Our boarder, Sue Ann Smith—Sassy, everybody called her—strolled out onto the porch wearing some type of silky lounging suit. Sassy had lived in California the last few decades. She was forever strutting around in urban hippie attire. Large red roses bloomed in swirls around her body. Her face was done up like it was date night. She was wearing false eyelashes and a push-up bra that lived up to its name. She sat down in a rocker facing the sidewalk so she could see who strolled by. She'd recently moved back to Knobby Waters and was surveying the pickings for a man to sink her fangs into. Her last husband, Doogie Duval, a LA real estate developer, had recently won an all-expense-paid trip to Club Fed, in Terre Haute, leaving her destitute. Rumor had it he was involved in a real estate scheme that had to do with selling desert lots to dim-witted Mid-westerners.

Sassy claimed she hadn't known anything about her husband's shady businesses. She claimed he left her just enough money to hightail it back to Knobby Waters. The California attorneys, however, felt Sassy must have had money squirreled away. They called the house all hours trying to get Sassy to fess up. When Veenie caught one of them peering in her bedroom window, she gave him an awful eyeful. He never did that again.

Sassy pulled out an emery board. She dragged it half-heartedly across her nails. "The Passion Pit open again? Lordy, but we had good times there, didn't we, gals?"

"You and the entire Knobby Waters basketball team." Veenie clicked her false teeth.

Sassy inspected her nails. Not satisfied with the results, she started raking again. "Veenie, you know full well I was born to entertain."

Veenie propped her tiny feet up on a white ceramic stool that was shaped like an elephant—a two-dollar Goodwill steal. "I plum forgot. How many Oscars was it you dragged home for your performances down in the passion pit?"

Sassy ceased filing. "It's a woman's rightful place to seduce a man. It's all right there, plain as gospel in the Bible. It's how people get begat and all."

"You read the Lord All Mighty's word, and *that's* what you came away with?"

"I'll have you know that I had an important position once, out in LA, in the Church of Scientology."

"What position was that? Missionary?"

Sassy raked a nail with a grand flourish. "I've seen that little hottie Dickie Freeman hanging around here. You two exclusive?"

Oh boy. I could see the fur flying. "Veenie's dating Dickie Freeman right steady. Hands off, Sassy," I felt compelled to say.

Veenie crossed her arms and hugged herself tightly. "All other body parts too."

Sassy studied the sky like she was pulling down memories about Dickie. "Those Freeman boys were all cute as buttons. All sandy hair and dimples. Don't Dickie love to dance? Don't he own that humongous gorgeous old house over on Maple Street?"

Veenie nodded. "Same house. Hair nests above his ears like baby bunny tails. I think he looks better now than he did in high school. What do you think, Ruby Jane?"

"Agreed."

Sassy screwed up her face. "Didn't Dickie marry Ruth Rucker?"

"Married. Buried."

Some days it felt like we weren't growing older. It felt like we were aging backward. The women fought over boys. The men just wanted to cop a feel. We'd returned to middle school, which had not been that swell the first time around, at least not for me. Sassy, on the other hand, had reigned over the tongue-tied farm boys like a backwater Cleopatra.

I chewed on my cheek as Sassy recalled memories of Dickie Freeman. I knew that look in Sassy's eye. I'd seen that look back in 1965 when she made me, the tallest girl in the class, hold the rabbit ears in place on the Zenith TV in her mother's basement. The goal then was for us girls to get an educational eyeful of *Peyton Place*.

Peyton Place, the book, had been banned from the Pawpaw County Bookmobile. Sassy had, therefore, been determined to watch it on TV. She mined a good bit of her ideas about seducing men from that show, most of which she reenacted with flair on the Daulton brothers at the '65 Spring Hop. Too bad there hadn't been a Facebook back then.

I could feel it brewing. A sixties redux. I wouldn't be surprised if I came home one day to find Veenie in the downstairs toilet treating Sassy to a well-deserved swirly. Yep. It was spring in Knobby Waters. All God's creatures, except for me, were on the prowl.

CHAPTER SIX

I unlocked the office Monday morning and stepped over a pile of letters that the postman had poked through the brass slot on the door. I stooped to gather the mail. Ackerman's Tanning, Fence, Catering, Stump Removal Service (they had diversified over the years to stay afloat) was offering a two-for-one spring stump removal special. It was such a good deal I regretted that I couldn't use the coupon.

At the bottom of the pile I found a postcard that read "Lookout Mountain, Tennessee." The photo was of Lover's Leap, a stone terrace on the trail up Lookout Mountain. Flipping the card over, I recognized the boss's ratty handwriting. "Don't tell Shap!"

I pinned the card to the corkboard along with a dozen others, now all curling at the edges. Every time Harry went on the lamb, he sent a postcard. He might or might not be in Tennessee. Hard to tell. Last time he'd gone on the lamb, we'd received a mermaid postcard from Weeki Wachee Springs, Florida. Harry had, in truth, been hiding out just down the road at the Winkin', Blinkin', and Nod Motor Court in the town of Toad Hop. Harry liked to plant red herrings in case some ticked-off husband was trying to track him down.

The office door squeaked open, and Veenie shouldered in. She'd been at the bank making the week's deposit. She carried a white bakery bag, which I imagined held half-price day-old cinnamon twists from the Roadkill Café. When she saw me pinning up the postcard, she said, "Harry?"

"Uh huh."

I sat down at my desk and fired up the computer. Now that Avonelle had authorized us to snoop into Bromley's death, I had some items to look up. I started with arrest records. In my experience, if people had secrets, they were usually about love or money. I wondered which had been the issue with Bromley Apple.

Veenie put on a pot of coffee and split open the white donut bag while she waited for the pot to drip perk. She squinted at Harry's postcard. "Remember when we took the kids to Lookout Mountain, down in Tennessee? Remember the shenanigans Eddie and Joyce pulled?" Eddie and Joyce were my grown children.

"Not easy to forget."

Veenie tore a square off the paper bag, placed a donut on it, and slid the donut across my desk. She poured a cup of black coffee into my yard sale mug, which read, "Hello darkness, my old friend."

"Those two were always poking at each other," I said. "They were on that swinging rope bridge over the chasm at the top of Lookout Mountain. Joyce smacked Eddie for doing something stupid. Think he stuck his pointing finger in her eye so she couldn't see the view." On a clear day, Lookout Mountain boasted a view of seven states. Hard to beat entertainment like that back in the sixties.

"And then Eddie fell. Got his foot caught in one of those rope loops on that swinging bridge," said Veenie. "He hung upside down by one foot, arms flapping. He was scrawny. With that white feathery hair, he looked just like a scalded chicken hanging off that rope bridge."

I gulped a sludge of coffee. "Squawked like one too."

"Well everything turned out all right in the end."

"Well, some of it anyway," I said.

Eddie and Joyce had not killed one another. Eddie, now almost fifty, still wore white bell bottoms and Aerosmith T-shirts, lived in a refurbished Bunny Bread truck, and push-mowed yards for a living. Joyce lived on the edge of Bloomington in one of those new uppity theme-oriented suburbs. Tara was her theme. The place was filled with imitation plantation houses with Greek columns and carriage turnarounds.

Joyce was married to an insurance salesman from Atlanta who had his face glued to every inch of billboard he could rent along the back roads. He even had a full length of himself dressed in a Southern Civil War uniform painted onto the limestone ledge just outside Tunnelton, right next to the "Jesus Saves" graffiti. Smart move because locals always slowed to gawk when they approached the Jesus graffiti. No one dared paint over the graffiti, just in case it was a true sign from the Holy Ghost. The "Jesus Saves" graffiti even had its own graffiti. Below it someone had slop-painted with a brush, "Moses Invests."

Joyce was a bit uppity, so her home fit her attitude. She sometimes pretended not to know her Knobby Waters kin when we crossed paths at the Golden Corral all-you-can-stomach Monday night smorgasbord on State Road 36. Her Facebook page claimed her hometown was Bloomington, not Knobby Waters.

When it came to children, I'd long ago decided you got what the good Lord dished out. It was all potluck. A mess of genetics, I reckon. It was like God was a blind man trying to bake a cake with whatever was leftover in the cabinet. The ingredients were all there, but the proportions might be way off. You didn't know that, of course, until it was too late.

I had somehow expected more of motherhood. What I had expected I couldn't quite say. Of course, next to Veenie, I was blessed. Veenie's ex, Fergus Goens Senior, wasn't worth the clay and spit it took for the good Lord to mold him. Fergus owed

Veenie forty-plus years of child support for their son, Fergie Junior, who was holed up in my cellar next to my canned goods. He slept all day and roamed the house all night like a sick possum. He had two college degrees in musicology, some talent, and not a spit bit of ambition.

Veenie had once tried to run down her husband, Fergus Senior, but not lately. Lately she was resigned to the fact that Fergus was wasted space. She saved her strength these days for important stuff, like binge eating deep-fried Twinkies on a stick at the Pawpaw County Fair. She'd given up trying to get Fergus, whose greatest career achievement had been a year of sobriety spent drilling holes in the paperboard backs of TV sets at the Sylvania plant to pony-up and support his progeny.

Fergus liked to drink Pabst Blue Ribbon, drunk dial Veenie, and shout at her that she should be grateful because he had given her the gift of her life, Fergie Junior, and that she should be paying *him* for that.

To which Veenie always replied, "Well that's debatable."

Finding something of interest about Bromley online, I stopped cold in my scrolling through web pages.

Veenie scooted next to me on her roller-powered office chair. She peered over the top of her thick glasses. She munched on a day-old donut with one hand while popping Tums with the other.

"Will you look at that," I said to Veenie, my finger pressed against the screen. We were staring at a photo taken at the Knobby Waters Christmas Parade last year. Avonelle was the grand marshal. She was sitting up on the back seat ridge of a red convertible, courtesy of Sammy Spray's Ford Dealership over in Salem, waving like the queen with one white-gloved hand. She was wearing a fur coat that made her look like a well-groomed bear. A tall fur hat covered the crown of her apricot hair. She was scowling into the camera. A gathering of red roses was tucked into her left arm crook.

It wasn't Avonelle who I was pointing at though. It was something blurry in the background, along the sidewalk in front of the bank parking lot. There stood a man, also wearing a fur hat. It had fur earflaps, like the kind of hat a Russian might wear. It was cold, so his face was hunkered down inside his coat collar. He was breathing a frosty cloud. He was clearly talking with a woman who stood pressed up against him in the crowd. The woman wore gunmetal glasses and had dark hair stuffed under a hand-knitted grass green hat that had a shawl knitted in, making it a one-piece winter ensemble. Sheriff Boots Gibson, dressed as Santa Claus, was strolling by, throwing out penny candy and candy canes.

Veenie whipped off her glasses and tilted the computer screen closer to her nose. "Holy corn dog. Is that ...?" She looked up at me.

"I think so. Looks to be."

"Well, I'll be."

We agreed that they were looking at a photo of one of the Apple twins engaged in a heated discussion with Barbara Skaggs. The question was which one?

Half an hour later, Veenie was off to the traveling Medicare RV, which parked behind the Wal-Mart the middle of every month. It was time for her annual heart checkup with Dr. Doohickey. I was sitting in a molded plastic orange chair in the waiting area at the Apple Dental Care Clinic. I always wondered whose butt they used to make molded plastic chairs. Certainly not mine. I did a good bit of twisting trying to find a comfortable spot.

The place was crawling with children throwing crayons and Legos at one another. One especially adventurous girl stuck crayons up both her nostrils. She was panting like she might be in need of a medical intervention. There was another adult woman in the waiting area, but she was plugged into her iPhone pretending she didn't know the children, who screamed

"Mom!" at her every now and then. The gum-snapping receptionist was chatting on the speakerphone with a patient in pain, while trying to type a new patient's medical billing data into a computer. She looked up at me and pointed down a hallway. "He'll see you now," she said. "Door at the end of the hallway."

I scooted toward the hallway, stopping to pull one of the crayons out of the girl's nose along the way.

Bert Apple was a tall man with his mother's overgenerous nose and icy blue eyes. His teeth were the color and size of Chiclets. His hair was thin, wheat brown, but graying. It covered his head like a helmet. His ears were long, shaped like narrow sandals. They lay neatly flat against his head. He wore a white lab coat with a red plastic pocket protector that had Apple Dentistry printed on it in old English script, with a caricature of a giant red apple that also had a Chiclets smile.

"How can I help?" he asked.

We were seated in Bert's office. On the desk was a paperweight/pencil holder combo shaped like a giant set of dentures. A gold-gilded photo of Avonelle sitting on an upholstered fainting couch surrounded by her two sons, their wives, and their children, sat prominently next to the giant dentures. The photo was maybe ten years old. According to the rumor mill, Bert's wife had packed up their three kids and scooted back north to Gary, where she'd come from, a few years back. Bromley's wife and one daughter were still in town.

I nodded at the photo. "My condolences about your brother. Terrible shame. So young."

Bert sighed and thanked me. He looked tired, weary even. "Not everyone shares your sorrow."

I pondered that. "Do you?"

He straightened his denture pencil holder and looked at me a little sad-eyed. "Course I do. Bromley was a great dentist. Neat. Precise. Like Mother."

"But not such a great person?"

He shrugged.

"Can you think of anyone who'd want to harm your brother?"

"Honestly? Loads. Did you talk to his wife, Gretal? I'd start there."

"Was he unfaithful?"

"Nothing but."

I was regretting now not keeping up on the town gossip. I could see I had more research to do. "Did your brother know Barbara Skaggs?"

"The porch glider lady?"

"Yes. In Hound Holler."

"My brother knew everyone who wore a skirt. Don't recognize that name though. He rarely kept a mistress long. His wife chased them away. It was a game they played. I think they both enjoyed it."

"Were they swingers?"

"Bromley certainly was."

"Your brother lived out at Camelot?" Camelot Court was the largest and most expensive addition on the east end of Knobby Waters. The houses there had been built in the late eighties. They were marketed to professionals and factory managers who commuted east to Seymour or west to Bedford. The development had a fake pond at the entrance with an equally fake gaggle of geese floating on the pond. The gatehouse, which was really just a storage unit for lawn-care equipment, was shaped like the turret on a castle. When I was growing up, Camelot had been an endless rift of limestone ledges and mud wallows, site of the Weeselpleck family pig farm. Despite the Camelot name, I knew for a fact that neither King Arthur nor Guinevere had ever spent a night there. Porky Pig, maybe.

Bert cleared his throat. "Bromley has … had … the largest house out there. 175. Mine's next door, 177."

"You know the names of any of your brother's mistresses?"

He shrugged his shoulders. "Read the phone book. Doing that would be about the same as reading his little black book."

"He had a little black book?" I always thought that term was just an expression.

"Prouder of that than his dental degree."

"Do you have it?

He shook his head. "Think he kept it on his cell phone."

I glanced over Bert's shoulder and studied the professional portrait of him and his brother standing back to back, arms crossed, in freshly pressed white dental coats. I wondered what had made Bromley so irresistible. He certainly *thought* he was a stud muffin. That had probably been enough in a town as sleepy-eyed as Knobby Waters. People ran off with each other all the time, mostly hoping to escape the boredom. Just this past winter, on Valentine's Day, three-hundred-pound Shirley Hill, the bookmobile librarian, and four-foot-tall Peanut Gilstrap, the sweep-up guy at Pokey's Tavern, stole Shirley's husband's Harley and roared away together. No one saw that coming, least of all Shirley's husband, Owen. He made the state police put out an APB on the Harley. When they asked about Shirley, and if he wanted to put out a protective order on her in case she'd been kidnapped, he said, "Hell no. I want that Harley back. The wife's on her own."

Bert stood up. "You want a cleaning while you're here, Ruby Jane? On the house, seeing as how you're helping Mom out, and all."

"I'll call," I promised, hightailing it out of the office.

It was lunchtime, so I loped on home. I found leftover deer chili in the refrigerator. I found Sassy sitting cross-legged on the floor in the living room. She was wearing a silver lamé mini dress and gold lamé gladiator-style sandals that laced up to her knees. Her hair was teased and held up in a Grecian style gold-toned headband adorned with tiny olive leaves. She was sucking on a Camel Non-Filter cigarette. On the floor in front of her was a metal ashtray shaped like Elvis in his heyday. Also, stacks and stacks of Knobby Waters high school yearbooks.

I waved away the smoke. I'd grown up locked in cars and houses and PTA meetings with everybody puffing, and I was still alive. I wasn't going to get my undies in a bunch about the health dangers of secondhand smoke this late in the game.

"What in tarnation are you doing?" I asked Sassy as I plopped down on the couch with a mug of deer chili. I'd sprinkled Velveeta over the deer chili and was waiting for the cheese skim to cool so I didn't burn my mouth. I had a cold bottle of Big Red soda pop to wash it all down.

Sassy pointed to the 1967 yearbook. Next to it was a green spiral stenographer's notebook that dated back to when we all took high school shorthand together. "Making my senior hottie list, sugar. Need your help."

"For?" I blew across the top of my chili mug. The Velveeta quivered like pudding skim. It was cooling nicely.

"Dating, silly. Miss Sassy is back in the game. I've been lonely as a heartbroken hen ever since Melvin got called back to DC for work. Hoping to find a local who has a bit of spit and shine to them. Can't everybody in Pawpaw County be a hillbilly."

Melvin Beal had been Sassy's last man. He was a right nice gentleman from Louisville she'd lured up to Knobby Waters after she lip-locked him at a VFW shindig on the *Bell of Louisville* river boat. I had half a mind to point out to Sassy that she was born and raised in the hills just like the rest of us, but I needed Sassy's extra forty bucks a week in rent to buy tires for the Impala. Dickie, who had just retired from the Lube It Up, had done the Chevy's last state inspection. He'd looked the other way when it came to my tires. They were balder than Kojak. Now that Dickie was retired, I was bound to get Spike Hill, that grumpy young idiot with the fishing hooks pierced through his lips, at my next inspection. Without Veenie to sweeten the deal by flirting with Dickie, I'd be needing four new tires, God knows what else, just to keep the Impala street legal.

Veenie strolled into the room carrying an orange plastic bag from the Hoosier Feedbag's deli department. She pulled out two quart containers that looked to hold ground pink meat sprinkled with chunks of white fat. "Ham salad. Twofer," Veenie explained when she saw me studying the container.

Ham salad never went on sale, except on the Fourth of July, so this was a real score.

Sassy had a package of black dot stickers and was turning the pages of the yearbook. She looked up and waved at Veenie.

I explained. "Sassy is trolling old yearbooks for dates."

Sassy flipped open the notebook. "Let's start with the live ones."

"You always did have high standards," Veenie said as she scooted back to the kitchen to make herself a ham salad sandwich.

Sassy asked me to point out who was deceased in our graduating class. She then placed a black dot sticker on the foreheads of each of the dearly departed. When she was done, it looked like most all the men in our class had converted to Hinduism.

"Dear Lord, these here all that's left?" Sassy sounded disappointed, like she'd arrived too late at what she'd hoped would be a promising yard sale.

Six men were still aboveground and upright in the class of 1967. Dickie Freeman ("spoken for," squeaked Veenie from the kitchen.), Boots Gibson ("still crushing on RJ," Veenie advised), and Bernie "Twinkles" Tatlock, (gay and married to a short-haul truck driver from Tennessee, explained me and Veenie simultaneously). Number four, Tubby Thomas, was career Navy and rumored to be living in a retirement nudist commune in Pensacola, Florida with three wives.

Number five, Petey Newkirk, was the best looking of the bunch, with wavy hair and Kirk Douglas dimples. Rumor had it he was doing time for robbing pop machines outside convenience stores around Chicago. He was cute all right but like all the Newkirk men he had dog kibble for brains.

"He ever rob anything bigger than a pop machine?" asked Sassy.

"Nope," I said. "Started at the bottom and stayed there."

Sassy slapped a black dot on Petey's forehead.

Only the sixth man, Bruce "Fussy" Jones, a local contractor, was single. Better yet, he was recently divorced and owned the prime show house in Camelot Court. Also, as the contractor who built the Leisure Hills retirement community, he held controlling interest in that project. He drove a shiny new canary yellow Lincoln Continental and captained a tricked out pontoon boat that all the men lusted over out at the White River Boat and Gun Club.

"He have health issues?" asked Sassy.

Veenie took a hit off my Big Red to help her swallow a hunk of ham salad. "He can walk. He can talk."

"Still drive at night? I like for a man to pick me up. Take me out to eat. I don't want to be racing around with some sour old pickle in a wheelchair rushing to hit all the early bird buffets."

"Sure, he drives all hours," I said. "I've seen him whizzing by here in the evenings on his way to the Boat and Gun Club. He's the Lord High Admiral." In a bigger place, The White River Boat and Gun Club might have passed for a yacht club. In Knobby Waters, being a small river town, you didn't need both a boat *and* a gun to join, either would suffice, but most respectable members had both. And any fool who aspired to a position of leadership mounted a motor on their boat. Fussy's pontoon boat was top drawer. He had a power harpoon rig mounted on the bow for gigging at carp, gar, buffalo, and shad.

The pontoon also had a little metal shack where Fussy kept a mess of high-powered BBQ equipment. All that glitz pretty much insured him the lead spot in the annual White River regatta.

Sassy's face lit up. "He got a girl?"

Veenie and I exchanged glances. "Nope," I said. "Nope, don't believe he has one of those." What we didn't tell Sassy was that Fussy Jones was rumored to have a few other issues when it came to women, but heh, that was unsubstantiated gossip. We were all adults. Anyone with an ounce of brains might have figured out in advance that a couple nicknamed Sassy and Fussy were destined to have some hair-tearing issues.

Veenie and I left Sassy to plot out her manhunt, and after finishing our lunch and gassing up the Impala, squealed on over to Camelot Court to interrogate Bromley Apple's widow.

CHAPTER SEVEN

I t was late afternoon before Veenie and I arrived at Bromley's house in Camelot Court. We were hoping to catch Bromley's wife, Gretal Apple, unawares. Being Bromley's wife, and a disgruntled one at that according to Bert, we were hoping she might have the lowdown on who might have sent her husband into an early retirement. If Bert were to be believed, the list of suspects might be longer than our life expectancy.

Gretal Apple wasn't home. Her daughter, Kimmy, answered the door. She told us that her mother was shopping over in Bedford. Kimmy looked to be about twenty years old. She wore thick eyeliner, purple lipstick, and an all-black wardrobe with a purple velvet cape that put me in mind of Vampira, the late-night hostess on the local cable channel's movie night *Fright Fest*. It wasn't anywhere near Halloween, so I figured Kimmy might be a little odd. Or maybe she was normal, and that was the way hip girls dressed these days. I'd given up on tracking fashion trends back when boys started wearing their underwear on the outside of their pants. When it came to fashion, I relied on Veenie to keep me in the know.

Veenie asked Kimmy, "You one of them steampunks?"

"Might be. What are you?" Kimmy's eyes swept across Veenie. Today she was wearing a Day-Glo orange poncho with wool argyle knee socks and purple dotted capri pants. It was seventy degrees, but Veenie's internal thermostat had cracked at menopause. Her little wave of white hair was moussed up

Kewpie doll style. Her tiny feet were clad in rubbery white cross-training shoes that looked like melted marshmallows.

Veenie stared Kimmy down. "This here is my Monday casual wear. I like to start the week off relaxed."

Kimmy looked at me. "She on meds?"

"Loads of them."

"But she's safe, right?"

"Long as you don't poke at her."

"Believe me, I'm not touching that."

"Hey," cried Veenie. "I'm right here. And my ears ain't busted."

"Sorry," said Kimmy. "Old people kinda creep me out."

"That makes two of us, sweet pea." Veenie ducked under Kimmy's arm and darted into the living room. The room had a cathedral ceiling with a floor-to-ceiling limestone fireplace on one end and stairs that led up to a second-floor landing with a railing that probably branched off into three bedrooms. "Nice crib," said Veenie. "Got anything solid to drink?"

"Diet Coke. My mom drinks it."

"That stuff will kill you. Mabel Beavers been drinking that since the seventies and now she sees Nazi U-boats coming up White River." Veenie busied herself snooping around the house. She found a desk over in the corner and began rifling through the papers.

Kimmy swooped forward, cape and all. "Hey, you can't do that!"

"Course I can." Veenie rifled some more.

"I'm calling the police."

Veenie opened a checkbook and scanned the register. "Ask for Sheriff Boots Gibson. He has the hots for Ruby Jane."

Kimmy looked at me, perplexed. "Who are you people?"

I gave her the 411 on why we were there, representing the agency and her grandmother. "We're investigating your father's death. Anyone you know might want to harm him?"

"My mom."

"They fought?"

"Duh. Like all the time." Kimmy sprawled out on a white sofa, careful to pool her cape to one side. "She tried to run him down once. In broad daylight. In our driveway. Claimed her high heel got stuck on the gas pedal."

"What did they fight about?"

"Daddy was a big old man ho."

"Was that a problem?"

"Not for him."

"Did you know any of his girlfriends."

"Ewww! He never brought them home or anything kinky like that."

I heard a garage door roll up. Kimmy looked through the kitchen and what appeared to be a laundry room toward the back garage door. "Bet that's her."

"Your mom?"

"Hey, you catch on quick."

A tall redheaded woman came into the kitchen cradling a canvas bag from the organic grocery. The place was called Healthy Living, but Veenie called it Wealthy Living. They charged an arm and a leg for good, old-fashioned poor people food like dandelion salad and bone marrow broth.

"We got company, Kimmy?" Gretal shouted the question into the living room as she put the groceries away in the kitchen.

Veenie popped up in the kitchen door. "Law enforcement. Investigating your husband's murder."

Gretal was wearing half-glasses hung around her neck on a jeweled lanyard. She was dressed in black yoga pants and a black sleeveless turtleneck. Her red hair was short, swept up against her head like a duck's tail. She eyed Veenie. "You don't look like the police. You look like an escapee from *Game of Thrones*."

Gretal brushed past Veenie into the living room. She carried an open bottle of red wine and two wine glasses upside down by their long stems. "Why on earth are you questioning me? I haven't touched Bromley in years. But say, let's drink to whoever did."

I declined the wine. "You don't look grief stricken."

She kicked off her high heels. "I'm not. Besides, what makes you think he was killed? He ate like a pig. Donuts and Diet Coke for breakfast." She poured two glasses of wine. When everyone refused one, she drank from both of them.

Kimmy spoke up. "These are the detectives Grammy hired."

Gretal eyed us as she rubbed the arch of her right foot. "Aren't you two a little old to be playing Nancy Drew?"

Veenie plopped down on the couch next to Gretal. "Social security is for shits. We need extra money to buy Twinkies and stuff."

"That's awful," said Kimmy. "Don't you have husbands to look after you?"

"That what you think husbands do?"

"I'm not having a husband," said Kimmy, glaring at her mother. "I'm making a baby in a test tube."

Gretal knocked down another glass of wine. "Can't argue with that."

I jumped in. "Any idea who killed your husband?"

"God no. Could have been anyone, but who says he was murdered?" She set aside the glasses. She was drinking out of the bottle now.

"Good point." April, the coroner, wouldn't issue an autopsy report for another day or two. Bromley could have died of natural causes, but then why was he wearing a scarecrow's outfit and sitting on a porch glider? Nothing about his death looked natural to me.

I asked Gretal, "Did you know Barbara Skaggs?"

"No."

"Know your husband was involved with her? Maybe having an affair with her?"

"Was he? That *would* surprise me. He never could keep his zipper up, but I saw that woman's photo. Not his type."

"Then why was he found dead on her porch? Did he know anyone from Hound Holler? You have family down there?"

"Oh, please. I've never been to Hound Holler. My people are from Columbus. I only live in this hillbilly haven because Bromley insisted, and his mother staked him to that dental practice. I'd have left him eons ago, but Avonelle, that old hamster, made me sign a prenup that was in force until we had children. That's pretty much how Kimmy came to be."

Veenie jumped on that one. "So you inherited everything when Bromley kicked?"

"Pretty much."

"Sounds like motive to me."

"Oh, please," she rolled her eyes. "Everything Bromley owned was wrapped up in that dental practice. The only thing he owned much of was debt. What am I going to do with half a dental office? And this house is underwater, double mortgaged. Should have started a denture lab like his cousin over in Salem. That's where the big bucks are in this neck of the woods."

Kimmy spoke up. "I know Barbara Skaggs."

Gretal looked surprised. "How's that?"

"She and daddy weren't involved. She was Grampy Will's lust bunny. He was gaga over her. He used to take me down there with him on Sundays when you left me with Grammy and Grampy Apple to go to the Ashram meetings."

"I thought he was taking you to the Pancake Palace while Grammy went to church."

"Barbara worked at the Pancake Palace. We'd pick her up. She'd make us pancakes down at her place. Then she and Grampy would sit on her porch glider and play a game they called find the bald gopher."

"Hey, I know that game," said Veenie.

"That's disgusting," said Gretal.

Kimmy disagreed. "Actually it was kind of sweet, in an old pervert kind of way. Gramps was gaga over Barbara. I think he was in love."

Gretal finished the wine and uncorked another bottle. "Was your father involved in any of this hillbilly hanky-panky?"

"Nah. He was busy with his own women. He always met them out on Lover's Lane, over at the Moon Glo Motor Lodge, down by the covered bridge. I could tell when he'd been out cruising because he came home with corn stalks stuck up like giant matches in the back bumper of the Lincoln."

"Figures," grunted Gretal. "He stuck his little pale stalk everywhere."

It was getting late. Time to knock off for the day. Harry didn't pay overtime. We left our calling card with Kimmy and Gretal and asked them to call if they remembered anything important. Kimmy said she would. Gretal mumbled.

Back in the Impala, Veenie popped open the glove compartment to get a little light going. She ruffled something between her fingers. She had her neck down, nose to the thing.

I put the Impala in gear. "What in the Sam Hill are you doing?" I asked.

She peered up at me. "Reading Bromley's checkbook register."

I stomped the brake.

Veenie bounced off the console like a Day-Glo orange Super Ball. "Why'd you do that for? I'm old. Got bones like Jell-O. You could have broken my hip." Her glasses were wobbly on her face. Her nose bridge was a bit red, like I might have bruised it a tad.

"You stole evidence? From Bromley's desk?"

"Don't be a wiener. His checkbook was sitting out there in the open, calling my name. Besides, he's dead. Dead people got no rights. Everybody knows you can go through dead people's stuff."

"What's in that check register?"

Veenie flashed the black leather register my way. I flipped on the overhead dome light. Her fat, little pointy finger was poking at an entry penned last week. One thousand dollars, paid to the order of Ms. Barbara Skaggs. That check was proof positive that Bromley Apple knew Barbara Skaggs. It proved something else too: people had been lying to us. That idea burned my bacon. I squealed out of Camelot so hard the fake geese rippled across the pond trying to make a break for it.

"Maybe it was Bromley who was having that affair with Barbara, not his dad?" I said, reasoning out loud.

Veenie fiddled with the eight-track tape player that her boy toy, Dickie, had installed in the Impala for us. "I saw this show on YouTube where the old men handed their mistresses over to their sons when they were done with them. Men are pigs like that sometimes."

"Were they Mormons?"

"Nah, just normal men."

I chewed on that idea for a while. Barbara Skaggs didn't look like much of a catch to me, but then I'd known men to do some pretty weird stuff in the name of lust. Ever since Great Aunt Shish told me what Great Uncle Moose really did with that dancing standard poodle of his out in the barn—Ms. Eva, he called her—I understood that a man's desires can run pretty muddy. I also understood why no one in the family would open Uncle Moose's barn door without first yelling "I'm coming! Here I come!" before storming into the stalls. As Grammy Titsy always said, you don't really need to know every little thing about your kin or neighbors.

While I was chewing my cheek over why Bromley would have given Barbara a thousand dollars the week he died, Veenie, who loved to cruise with the tunes cranked, popped in an eight-track tape of Dolly Parton promising to always love everybody. The bass was thumping so loudly that everybody who lived on the east side of Knobby Waters got to enjoy the sixties with us again. The eight-track player worked most of the time, if you poked at it. Veenie kept a Philips head screwdriver in the glove compartment so we could rewind tapes by hand as needed, because the rewind doohickey was busted on the tape deck. Our selection was limited, but we'd found even the most heart-wrenching things in life could be set to a soundtrack from Hank Williams or The Eagles or Dolly Parton.

We rumbled on home, stopping at the Go Go Gas to get a family-sized bag of pork cracklings. I was so frustrated I picked up a double pack of pink Hostess snowballs on my way out the door just to calm my nerves before bedtime. When I exited the Go Go, snacks in hand, the Impala wasn't parked out by the pumps where I'd left it. Veenie had taken the wheel—she isn't supposed to drive, long story—and was laying rubber up and down the edge of the driveway. I had to dangle the pink snowballs Veenie's way before she'd zoom over and hand the wheel back to me. Once she sank her teeth into a snowball, she was sedated. After gobbling down the cupcake, she fell asleep in the front seat. She was deep in her dreams, snoring like a hound dog, by the time we reached home.

CHAPTER EIGHT

B oots visited the office bright and early the next morning. He fiddled with his gun belt as he fired questions at me. "Were you and Veenie cruising in the Impala last night? Listening to Dolly Parton cranked up high? Cutting donuts over at the Go Go Gas?"

"No," I lied.

"Well I got several complaints says you were." He pulled a pile of yellow sticky notes out of his shirt pocket. They fluttered onto my desk like butterflies.

I eyed the notes. "People are petty. They like to complain. You ought to know that by now."

Boots hitched up his belt. He placed a booted foot on my chair rung. "What got you all riled up last night, Ruby Jane?"

"Listening to Veenie rattle on about what random body part fell off her this week."

"Really, because I heard tell you were out at Camelot visiting Bromley's widow, Gretal. She tell you anything you ought to be sharing with the law?"

I squirmed, mostly because Bromley's stolen checkbook was on my desk in plain sight. I'd had way too much Sunday school as a kid. I sweated when I lied to authority, even Boots Gibson, which was silly because I'd seen him looking awfully unofficial back in VBS long about 1953. He was five at the time and had been messing with the grape Kool-Aid powder in the church kitchen, stealing it straight out of the packet by wetting his fingers and running them through the purple sugar packets. The little fool stained all his fingers purple. His fingers, in turn, stained his privates purple when he latched on to relieve himself in the outhouse behind the rectory. Veenie had taken to calling him "Grape Nuts" Gibson after that, whenever she wanted to get his goat.

Not much authority in that.

I pecked at my keyboard, trying to look busy in the hope that he'd go away. "Gretal said she knew nothing."

"And you believed her?"

"Dang it! I didn't say that, Boots."

He grunted. "Don't lock those cute little lips. This is a police investigation. Might be murder. You can't be obstructing justice, Ruby Jane."

"Stop fussing at me. I don't have to share anything with you. We don't even know if there ought to be an investigation. Maybe Bromley just up and died. It happens." I was thinking of my husband, Charlie, who'd been about Bromley's age when he went facedown into the potato salad.

The door squeaked and Veenie stepped in. She glanced at Boots but kept quiet. Guilt screwed up her face when she spied Bromley's check register on my desk, right out in the open. "Excuse me," she said, grabbing the checkbook off the desk and running off to hide in the ladies' room.

Boots blew out a huff. "I'm going now, but if you hear anything about Bromley's death, you need to be calling me, you hear?" He shuffled out the door.

Veenie came out of the restroom drying her hands on a dish towel. "What did old Grape Nuts want? He still after you for a date?"

I eyed her and ignored the last part of her question. "Boots heard we were out at Camelot Court interrogating Gretal Apple. He was nosing around to see if we were doing his job. It's your day off. Why you here?"

"Pappy."

Pappy Tuttle was Veenie's dad. He had retired from the brick plant after fifty years of feeding coal into the giant kilns. Luckily he had a fireman's pension that kept him swimming in corn dogs and Schlitz up at Leisure Hills. "What's up?"

"His little red choo-choo done chugged around the bend again. They want me to stop by. See if I can jog his brain back on track."

Pappy Tuttle was ninety-eight years old some days. Other days he was nine. It didn't seem to matter much to him. The nursing staff got all riled up when he slipped a decade or two. Veenie didn't mind the slippage, but the nurses called her when Pappy's screws started popping. They didn't want to be liable if his mind chugged down the tracks never to be seen again.

I had taken the Chevy to the office that morning. Leisure Hills was out by the river. Veenie needed a lift. Her macular degeneration had gotten so bad she wasn't technically allowed to drive. She had a go-kart, custom built for her by her boy toy, Dickie, but the thing only had a lawn mower engine and no shade roof. She'd have been a red boil ready to pop by the time she reached Leisure Hills, either that or dead in a ditch. If she knocked off dead, I'd never hear the end of how I could have saved her, but no, I'd sent her to an early grave. No way I was letting her hold something like that over my head for the rest of our earthly days. I grabbed my messenger bag and the keys to the Impala, and we were off.

I gunned the Chevy up the private gravel drive to Leisure Hills, which was lined with ragged marigolds and weeping sycamore trees. Leisure Hills sat on a hill high above a bend in the White River. Visitors were welcome but were supposed to stop and sign in at a security gate. Spying the gate, I honked at Jed, the gatekeeper, whom I'd known for a coon's age—third cousin on my mother's side—and he lifted the mechanical arm, letting us zoom on in with a quick wave.

We shot under a giant Disney-like archway at the entrance to the home that promised "The Time of Your Life for the Time of Your Life." The old folk's home itself was big and bright yellow, with a wide, well-shaded front porch. The porch was lined with oldsters in scooters and wheelchairs. Seniors bundled in afghans sat in a pair of porch swings at each end of the porch reading books and swiping at computer tablets. Most folks took rooms at Leisure Hills because they couldn't quite hop around like they used to and needed some type of assistance with walking. That's how Pappy Tuttle ended up there. His spine was all squeezed down with age.

Pappy didn't mind being "a man of Leisure" as they called the residents. They gave him biscuits and gravy for breakfast, fried chicken for lunch, pork chops for supper, and a new tub of chaw every Friday night. All that was fine and dandy with him. As far as he was concerned, he'd died and gone to heaven.

Veenie and I entered the lobby to find it crammed with old ladies in floppy straw sun hats and baseball caps engaged in a heated euchre tournament. The loud speaker system was playing the Statler Brothers. Everybody threw us a wave as we loped back along the hallway toward Pappy's place. We headed to the back, then out onto an interior brick patio where Pappy was usually parked this time of day.

Pappy was sitting in his motorized chair when we arrived. He had been a decent enough looking fellow back in the day, but age and hard living had sucked him down into himself like a lump of warm mashed potatoes. The aides wheeled him onto the patio every day to get some Vitamin D, whether he wanted it or not. Mostly he did not. He preferred to sit in the dark and watch *Mr. Ed* reruns on his portable Zenith.

It was a bright and sunny day. When we arrived, they'd left him out in a puddle of sunshine on the patio next to a bed of purple petunias. The petunias were arranged in circular patterns inside a pair of old tractor tires that the Ladies of Leisure, the retirement village's ladies auxiliary, had slop-washed white.

He tossed his aluminum grab-it stick in the air in a one-handed hello as we approached. He wore yellow Crocs and knee-high wool argyle socks pulled up over the legs of his overalls. He wore a red woolen shirt under all that. He'd stretched a red Indiana University sock cap over his head to block out the sun, as he did every morning. The top of the hat was pointy, making him look like a garden gnome. He looked perfectly sane and normal to us.

"Them there nurses are trying to boil my brains," he complained as we reached his scooter.

"You misbehaving, Pappy?" Veenie asked.

"Them idiots stole my horses," he sniffled.

"You don't have no horses."

He spat chaw into a Mountain Dew can. "I know. They took 'em."

Oh boy. This could go on for hours. Veenie asked him what year it was.

He ignored her and started cleaning out his ears with a bobby pin. A large, yellow hairy glob popped out of one ear canal.

I said, "He might be digging out more than ear wax."

Veenie squatted down and peered into his ears, then his eyes. She took her thumb and finger and spread open the lids, which drooped, exhausted with age. "What year is it Pappy? You know the year?"

"1947," said Pappy.

"Close enough," Veenie said. She patted his speckled hand.

The head day nurse, Mrs. Pruitt, came out looking all prim and proper in her peach nursing outfit and marshmallow shoes. "He's been addled like that since breakfast."

"What'd you feed him?" Veenie asked.

"We didn't do this," huffed Nurse Pruitt.

Veenie shrugged. "Seems ok to me. Normal as he ever was."

The nurse objected. "He thinks it's 1947."

"Lucky him," Veenie said. "He's gonna be real excited when you wheel him in and he discovers color TV and air conditioning."

I watched a kid with a nose ring, his shoes untied with tongues gagging out, slink by at the edge of the patio. It was a Sneed. I'd know a Sneed anywhere. That whole bunch had arms so long their knuckles dragged the ground. They had a grandmother, Sally Sneed, in Leisure Hills, who roomed across the hall from Pappy. She was a notorious bingo shark and heartbreaker. She and Pappy had done the dance with no pants in the petunia beds last Fourth of July. They both claimed they'd been sleepwalking. Blamed it on the meds. Veenie and I both thanked Jesus that she wasn't fertile. The Tuttle gene pool didn't need even a whiff of Sneed dumped into it.

Veenie pulled a butterscotch candy out of her pocket. She unwrapped it and popped it into Pappy's mouth. "Sugar might be a little low."

Pappy brightened a bit. His head popped out of his lumpy mashed potato torso. "Why you here, Lavinia?" he asked. He looked around like maybe he'd been caught doing something. "It Saturday?" On Saturdays, Veenie often took him out to the covered bridge fishing. Mostly they spun around in circles in a rowboat in the muddy water catching cat tails. Neither of them could cast worth dog crap, but they both enjoyed the father-daughter time.

Veenie patted Pappy's hand. "Your mind was sliding around."

"Shoot. My mind is fine. Rest of me is a mess. Wheel me back in before the buzzards get me."

He meant the turkey buzzards. There was a family of them living in the big sycamore trees along the river behind Leisure Hills.

"Okeydokey," said Veenie.

CHAPTER NINE

A vonelle called several times demanding updates. I was embarrassed to confess that Veenie and I were spinning our muddy mental tires. We'd been talking to people all week, waddling around in circles getting nowhere, like thick-headed possums. No one knew anything about Bromley or old William and his affair with Barbara. The whole town had a bad case of zip lip.

"You know anything about a thousand dollar check Bromley wrote to Barbara the week before he died?" I asked Avonelle. "You got any idea why Bromley wrote that check? What business Bromley might have had with Barbara?

"Lord no," she said.

It occurred to both of us at the same time that maybe Barbara had been squeezing the lemon at both ends, so to speak. "Maybe she was blackmailing Bromley, threatening to get chatty about his stepsiblings if he didn't cough up support money."

"Well, her kind has been known to do that sort of thing," reasoned Avonelle. "But then why did she write me asking for money straight out? Why not just take my son's money and be gone?"

"Got me. Doesn't sound right that she'd be sneaking around threatening to dirty the Apple family name while also asking you for legal support money."

I heard Avonelle sigh deeply. "Honestly, if William or Bromley were here right now, I'd whack them both up the side of the head with my purse."

I knew that feeling. I reckoned every woman did.

"I'm going to talk to Barbara again," I offered.

"Keep me posted. But let's get this wrapped up. I want to clear Bromley's name. The family doesn't need more gossip floating around town."

By the time I steered the Chevy toward the Pancake Palace, it was late afternoon. Only one car was in the parking lot, a white SUV with Illinois plates. I got a prime parking space up by the front door. Barbara was standing at the hostess podium when I came in the door. She was wearing a big plastic corsage shaped like an orange tiger lily with a banner that read, "Ask me about our waffle and wieners early bird extravaganza."

I was well acquainted with their waffles. Barbara, I knew, was well acquainted with the wieners of Knobby Waters. Being me, and not Veenie, I kept my clapper shut.

Barbara's face tightened when she saw me. "Booth or counter?" she asked politely.

"Booth," I said. Everybody always said the same thing, don't know why she bothered asking.

I followed her to an orange booth and listened while she gave me the ten-cent tour of the daily specials. I ordered a bottomless pot of black coffee and a stack of blueberry pancakes. "Can you sit a spell?" I asked as I handed back the menu.

She looked over her shoulder nervously. No one else was around except for a man at the counter eating some pie. I saw a bearded cook sliding back and forth in the serving window. He wore one of those tall floppy white hats. "Got a break coming up in twenty minutes," she said. "That do?"

"Yep," I said.

She poured the coffee and was back in a jiffy with my pancakes. They floated in a puddle of purple simple syrup. Not a blueberry in sight. I didn't know why people thought the twenty-first century was so dang blasted wonderful. Last century you could buy an entire breakfast for a quarter, and they gave you real blueberries to boot.

Barbara kept her word. She scooted into the booth across from me as I was enjoying my third cup of coffee. I got to the point quickly since she was at work and I was old enough to respect things like that. "If you didn't know Bromley, why'd he give you a thousand dollars the week before he died?"

Her eyes widened, like a polecat caught raiding the trash. She fingered her corsage, trying to get it a little straighter. "Okay, look," she fessed up, "maybe I did know him. A little bit."

"You were lovers?"

"God, no. Oh dear Jesus, no. What kind of jezebel you take me for? I'd never cheat on William like that. Me and him, we were in love."

It seemed odd to me that a woman who'd been sleeping with a married man would react so hotly to an accusation of cheating, but hey, morals were slippery little minnows. "So what was the thousand dollars he gave you about?"

She leaned back in the booth and chewed on her little fingernail. "I never cashed that check. You check with Bromley's bank. I never did nothing with that check. Still have it in my purse." She rose to get her purse.

I laid my hand on hers. "No matter. I believe you, but what was the money for?"

"He didn't want his mama to find out about William's children, his stepkin. I didn't ask him for that money. He knew about me and William. After William passed, he was afraid his mama would find out about me. He wanted me to move out of town. Claimed I made the family look bad. Me. After all his whoring—excuse my French—around town, he was afraid I might make the Apple family look like common trash."

"You turned his money down?"

"Course I did."

"Out of pride?"

"No. It was more because … well, how far was a thousand dollars going to get me? I didn't think it was a fair and right offer. I mean, I have to raise them three kids. That'll take a sight more than a thousand dollars." She checked her wristwatch. "Dinner trade will be parading in shortly. I got to wheel out the mini-pancake machine. The Baptist Ladies Missionary Society comes in promptly at four. They're addicted to the early bird wieners and beans. They get cantankerous if their wieners aren't warmed up just right."

"Wait," I said, "did you ask Bromley for more money?"

"Course not. I'm not looking to pull up roots and leave town. Took me almost ten years to work my way up at the Pancake Palace. I get medical. I get ten days paid vacation. No weekends or overnights. Where else am I going to get a deal like that?"

"Did he offer you more money?"

I heard the bell over the door buzz. Mabel Hudsucker and her party of Baptist soul saviors crowded into the foyer. They were carrying their Sunday purses and clucking like Rhode Island Reds.

"Yes," said Barbara. "He kept pestering me. He offered to set me up in my own little apartment out in California somewhere, but like I said, I wasn't interested. All my kin are close by, down in Washington County. I want my boys knowing my family, since Avonelle don't seem in no hurry to add extra pages to her family album."

"Did you talk to Bromley the morning he died?"

"No," she said. "Like I told you and that sheriff, I have no idea why he was on my porch. Reckon he came back to try and persuade me to move on for his mama's sake. But I never saw him or touched him that morning. And I didn't take his filthy hush money either."

Mabel and her hens were beelining it to the back curved corner booth. Barbara had to scuttle to keep up. She scooped up an armful of menus and a fresh pot of coffee. She was flinging menus right and left by the time I left the place.

CHAPTER TEN

I was at the office poking at the computer, checking databases for financial information on Bromley. Gretal had said he was in debt up to his floppy ears. What I was finding online screamed the same. Greed and lust had been dragging people kicking and screaming to an early grave ever since the good Lord shouted, "Let there be light." Bromley had been abundantly blessed on both counts. If money had been the motive behind Bromley's early demise, it surely wasn't his wife, Gretal, who'd offed him. She told the God's honest truth when she told me and Veenie that all she stood to inherit was debt. Heaps of it, I'd come to discover.

While mulling over who'd have motive to see Bromley strap on his angel wings early, I decided to ring the coroner, see if she had a cause of death or other interesting tidbits on Bromley from the autopsy yet.

April answered right away, but she sounded a little out of breath, distracted. "I was just getting ready to hop on over to the funeral home, take the official paperwork. Meet me there?"

"In a jiffy," I said.

I bumped into Veenie on my way out the door as I locked up the office. She'd been down the street at the VFW catching up on the local scuttlebutt. Well, I called it scuttlebutt, but Veenie called it "intelligence gathering" now that we were paid professional snoops. Chin wagging at the VFW was one of Veenie's favorite professional activities. Also, just about her only form of exercise.

"Learn anything important?" I asked.

"Sure did." Veenie's tiny blue eyes were twinkling.

"Let me have it."

"Nurse Pruitt, you remember her?"

"Ada Pruitt? Pappy's nurse from out at Leisure Hills? Married to Jimmy, who farms over around Fort Ritner, couple of years behind me in school?"

"Yeah, her. Well, anyway, besides working out at Leisure Hills, she works here in town, part time for Doc Scarborough. Sees a lot of town folks right regular. She claims Bromley came into the doc's more than once with one of them sexual diseases. John-Or-Rhea, I think it was."

"You mean gonorrhea?"

"Something like that."

"She have any idea who he got it from?"

"Well, he was supposed to draw up a list of his partners and all for the public health folks, but he claimed his wife, Gretal, was the one and only, and then he slipped Nurse Pruitt a gift card for two free porcelain crowns. And then the VD report paperwork accidently got lost somewhere in her wastebasket."

"You reckon that's important?"

"Could be. If some fellow gave me crotch critters, I'd be mad enough to take a swing at him."

Veenie was right. Love spats and money problems were the top motives for murder. I filled Veenie in on Bromley's dire financial situation.

"Bromley being in debt don't surprise me none," said Veenie. "The high and mighty are often the same ones ain't got a pot to piss in. You still think Barbara ain't involved in all this?"

I told Veenie about my meeting with Barbara out at the Pancake Palace and how Bromley had tried to pay her off to disappear to California, taking the kids with her.

Veenie shook her head. "You believe her?"

"Think so. What she said rang true to me."

"And she's got no idea why Bromley was found dead at her place in that scarecrow getup?"

"Not a clue. Look," I said, changing the subject to a more hopeful possibility, "I'm going over to the funeral parlor to see April. She's got the results of Bromley's autopsy, and she sounded excited about it."

I didn't have to ask Veenie if she wanted to tag along.

It was lunchtime by the time I swung the Impala into the gravel parking lot behind the Reddy Funeral Home. Locals knew the name wasn't pronounced "ready," but "reedy," as in Moses and the bull rush reeds, but derelicts had fun with the name anyway. At present, some smartass had marked up the sign in the back to read "Reddy—OR NOT—Funeral Home."

April's white coroner van was pulled tight to the back entrance. There was a green-striped awning over that entrance and a cement rolling ramp so ambulances could pull up and unload the dearly departed without the body getting all wet or covered with foul weather. I thought it was a nice touch.

Reddy Funeral Home had been doing send-offs for Knobby Waters residents for close to a hundred years. The Reddy family still owned the enterprise. Beryl Reddy III arranged the services and comforted the families, as did his pappy and grandpappy before him. Like all businesses, they had diversified to keep up with the times. They offered cremations, and green funerals. If you went green they'd tie you up in the root ball of a tree and plant you just about anywhere you might care to take your eternal slumber.

Most folks in Knobby Waters preferred to be stuffed and displayed the old-fashioned way. The White River Cemetery was dotted with Waskoms and Reynoldses. I was pretty much planning on it being my eternal bedroom. I kind of liked the idea of having familiar neighbors in the Holy Hereafter.

Veenie, who loved a great send off, was wondering what method of burial Bromley had chosen. "If Gretal's right about Bromley's debts, Avonelle will be paying for the services. I reckon she'll go traditional. On the other hand, I heard tell being roasted is a heck of a lot cheaper. Whole town knows Avonelle is so tight she squeaks when she walks."

"But it would look mighty bad," I mused, "penny pinching on a family funeral, for your prized son to boot. And you know how Avonelle is about appearances."

Curious to see how Avonelle might have resolved her dilemma, Veenie and I scurried in the back door of the parlor in search of April. We didn't find April, but we did run into Bernie Tatlock, who worked as the Reddy cosmetician, gussying up the dearly departed, getting them presentable for their last big public to-do.

Bernie was the youngest of the Tatlock boys. His oldest brother, Pokey, owned the tavern and pool hall, while his mother, Dolly, was the chief cook at the same. Most folks referred to Bernie, the baby Tatlock boy, as Twinkles Tatlock. If you ever saw him straight on, you'd not have to ask why.

Twinkles sat with his legs crossed at the ankles at the white French provincial reception desk. He wore a red jumpsuit with flared white legs and a rhinestone collar studded into the neckline. His whole look tended toward Elvis. His dyed black hair, a Miss Clairol number 124 job if ever I saw one, was piled atop his head, topped with a bun wig. Cute little corkscrew curls fell down to cover where most men might have sideburns. His makeup put me in mind of Elizabeth Taylor in her prime, except for the gray five o'clock shadow.

He was enjoying lunch. He had a cheesy mystery meat sandwich, a specialty of Pokey's Tavern, on a paper plate, along with a mess of onion rings. The onion rings were swimming in a pile of ketchup. He had cut the sandwich into dainty finger bites, which he was eating with a tiny plastic knife and fork. He was using a linen napkin to wipe his lips in between bites.

"Come on in, ladies," he said. "Just finishing lunch. Got Bromley in the back. April's with him, finishing his paperwork. You gals come to visit him?"

"Nah," said Veenie, eyeing the mystery meat sandwich—I swear I heard her stomach rumble—"we're after April."

"Oh right," said Twinkles. "Saw in the *Hoosier Squealer* you two are working the Apple case." He noticed Veenie's drool and held out his plate, offering her a bite of his sandwich. "Help yourself. Can't nobody resist Mama Dolly's cooking."

"Much obliged," Veenie said as she wolfed down the itty-bitty bite.

I asked Twinkles how work was going.

"Splendid," he said. "I just love, love, *love* working on dead people. They never complain. Never a bad word. And I just got some new face paints in from Louisville, so Bromley's got this nice warm apple glow about him. Avonelle was right pleased."

"You always do everybody up so nice."

"Lord knows I try. It's their last big shindig."

In truth, Twinkles was the best beautician and cosmetician in town, better even than Tinky Sue Knute, who ran the Curl Up and Dye. A lot of folks went with the Reddy Funeral Home when their time came because of Twinkles' mastery of makeup and hair. With Twinkles working on you, you'd look sharp even if you spent your whole ordinary life looking like you fell out of an ugly tree and hit every branch on the way down.

Veenie was already booked with Twinkles. She'd splurged on the down payment for a big send away last spring when Beryl had offered a one-time-only senior layaway plan. Veenie loved a good party, so she'd selected her package up front, sparing no expense.

The back door to the body prep lab swung open. April peeked out. She wasn't wearing her customary black sock cap, so her natural salt and pepper curls puffed out like Shirley Temple. "Hi there, gals. Come on back. We can sit and yack in Beryl's office. He's out on a pickup. I can fill you all in about the autopsy."

We said our good-byes to Twinkles and followed April into Beryl's office. The room was filled with more white French provincial furniture and red satin drapes. The walls were covered with paintings, mostly of Jesus and angels. A white leather Bible big enough to brain the devil himself was spread open on the desk. The biggest thing on Beryl's desk was a gold-tinted triple box of tissue. Veenie helped herself to one. When she was done honking, April started in. She didn't really have a lot to say. And what she did say took us both by surprise.

CHAPTER ELEVEN

"Bromley died of natural causes."

"Come again?" I sputtered.

"Natural death," April said as she signed and stamped the last of her paperwork and slid it into the white leather inbox on Beryl's desk. "Heart stopped."

"His ticker popped?" asked Veenie.

"Not quite. He had a heart defect. Hypertrophic cardiomyopathy. Abnormal thickening of the heart muscles. It's genetic. The muscles of his heart had been thickening up for some time. Found evidence that he'd had at least one minor heart attack. Recent. Probably thought it was indigestion. May have fainted once or twice. Probably ignored the signs, thought he was getting old, out of shape. People do it all the time."

"What about the clothes he was wearing?"

"What about them?"

"They came from the scarecrow out in Barbara Skaggs's garden. Veenie and I saw the scarecrow wearing them when we first arrived that day. An hour later, Bromley was dressed in those same clothes, dead as a pumpkin on the front porch."

"Well," April stood up and closed her medical bag, which had held the paperwork, "I certainly can't explain that."

Veenie asked if Bromley had been wearing normal underwear.

"Yep. Blue boxers. Why?"

"Just curious."

I asked if Avonelle had been informed about the cause of death.

"Called her about an hour ago. She didn't answer her phone. Didn't want to leave a message or a text. Like to show respect. Do these things in person." April checked her watch, a cute little red acrylic number with white stripes, kind of like a candy cane. "I'll swing by the bank, then her place on my way home. If you gals could keep this quiet until tomorrow, I'd appreciate it."

"Sure thing," I said.

"You believe that?" I asked Veenie as we climbed into the Impala.

"Nah," she said. "Something's all cattywampus here."

I had to agree, but I had no clue what was going on with this case, and once Avonelle heard the official news from April that Bromley's death was natural, I was pretty confident she'd pull the plug on our nosing around. She wasn't one to throw away fistfuls of cash out of sheer curiosity. It didn't sit well with me, but Avonelle was the client, and it was her dime we'd been dining on.

By the time we reached home, it was dinner time. We'd stopped at Pokey's Tavern and picked up a to-go bag of mystery meat sandwiches. We'd recently solved a mystery for Pokey. To pay us back, he gave us an open tab on food items at the tavern. Any drinks we wanted we had to pay hard cash for though.

Veenie rushed in to have at her sandwich while it was still hot and gooey. Also, it was time for the *Grand Ole Opry* rerun show. Tonight it was Lester Flatt and Earl Scruggs on the dueling banjos. Veenie was a sucker for country boys who loved to pick and grin. Her pappy had been a barn dance fiddle player back in the day. She could still shake a leg when she had a mind to. Truth be told, Veenie knew about every dance from the waltz to the mashed tater. Lately she'd been brushing up on twerking and flossing. She was saving her big moves for the barn dance at Ma and Peepaw Horton's annual Chickenlandia Festival in a couple of weeks.

The first thing I saw when we arrived home was Sassy. She sat on the porch swing, all dolled up. She waved at people as they strolled by walking their dogs or strutting it up to whatever marching music they had stuck in their ears. And she wasn't alone. Fussy Smith was parked next to her. He was dolled up in a navy blazer and a blue button-up dress shirt with a red tie. He wore navy dress trousers with a slick white belt.

Back in my day, that kind of dress meant a fellow was serious about impressing a lady. I didn't know when it became ok for men to prance around in sloppy shorts and tongue-wagging tennis shoes. Probably the seventies did that. Fashion went hog wild back then. Most people never recovered. Fussy, who graduated high school with us, was still doing it up old school.

"Evenin' Ruby Jane," Fussy said. He stood up and shook my hand. His silver-gray hair was slicked back, trimmed nice and tight above his ears. He wore shiny white penny loafers, the kind most men in these parts pulled on for weddings or Sunday school.

"Evening Fussy. You still out there at Camelot?"

"Still there. Real shame about Bromley. Lived across from me. Right nice fellow. Never gave none of us out at Camelot a lick of trouble."

"Not sure his wife would agree with you."

Fussy straightened his belt buckle. "Well now, sometimes a fellow has to sow a few wild oats."

"You know Bromley well?"

"Oh, sure. Sure did. Did some investments together. Real estate. Construction. You know."

I nodded, though I didn't know. None of those things seemed very exciting to me.

Sassy spoke up. "Fussy here is taking me down to the yacht club tonight. We was just sitting here enjoying the breeze before we hightailed it down there for supper. It's steak night. A private to-do."

By Yacht Club I was pretty sure she meant the White River Boat and Gun Club. Sassy was like that, always sprinkling fairy dust all over everything. Fussy was a bit like that too. The boats most folks put into White River had to be rowed. Nonetheless, Fussy called the place a yacht club and the annual river parade a regatta. He enjoyed swooning around town in a white captain's hat and navy sailor's jacket most of the summer.

Fussy cleared his throat. "It's a special dinner. Regatta planning committee. Sassy here is my plus one."

Sassy messed at an imaginary piece of lint on Fussy's navy jacket. "Fussy here is the High Commander."

"Still got that tricked out pontoon boat?" I asked Fussy.

"Sure do. Hey, maybe you and Boots can come over. Take a river cruise with me and Miss Sassy. Make it a double date." He patted Sassy's hand.

"Boots? Boots Gibson? Why you bringing him up?"

"Sassy here told me you two were an item now."

Sassy nodded so vigorously that her hair, which was piled high atop her head, bobbled a bit. "We could make it a double date, Ruby Jane, like in high school."

"I am *not* dating Boots Gibson. Where'd you get that silly idea?"

"Veenie told me. Besides, I seen the way he looks at you, all moon-eyed." She rolled her eyes and giggled.

And that was that. Our conversation smacked into a brick wall, probably just as well, as my cell was vibrating and wobbling like the Impala trying to climb the knobs. I looked down to see a whole mess of texts with a bunch of squiggly sad faces and exclamation points from my grown daughter, Joyce.

Odd, because mostly she kept to herself with her high-powered insurance salesman husband up in the big city of Bloomington.

"See y'all later," I said to Sassy and Fussy as I ducked into the house to see what had Joyce's tail in such a twist.

CHAPTER TWELVE

"**B**oy, oh boy," said Veenie when I showed her Joyce's texts. There must have been fifty of them. "That girl done wrote you a novel. Looks like a *Gone with the Wind* thingy to me. She okay?"

"Dunno. Near as I can tell, she thinks her husband is cheating on her."

"Never did like that fellow. His eyes are too close together." Veenie slapped a hand to each side of her face and squished her cheeks up. "He's got a face like a chicken hawk. He's all squinty-eyed, sneaky-looking, and a southerner to boot. You gonna get involved?"

"She sounds pretty shook up."

"Ruby Jane, that daughter of yours is always upset. She's wound tighter than a two dollar watch. Always has been. Her life is one big swirling toilet of upset and emotion. Why you want to go swimming in that?" Veenie offered me some of her bag of BBQ pork cracklings by way of comfort, and I popped a few.

"She's kin," I said between crunches. "My only daughter, and you know she only gets so darned upset because her heart's so big."

Veenie shook her fingers at the cell phone. "Put that thingy on speaker then. Let's get this soap opera going."

"I'm too tuckered out," I said, moving Veenie's little feet over on the couch and plopping down. "Imagine whatever all the fuss it about will hold till morning."

I shut off my cell phone and stretched out in the recliner. Veenie and I snuggled into some afghans and kicked back over a bowl of popcorn as Lester Flatts and Earl Scruggs plucked out "Foggy Mountain Breakdown" on their dueling banjos.

The next morning, Veenie and I got a surprise when we went to unlock the office door for work. The door was already unlocked. Harry was sitting at his desk, feet up. His fedora hat was still on his head, so I reckoned he hadn't been there all that long. "You gals are late," he bellyached, making a to-do out of squinting at his wrist watch. "I need coffee."

"Well, well," said Veenie. "Look what the devil dumped on us. It's Harry, the man ho."

Harry's face tightened. His little pewter-colored mustache danced in grim disapproval. "Why you always have to sass me, Lavinia?"

"Why you always have to leave us here to get shot at, Harry?"

"Shap been sniffing around?" Harry's eyes darted around the office, across the big plate glass windows in the front. "Shap in town? You see him out there?"

Veenie put some coffee on to brew. "We told him you were out of town, so he's leaving us alone, but if we get killed because of your weak zipper, the law says you'd be responsible. It'd be a crime. Testicular manslaughter."

Harry puffed. "*That* is not a real thing." He sat upright and tightened his tie. "Besides, it's not my fault. It's that wife of his. Dottie won't leave me alone. She keeps following me around, wanting a piece of me. What am I supposed to do?"

I made a suggestion. "Behave yourself?"

That got me a snort.

Veenie was pouring us coffee when Dottie Reynolds blew in the door. She was a holy mess. Her hair, which was a white-blonde wig, was a wee bit sideways. She was wearing bug-eyed, lime green sunglasses and a yellow mini-skirt. Her legs were skinny as matchsticks, and she was more than a little pigeon-toed. She ripped off her sunglasses and lit into Harry like it was time for Sunday dinner and he was the pot roast.

Veenie made a gagging sound with her fist pressed to her mouth.

Dottie hugged Harry so tightly I thought she was going to squeeze him right out of his three piece suit. "Sugar buns," she said, "Dottie has been dying for you. Why'd you up and leave town?"

Harry squirmed loose. He stood on tiptoe, trying to see out the front office window over Dottie's shoulder. "Shap with you?"

"Heck no. Old fart is gone for the day. Went to Seymour to pick up some seed."

"You sure?" Harry ran to the window and checked the street in both directions.

"Sure, I'm sure. We got time for a quickie." She tugged at Harry's hand, pulling him toward the back staircase that led up to his bachelor pad above the office.

Harry looked hesitant, but after Dottie slapped a few kisses on him, hoovered his neck, and yanked off his tie, he crumpled. The two disappeared up the stairs, clothes flying off as they headed up to Harry's love nest.

Veenie smacked down her coffee cup. "I ain't sitting here listening to Harry get his banana peeled."

The building was old—used to be a Rexall drugstore, back in the day—so neither the floors nor the walls had much insulation. We'd learned from experience that if Harry had sex upstairs, we were going to get treated to some free, cut-rate porn.

I grabbed my messenger bag and the keys to the Impala. "Let's see if we can find Avonelle. Imagine she's heard from April by now. Reckon she's going to fire us, but we should hear it from the horse's mouth." I wasn't all that eager to lose the

Apple case. We didn't have work to replace it, and gosh darn I was certain Bromley's death was not natural. I just hated to leave a case open with so much doubt poking at me.

We drove across town and checked Avonelle's house, a fancy Dutch Colonial with a wooden porch big enough to serve as a roller skating rink, but it was locked up tight. The morning paper was still tossed up on the steps, and no one answered when we rang the doorbell.

Veenie tried to peer in a picture window, but the drapes were closed tightly.

I eyed Veenie, who was on tiptoe trying to see in the big window. "Avonelle sees you, she'll call the law."

"Avonelle can bite me," said Veenie.

We were about to climb back in the Impala when Bert Apple pulled into the driveway. He drove a white Lincoln, same as his mother and brother, only a newer model. He wore a white dentist coat and gray flannel work slacks. "Can I help you?" he asked. He had his hand cupped over his eyes, shading them from the sun.

"Just us," I hollered as I stepped away from the house. I scooted to the edge of the porch into a spot of sunshine, waving. "Me and Veenie."

Veenie popped up next to me. "We was looking for your mama."

"Probably down at the bank. Quarterly director's meeting is this afternoon. She's doesn't work full days, most days, but she never misses a director's meeting, her being the president and all."

Bert hopped up on the porch and stood next to us. "Can I help you?"

I said we were there to check in about Bromley and the case.

"Oh," he said. "Thought that was all wrapped up. Coroner told Mom and me he died of natural causes. Some kind of genetic heart condition. Told me it there was a fifty-fifty chance I might have it too. Me and the kids, we all have to be tested."

Bert plopped down on the porch swing. He looked tired, and his face was a little puffy. His hair had been whipped up into forked gray fingers by the wind. "To tell the truth, it's got me a little spooked." He smoothed his tie, or maybe he was patting at his heart.

"I'd reckon so," I said. "They have a test for it though?"

"Seems like it. Doc Scarborough said they do. When I leave here, I'm going down to his office to let them draw some blood and give me a heart monitor to wear. They can tell from that." He pulled a kerchief from his pocket and mopped at his forehead. "Man, you just never know."

Bert stood up and pulled a key out of his pocket. It was a single key with a spot of red nail polish on the head. He headed to the front door. He turned to face us after he keyed the door open. "Anything else I can do for you?"

"No," I said. "We'll go on down to the bank. See if we can catch your mama."

"You hang in there," said Veenie.

Once we were back in the Impala, Veenie turned to me. "If he knew his mama wasn't home, why you suppose he came over to her house? Don't that seem suspicious to you?"

I shrugged as I fired up the Impala. It was getting hot, so I cranked a window down and popped open the wing on the window to let in extra air. Veenie did the same, but then her door knob came off in her hand. She pulled the Philips head out of the glove compartment to screw it back on. She had it fixed in a jiffy.

"I dunno," I said. "Maybe she asked him to look in after something or maybe he keeps his lunch at his mama's place. He's got no wife or kids around here. Lives alone in that big old place out at Camelot. He is kind of a mama's boy. Nothing criminal about that."

"He seemed kind of shifty to me. Didn't he seem shifty to you?" Veenie pointed to the porch. "And lookie there! He's peeking out the window, checking to see if we're still out here."

I looked up just in time to see the curtains flutter. I didn't see Bert though. For all I could tell, it was the air conditioning blowing the curtains around inside.

"Lord All Mighty, Lavinia, you watch too many murder mysteries on the Hallmark Channel. Maybe he just didn't like you snooping in his mama's windows. A lot of people would find that kind of behavior peculiar and nosey."

"I'm not nosey. I'm a paid professional."

"You were hoping to get some dirt on Avonelle. Admit it."

"I'm telling you, Ruby Jane, there is something odd about this whole case. I don't think we should stop snooping."

"Well," I said as I keyed the Impala, "I agree with you on that." I checked my wrist watch. It was late morning. If Avonelle had an afternoon board meeting, it'd probably be best if we left her to her work. I said as much to Veenie. She agreed and suggested we go out to Camelot Court to visit Gretal, see what she thought of her husband's official cause of death.

I put the pedal to the metal, and we gunned it that way.

CHAPTER THIRTEEN

G retal was home, but she didn't look to be home for long. Her fancy red leather suitcase sat open on the bed. She was throwing clothes into the case with mad abandon. "Frankly, I don't care how he died. Like I told you, we weren't that close. I stayed with him for appearances' sake. He's gone now, so I'm out of here, and damned happy about it too."

I asked if she'd ever seen Bromley faint or heard him complain about heartburn or shortness of breath.

"He ever wheeze when he walked?" Veenie asked. "I do that sometimes when I feel a spell coming on. Got a bad ticker myself."

Gretal eyed Veenie. "Not that I can recall, but you're asking the wrong person. I didn't spend that much time with him. Why not ask his girlfriends?"

Veenie asked Gretal if she had a list of them.

"No." Gretal went back to the closet and pulled a few things off hangers. She flipped these things into log rolls and stuffed them into her bag.

Remembering that Bert had told me that he thought Bromley stored his little black book on his cell phone I asked Gretal if she had her husband's cell phone. She went over to the bedside table and pulled an iPhone out of the drawer. "Help yourself." She tossed the phone my way, and I pocketed it.

I asked if she had any idea why Bromley had been dressed in a scarecrow outfit.

"God, no. Don't know. Don't care to know. Probably hillbilly hanky-panky with some farm girl. Dressing up. Role playing. He liked a lot—and I mean *a lot*—of weird stuff. He was probably going at it with some skank who had a wet spot for scarecrows. Maybe she was Dorothy, and he was the big bad scarecrow. Who knows?" Gretal stuffed a couple more pairs of pricey shoes into her suitcase and zipped the bag shut.

"That a real thing?" Veenie asked. "I mean, a scarecrow fetish? I guess that could be a real thing. But if it was me, I'd be going after the lion. I like a man with hair, especially on the chest. Not on the rear, though. If a fellow has too much hair on his rear, count me out. How about you, RJ?"

I definitely wasn't getting dragged into that one.

Gretal shrugged. "Around these parts, nothing would surprise me."

I wondered what I was missing. Bromley was found at Barbara's house, on her porch, dressed like her scarecrow. Barbara seemed like the logical choice for a hanky-panky partner with Bromley, but she'd been inside with us the whole time between our seeing that scarecrow and Bromley ending up dead on her porch swing. Besides, I tended to believe her when she said she loved old William, the Pappy Apple. As far as she was concerned, she and William were family, what with the kids and all.

Gretal rolled her suitcase toward the door. "If you ladies will excuse me, I'm headed up to Columbus. My sister has a condo up there. I'm done hanging out in Hooterville. Kimmy's back in college over at Bloomington. Avonelle can have this drafty old house. Thing was built on the cheap by old tight-wad Fussy Jones, anyway. It's Avonelle's name on the mortgage. Bromley never could hold onto money."

Veenie and I followed Gretal out the front door. We waved good-bye as she climbed into her red BMW and squealed out of the asphalt driveway.

"She seemed kind of in a hurry to me. She seem in a hurry to you?" asked Veenie.

"Not everybody's made for country life," I said.

A door flew open across the street, and Fussy strolled out. Sassy popped out of the doorway behind him. She waved at us with both hands, like a windmill. "Yoo hoo! Gals!"

I heard Veenie's false teeth click. "That woman burns my bacon."

"Really? You hide it so well." I waved back at Sassy before reluctantly loping across the street to see what she wanted.

Veenie climbed into the Impala and stuck an eight-track tape into the deck. Loretta Lynn's "You Ain't Woman Enough to Take My Man," rolled out the open windows.

Sassy gave me a big old hug. "Veenie ain't coming over?"

"She's catching up on her Facebook."

Fussy was dressed in his Commodore's outfit, except his jacket was white now, with a little gold anchor stitched on the pocket. Sassy had changed into a new outfit that I'd never seen before. She was dressed in a long, red silk Chinese tunic with a Chairman Mao collar and black, stretch pencil pants. She had on a topknot hair piece with chopsticks stuck in her hair. She slipped one of her arms around Fussy's waist and held him tight, like she was afraid a tornado might swoop down and suck him away. He didn't seem to mind.

Fussy asked me what was up with Gretal. "Boy, she really tore out of here. Came out to see what all the commotion was about."

"She's going to stay with her sister up in Columbus for a spell."

Sassy nodded and looked sympathetic. "She all tore up about the hubs passing?"

"Yeah. Something like that." I saw the pontoon boat in the driveway. It was spit clean and shiny. The harpoon rigging glinted like a row of silver swords along the bow. The contraption was so big you would have thought Fussy was outfitted to drag Moby Dick ashore. The pontoon boat was yoked to a sparkling, yellow Ford double cab truck. "Truck new?" I asked.

"Just bought her from Sammy Spray over in Salem. Was thinking of hauling the pontoon up to Lake Monroe after the regatta. I'm a member of the yacht club up there. Got an annual pass. Sassy's never been."

Sassy beamed. "You and Boots ought to drive on up to Lake Monroe. We could have us some cocktails on the lake. Watch the sunset."

It seemed no matter what I said, Sassy and half the town was determined to mate me up with Boots. "Thank you," I said, "but Boots and I are *not* an item."

Sassy nudged me with her elbow and said, "Right. Wink. Wink."

"No," I said. "*Really.*"

Veenie laid on the horn of the Impala.

I tried ignoring her.

Fussy shaded his eyes and looked over toward the Impala. He said, "I think your friend is trying to get your attention."

"You go on," said Sassy. "We're headed over to Salem soon as we put the boat in down at the White River Yacht Club. They got a new German sausage house opened up down there. Fussy here is taking me out for dinner. I'm probably not going to be home until real late tonight, so don't you and Veenie wait up." She winked at me.

Veenie horned me again.

"Hold your horses!" I cried over my shoulder at Veenie. "Nice seeing you again," I said to Fussy.

"Same," he said as I loped away.

Back in the Impala, Veenie bellyached about being left alone in the hot car. She fanned herself with a Hoosier Feedbag coupon flier and coughed like she had a hairball. "I got a bad heart, you know. Not supposed to get overheated."

"That was your choice," I said. "You could have come on over and said howdy to Sassy and Fussy with me."

"I don't care for Sassy or Fussy. Never did like him. He carries a purple umbrella with tassels on it when it rains. My God, what kind of man does that? You know as well as I do that he's got a right peculiar side to his personality."

"Some people say that about you."

"Yeah, but I'm peculiar in interesting ways. I've got character. People are always telling me that."

"Mostly what they say is that you *are* a character," I said. "There's a difference."

Veenie handed me my cell phone. "Thing's been buzzing like a nest of drunk bees. It's your daughter again. You were right. She thinks her husband is getting his corn dog battered on the side."

"You read my texts?"

"You left it here on the seat. I was checking to see if it was an emergency."

I scrolled through the texts. They were more frantic than the day before. "For Christ's sake," I muttered as I read the texts, "can't anybody in this state keep their zipper up or their skirt down?"

"Just you, Ruby Jane. The way you live, I don't see why you just don't turn Amish."

"It's the bonnets," I said. "I never did like hats."

I texted Joyce and told her to drive down to my place for dinner. I promised I'd whip her up some fried chicken and persimmon pudding, her favorites, and we'd talk about her problems. She lived a little more than an hour away. This way we could talk without her husband suspecting anything. He wasn't the sharpest saw in God's tool chest, but if he saw me rattle up to their house on a weekday for no good reason, he was bound to be suspicious.

Joyce texted back a mess of smiley faces and upturned thumbs and hearts.

I wished people would use words, but it was a losing battle. Everybody was illiterate these days. They talked in pictures. Maybe it was for the better. Nobody under the age of forty could spell worth a spit anyway.

"Fried chicken," said Veenie. "That's smart of you. Ain't nothing fried chicken can't fix. You making real gravy?"

"I reckon." I could tell by the look on Veenie's little face that she'd already invited herself to supper.

CHAPTER FOURTEEN

I had a mess of fried chicken forked onto the serving platter by the time Joyce blew into the kitchen. She looked more like her daddy's side of the family, the Waskoms, than my kin. She was just over five feet tall with a teased hairdo that added another five inches. She was plump. She'd gained weight since I last saw her at Christmas. Her blue blazer wouldn't quite close around the middle. She wasn't sleeping well. I could tell by the extra white cover-up she had slathered under her eyes. And her mascara was sloppy, not like her. She had some new eyeglasses, red plastic ovals that made her look like a chubby cheeked owl. Her hair was a new color, kind of auburn. She plopped her purse down on the kitchen table and climbed onto a chair. She was weeping by the time I got to the table with the platter of chicken. She yanked a chicken leg off the platter and started gnawing. She always had been a stress eater.

Veenie plopped down in a chair across from Joyce while I mixed up a pitcher of iced tea.

By the time I sat down, half the chicken was gone.

"Have some mashed taters and gravy," I said to Joyce as I slid the gravy pitcher and a steaming bowl of taters over her way.

Joyce shoveled a mountain of taters onto her plate, then mashed a valley in the middle and poured in a lake of gravy.

Veenie followed suit.

In no time flat, the bowls were empty.

Veenie licked the gravy bowl.

Joyce started weeping again. "He's leaving me this time."

"You sure?" I asked, mostly because with Joyce you never could tell if something was all that serious. A hangnail could make her go on like she was having her hand amputated.

"Mama, he's cheating on me. Cheating!"

Veenie sucked down some iced tea. "Men are like that, honey. Fergus Senior used to paddle up hoochie-coochie creek with every skank that shot him a smile."

"But Russell is refined. He's college educated."

"His willy never went to school," Veenie said. "And men think with their willies, don't they, RJ?"

"Mostly," I said. "What evidence you got of cheating?" I asked Joyce.

Joyce started bawling again.

I brought a plate of persimmon pudding to the table, topped it off with whipped cream, and handed Joyce a fork.

She lit into the pudding.

Veenie had to fight to get in there and yank out a piece for herself.

When the pudding was gone, I cleared the table and threw the dishes into the sink to soak with some warm water.

By the time I got into the living room, Veenie was comforting Joyce. Joyce had kicked her heels off and was sitting next to Veenie on the davenport. She had her legs tucked up under her, ripping through a box of tissues. Veenie was patting her hand.

I handed Joyce a cold glass of Big Red.

She gulped that down then sat up a little straighter. "Oh, Mama, why would Russell cheat on me? I've been a good wife."

"Wish I could tell you, honey, but Veenie is right. Men get awful addled about sex."

"Daddy never cheated on you."

"Your daddy wasn't like most men. Besides, back in our day, people didn't just pick up and get divorced. We stuck with it. None of us ever expected to be all that happy to begin with."

Veenie patted Joyce's hand. "It probably don't mean nothing. Rusty is getting to be middle aged. Men get insecure long about then. He said he's leaving you?"

"He hasn't said a single word about the whole thing." Joyce blew her nose and made a little sigh. She spread out on the couch.

"Probably a good sign," I said.

"Oh heck, yeah. That's a good sign," said Veenie. "If this was serious, he'd have been mouthing off about it by now."

I asked Joyce how she knew Rusty was having an affair.

"Oh Mama, I just do. He's staying late at the office. And he never wants to do *it* anymore."

Veenie nodded. "Male menopause. Saw it on the Discovery Channel. Men got hormones too. Are his nuts drooping yet?"

"Maybe a little." Joyce started bawling again.

I asked Joyce again if she had any hard evidence.

"Like?"

"Letters? Phone calls?"

"He isn't stupid, Mama. He's not going to leave handkerchiefs with lipstick on them lying around the house. I just know, that's how I know. I bet it's one of those junior agents he works with." Rusty ran an insurance agency up in Bloomington. In fact, he was Mr. Insurance of Southern Indiana. He was a successful pot-bellied little guy from Atlanta with a hawkish face who I'd always found a wee bit light in the loafers. He was one heck of an insurance salesman though. Old ladies liked to talk to him. He was smart enough to sit with them and compliment them on their looks and hairdos. It didn't take much of that kind of attention to get a woman in these parts juiced up. Most of them were married to husbands who never paid them much mind unless it was Valentine's Day. On Valentine's Day, a gal could count on a wilted bouquet of carnations from the IGA and some gas station chocolates. That was about as romantic as most Hoosier fellows ever got. That's pretty much how Joyce got here.

Veenie asked, "He around women all day?"

"All day. Every day. He's got twenty or more of them working for him now. Some college girls too. A veritable harem." Joyce's face cracked, and she started weeping again. She took to wringing her hands. "I don't want to lose him. What will I tell Katey and Riley?"

Katey and Riley were Joyce's kids. They were twin teenagers who attended college at IU. They were nice kids, down-to-earth, bookworms. Frankly, given all the fruits and nuts in our family tree, I didn't know how they turned out so stable.

Veenie scooched over on the couch and dabbed at the mascara trails that ran down Joyce's face with a tissue. "Don't you fret none, honey. Me and your mama will get to the bottom of this. If that skunk Rusty is cheating on you, we'll set him right."

Joyce looked up, her brown eyes big and pleading. She'd cried so much the inside of her eyeglasses were smeared with mascara. "You will?" she choked out. "I was going to hire you. You know, I mean you're detectives and all, and me and Russell, we have money. You do this kind of thing all the time now, chase down cheating husbands, right?"

"Yep," said Veenie. "Matter of fact, we've been working on a case that involves some fellow doing the hollow wallow down in Hound Holler."

"I read about that online. That dentist? Bromley Apple? Him?"

"The same. You know him?" I asked.

Joyce made a face. She was sitting up now, working on straightening herself up. She tugged at her jacket. "He was a year ahead of me in school. He asked me out once, junior year."

"I don't remember you dating him."

"I didn't. He was awful. Creepy." Joyce shuddered a little. "He was always following us girls around, trying to cop a feel. Cathy Phillips, you remember her, cheerleader, well she had to report him to the principal for following her into the gym shower. His mama gave some extra money to the basketball team to buy new uniforms, so they kept it all hush-hush. Is it true someone killed him?" She blew her nose. "Bet he deserved it. Old creep monster."

I told Joyce that Bromley's death had been ruled natural causes, but we had our suspicions.

Joyce excused herself to go to the toilet and put her face back on.

While she was gone, Veenie said she thought we ought to take Joyce's case. "We got no case now that Bromley wasn't murdered. Harry's not about to find us a case. He's too busy playing ride the bologna pony with Dottie. Joyce is our flesh and blood, and she needs our help something fierce."

"Thought you said I ought not to be casting myself in Joyce's soap operas."

"This here is a professional thing."

I eyed Veenie. "You still trying to save up enough to see Blake Shelton in concert over in Terre Haute?"

"Dang right. That boy is a hottie, dimples and all."

"Okay," I said. "We'll take Joyce's case, but if this goes south, I'm holding you responsible."

Joyce squealed when she came out of the bathroom and Veenie gave her the good news that we'd be snooping on Rusty starting first thing the next morning.

"I love you, Mama!" Joyce squeezed me, reminding me she'd always be my little girl. My crazy little girl.

CHAPTER FIFTEEN

V eenie woke me up bright and early the next morning. She was dressed for the day and bounced on my bed like a beach ball. She wore a new outfit: a fluorescent green and blue paisley poncho and a pair of screaming yellow stretch pants with red cowboy boots. I practically needed sunglasses to cut the glare. "Get up, Ruby Jane!"

"Why?" I asked as I rubbed my eyes, which were crusted shut. I'd been deep in a dream about this pet chicken I kept as a girl, Clucky. I'd loved Clucky. By mistake, my daddy had chopped Clucky up for dinner one night. In the dream, Clucky was sitting at the table in a bow tie talking dirty to me. Oh boy. Too much greasy fried chicken and gravy and yacking about sex before bedtime. "What's up?" I asked Veenie. I wasn't quite ready to get out of bed. It was almost an hour before my normal rise and shine.

"It's Sassy," said Veenie. Her blue eyes were huge and bright behind her Coke bottle glasses. "She's done been arrested for murder."

That got me to sit up straight. "What in the name of Sam Hill? You sure?"

"Sure. Sassy done called, wants us to come on down to the jail. Grape Nuts has her locked up tight."

"Who'd she murder?"

"Fussy Jones."

"You're putting me on."

"Nah. This is for real. They found ol' Fussy napping face down in the White River next to his pontoon boat. Sassy was the last to see him. Guess they had a hot date last night. I reckon things got too hot. Maybe they were playing one of them dress-up games. Everybody says Fussy loves them kind of games. Maybe Sassy got so worked up she lost all control."

I pulled a foggy memory out of my brain of Sassy telling me she and Fussy were going to drop his pontoon over at the White River Boat and Gun Club, then drive over to that new German sausage restaurant in Salem. And yes, everybody knew that Fussy loved to mess around and wear outfits in the boudoir. His ex-wife had made no secret about that down at the VFW after she divorced him. She told the best stories about Fussy and his peculiar love of women's lingerie to anybody who'd buy her a shot of Jim Beam.

I rolled out of bed and tugged on my jeans. I grabbed a shirt off the rocker and pulled it on, buttoning it up before sticking my feet into canvas sneakers. I ran my fingers through my unruly white hair and fluffed it up a bit as I followed Veenie through the kitchen and out the back door. "Boots got any hard evidence?" I asked.

"Lord, I hope so," said Veenie.

Sassy was pacing back and forth in her cell by the time we arrived at the jail. She'd taken her heels off and had a runner up the back of both of her stockings. Boots had taken us in to see her. He unlocked the cell door so we could go inside and sit with her. She looked a fright. Her face was all smeared from crying. Her hay pile of hair was mushed down on one side, like she'd been hit in the head by a frying pan. "I didn't kill him!" Sassy screamed. "Honest, gals. You know how hard I work to get a man."

True. Sassy loved getting all dolled up for men. I honestly couldn't see her doing anything that might reduce the dating pool.

I asked Sassy why they thought she'd killed Fussy.

"I was the last to see him."

"You went out to dinner last night?"

Sassy made a strange face. "Well, no. Not quite. We meant to go out to dinner, but we, er, got distracted. And then Fussy got a phone call that got him all excited. He said we had to wait around at the river awhile longer, so he could talk to a man about some business deal."

"Distracted?" said Veenie. "What in tarnation would make you forget to go out for a free sausage diner? Sausage talks to me, especially that German bratwurst. Might be talked into killing a man myself for a hot plate of that stuff."

"Well, if you must know, Fussy was hinting that he wanted some full-on nookie. He'd just shined up his boat real nice, and he looked so cute in his little captain outfit." Sassy broke down weeping.

I was thinking spring better end soon, or there wouldn't be enough tissue in Pawpaw County to comfort all the broken-hearted hens.

Veenie piped up. "Boots said Fussy was found floating face down with a fish gig through his chest. You do that?"

"Lord, Jesus, no!" she cried. "I told you I didn't touch him." Sassy pressed a hand to her chest. "I mean I really *didn't* touch him. We were on his yacht having some wine, a right nice Indiana peach wine with a screw top. We were watching the sun set through the sycamore trees. It was getting dark. He got a little frisky and started smooching on me. Then he told me to hold my wild horses while he ran back to that little cargo shed at the back of the boat. It's like a little shed where he keeps the grill and fishing tackle and whatnot." Sassy stopped and gritted her teeth. She got up and glanced out the cell bar doors, then scanned the hall to make sure Boots or Devon weren't around. "This part is kind of embarrassing."

That got Veenie's attention. "And?"

"Well, gosh darn, Fussy busted back out of that shed wearing nothing but underwear."

I was taken aback. "That got you upset?"

"You don't understand," wailed Sassy. "It was women's underwear. He was all trussed up in a red lace bustier, and he was wearing a Farrah Fawcett wig. And ... and ... he was wearing my lipstick and one of my best leopard bras." Sassy broke down completely. She buried her face in both hands. "He's one of them transvestites."

Veenie shrugged. "Whole town knows that."

"They do?" Sassy looked twice as mortified now.

"Afraid so," I said.

"Why didn't you tell me?"

I handed Sassy another tissue. "You asked us if he was healthy and could drive nights."

"And it never occurred to you to tell me he was kinky?"

Veenie shrugged. "There's always something. I dated a fellow once from over around Leesville who couldn't do anything with his willy unless I spanked him first. Once I whacked his behind. everything worked just fine."

"Who was that?" I had to ask.

"Spanky Ritter."

"Figures."

Sassy hugged herself. "I don't have many rules in this life. Lord knows I try to please my men. But if someone's going to wear lingerie, it darn well better be me. Lord, I felt like he was asking me to be a lesbian. That's all good and fine, lesbians, I mean. California is full of them. They're right nice, near as I can tell. A whole herd of them used to clean my pool. But, well, dang it, men don't look good in lacey things."

Sassy sat down and put her face in her hands. "You gals got to help me. I'm innocent. I got a couple of thousand laid away from when they arrested Doogie out in California. I could pay big time."

Veenie said, "Thought you didn't have anything to do with that real estate scheme your hubby cooked up."

"Might have had a wee bit to do with it. I mean, I might have hidden back some money for him, just in case he got in trouble."

"He *did* get in trouble."

"I know. That's why I left him. You going to help me or not? I got cash money."

Veenie and I looked at each other. "Sure," I said. "We need a five-hundred-dollar retainer. You got that?"

Sassy nodded yes and grabbed her gold lamé clutch purse, which she'd been using as a pillow. "I'll write you a check right now. Give you an even thousand just to show I'm serious." She looked relieved as she ripped the check out of her register and handed it to me. "Plenty more where that came from. Can you gals get me out of this drafty old cell now?"

"Probably not right away," I said. "You'll have to see the judge. He'll set bail. We'll talk to Boots. See what they have on you. You ever been arrested?"

"Course not!"

Veenie took the check and stuffed it into her bra. Said she was walking down to the bank to deposit the check as we left the cell. "Could be rubber," she said. "I'd not start working the case until we know we got the real thing here."

"You think Sassy killed Fussy?"

"I dunno. Maybe she's one of them black widows. You know, the kind what kills their mates just for fun."

I could completely see how a woman might want to off her husband, but Sassy didn't seem like a black widow killer to me. That woman lived and breathed men.

"How we know what Sassy is?" asked Veenie. "She showed up in town one day looking to rent a room. She was out in California all them years. You know how freaky they get out on the West Coast. She was probably hanging with a fast crowd of hippies. They smoke LSD. That kind of stuff."

"I don't think you can smoke LSD."

"Her husband was a crook."

"Don't mean she was a part of that."

"How'd she get the cash money for this check then?" Veenie patted her bosom.

She had a good point. All this time I'd bought Sassy's story about how her last husband, Doogie Duval, had swindled her right along with all those dim-witted investors with his fancy real estate scheme. For all I knew, Sassy herself had masterminded the scheme and left Doogie to take the fall. Boots had undoubtedly run an interstate background check on Sassy when he'd booked her. I'd have to sweeten him up a bit. That'd be the fastest way for us to uncover what Sassy had really been up to all them years out in California.

CHAPTER SIXTEEN

"You trying to sweet talk me, Ruby Jane?" Boots sat at his desk, his feet up. He'd just finished reading the *Pawpaw County Banner*. He rolled the paper into a tube and slapped it against the edge of his desk.

"We been friends a long time, Boots. I was thinking maybe Veenie and I could help you out on this case."

He grunted as he poured himself a cup of coffee from a glass pot. "Want some?" he asked.

I nodded yes. Veenie had yanked me out of bed mighty early. I was still trying to jump-start my brain.

Boots slid me a cup of black coffee.

It was thick, bitter, and as chewy as tar. "I think you need a new coffee maker," I said as I spat the coffee back into the cup.

"I'm not one to waste the taxpayer's money. Stuff tastes fine to me." He knocked back a slug of his own coffee. "Sassy tell you everything about her past?"

"She married bad. What's to tell?"

"That what she told you?" He leaned forward in his roller chair and eyed me.

"Pretty much. You telling me different?"

"She was married four times."

"So?"

"That's a lot of poor judgment for one woman."

"She's rattlebrained. You know that."

"Her mama, Mildred Smith, was a little off. Kinda odd about men."

"Mildred was a social climber. Some people are just like that." Sassy's mama, Mildred Smith, had sent her to all the best schools: Twinkle Toes Tap & Twirl and Miss Mamie's Conservatory of Music and Manners. She sent her to the Methodist church, although she herself had been raised a Baptist, because that was where all the town socialites congregated. The Methodists of Pawpaw County may not have been closer to God, but they were certainly higher up in the income brackets.

Sassy's father, a ne'er-do-well bottle sucker named Jakie Smith, either died or disappeared. No one knew for sure. He up and vanished one night. And not a single soul cared to ask after him.

Whatever happened, Mildred and her daughter were left to fend for themselves. "Mildred was a social climber," I repeated. "Wanted a better life for her daughter. No crime in that."

"Just saying, maybe it's genetic. The bad husbands. Disappearing husbands. All that."

"Oh for Pete's sake, Boots, we went to school with Sassy. She seem like a serial killer to you?"

He shrugged. "I got a report here from California says Miss Sassy is a person of interest in her last husband's crime spree."

"Everybody knows her last husband was a con artist. She told us that. No big secret. What's your point? You got anything there that proves Sassy committed a crime?" I tried to peek a look at the state police report sheet, but Boots yanked it back.

He teased me with the paper. "You know her husband is out of the pokey?"

"Parole?"

"A kind of do-it-yourself parole." Boots twirled his sheriff's hat around on his fingertips.

"He escaped?"

"Last week. There's an all-points out on him."

"That why you locked up Sassy?"

"Jealousy is a mighty strong motive for murder."

"You think Doogie has been hanging around town? That he saw Sassy dating Fussy and decided to gig him straight on?"

"I'm saying it sort of makes sense, don't it? A lover's quarrel. One of them love triangles. Maybe a three-way. And it got out of hand."

I rolled my eyes. "Don't you think we're all a little old for that kind of hanky-panky?"

"Age has got nothing to do with it. Some people just lack common sense. For instance, I have it on good faith that your friend Lavinia got kicked out of the drive-in last weekend for conduct unbecoming a senior citizen; and during a showing of *The Ten Commandments*, no less. She'd been putting on a show with Dickie Freeman, who used to be a right good Baptist boy. She tell you that?"

"Lavinia is a little odd. Don't surprise me a bit."

"Odd?" Boots white eyebrows shot up. "A two-headed cow is a little odd. Lavinia is …" The desk phone rang, and Boots took it. "Excuse me," he said as he turned around and muttered into the phone a few times. "Gotta go," he said, sliding the phone back in its cradle. "Business."

I knew a brush-off when it hit me. I was being swept out the door. No ifs, ands, or buts about it. I thanked Boots for his time and ambled on over to the Shades Agency office. Time to fire up the old desktop and start to snoop electronically for some answers about Sassy and her past.

Back at the office, Harry was pleased as punch that Veenie and I had brought in two new cash cases. Not pleased enough to work either of them though.

Veenie was a little peeved. "Why we got to do all the work?"

"I'm the boss." Harry hitched a thumb at his chest. "I'm licensed. You two are in training. Ought to thank me for giving you a crack at this. Could have hired a pair of cute gals with college degrees and great legs."

Veenie snorted. "Everybody knows that ain't true. For the chicken scratch you're paying us, the only applicants you got was me and Ruby Jane."

Dottie, who was still hanging around the office and working on her nails, echoed Harry's sentiments. "Harry is famous, you know. He solved that ghost busting mystery. They had him on TV. CNN. Just makes my skin crawl thinking about it."

"Yeah," said Veenie. "Harry makes my skin crawl too."

Dottie crossed her legs and wagged a skinny foot wrapped in a red, canvas wedge shoe at us. "He found that missing treasure. He's like a national hero." Dottie crossed the room and laid several sloppy kisses on Harry's cheeks. She tweaked his little pewter-colored mustache. "My hero."

Veenie stood up on her chair and craned her neck to see out the window. "Heads up, Dottie! I think I see your hubby coming down the sidewalk. And he's armed."

"Oh, hell," Dottie murmured. "Hell's bells. Oh, hell!"

She and Harry jumped up. She started to pull him up the stairs to his apartment.

"Not that way!" Harry cried as he grabbed his hat and mushed it onto his head. "We'll be trapped up. Fire escape is broken. Out the window. The alley."

Last thing I saw was Dottie's skinny legs scrambling out the alley window after Harry.

"Shap really out there?"

"Nope."

"Tired of hearing Harry and Dottie yack?"

"Yep."

I filled Veenie in on what Boots had told me about Sassy being a person of interest in Doogie Duval's real estate schemes, and how Doogie had flown the coop last week at Club Fed over in Terre Haute. I asked her about getting thrown out of the drive-in too.

She made a face. "That thing at the drive-in was not my fault. Charleton Heston in a skirt always gets me going. Dickie was a backsliding Baptist when we took up, and I aim to keep him that way. More fun for me."

She changed the subject. "You reckon Doogie is hanging around these parts?"

"Might be," I said. I'd found a bank of articles on Doogie and his background online in one of my crime-busting databases. "Doogie was born in Indiana, you know."

"Whereabouts?"

"Says here, Terre Haute."

"Sassy went clear across the country to hook her a crazy Hoosier boy?"

"Says here Doogie's upbringing was right common."

"My upbringing was right common. Didn't give me a desire to go around gigging people."

It was true. Lavinia, like me, had been born with a plastic spoon in her mouth.

My cell started jumping. I clicked it on to hear a voice mail from Avonelle. She asked if we could drop by the bank that afternoon to talk to her about Bromley and a few other issues that had come up.

It was already afternoon, so I printed out a heap of articles about Doogie and shut down the computer. "We got a summons from Her Majesty, Avonelle," I said to Veenie. "Let's roll on over to the bank and wrap up that case before we head toward Bloomington to check on Rusty."

"Oh boy," said Veenie. "Good thing the Lord Almighty gave men ding-a-lings, or we'd not have a gosh darn thing to do all day long."

And we were off.

CHAPTER SEVENTEEN

Avonelle was sitting behind her desk signing a mountain of papers when we arrived at the bank. Her great-great grandpappy in-law, Silas Apple, had founded the bank at the turn of the century—the twentieth century—1901, to be exact. A portrait of him hung on the wall behind Avonelle. He had a shriveled-up face like a crab apple and a set of gray side whiskers that looked like sweep-up brooms. Old Silas was so tight he could squeeze a buffalo nickel until the buffalo pooped, or so said Titsy, my Grammy Waskom. Avonelle was much the same. She was older and richer than me or Veenie but still enjoyed mashing nickels together to make ends meet.

Avonelle didn't look up when we were shown into her office. Veenie and I plopped down in a pair of red-velvet padded chairs and waited for her to get to the end of her paperwork. Veenie started fidgeting almost instantly. She was clicking her teeth, getting ready to bite. She hated being made to wait. I shot her a look. She pursed her lips at me and made a noise like a motorboat before busying herself playing Farmville on her phone.

Avonelle looked up after a while. She was, per usual, dressed to meet her maker. She wore a navy-blue suit with white piping and one of her giant, white Buster Brown silk bows. A good choice, I thought. The color scheme went well with her apricot hair and hand-drawn eyebrows. Ignoring Veenie, she asked me if I'd heard from the coroner about Bromley's cause of death.

I said we had. Assuming she was going to close the case, I'd brought with me a detailed invoice of our hours, with a balance figured on the account. Avonelle only owed us a couple of hundred. Since we were always short on cash, I found it best to hand deliver our bills on check out. On our way over, I'd received a text from the genetics company we used informing me that William Apple was indeed the father of Billy Skaggs. Avonelle could use us to settle up with Barbara, or call on her herself. I'd already forwarded the genetic test results to Avonelle.

Avonelle shook her head at the bill. "What's this?"

"Assuming you want to close out the case on William and Bromley."

She slid the bill back across the desk. "Well, I don't." She stood up, yanked her jacket down over her bowling-pin hips, and strolled over to the window. She looked out through a nice cluster of maples, over across Main Street. "Something else has come to my attention."

Veenie stopped thumb wrestling her phone and looked up.

I asked Avonelle if she doubted the results of the autopsy.

"No," she said. She was holding her lips so tightly they started to quiver. "I had an aunt who probably died of the same thing. They didn't have tests back then. Just glad they know what it is. Hoping Bert and the grandkids didn't inherit it."

"You got my text about Billy Skaggs?"

Avonelle returned to her desk and sat down in her chair. She folded her hands on the desk blotter in front of her. "I did."

"You want us to arrange some sort of payment plan for child support with Barbara?"

She heaved a sigh. "I suppose that's the only decent thing. I've talked to my lawyer. He'll set up a small trust for the children. I don't want Barbara wasting my hard-earned money buying press-on nails and cheap liquor. The lawyer will keep a tight hold on the purse strings. That's what William would have wanted."

I was mystified why Avonelle would still need our services, and I said so.

"This," she said. She drew a piece of lined yellow paper out of a drawer on her desk and slid it across to me.

I plucked up the paper and read it.

Veenie craned her neck over my way to get a good gander.

The message on the paper was spelled out in letters cut from magazines and newspapers, like in one of those 1950s detective movies. It read, "We know your secrets. Buy silence. $20,000. Will contact soon."

That raised my eyebrows. "Any idea what this message means or who sent it?"

"Of course not. Probably some kin of that Skaggs woman hoping to suck cigarette money out of me." She straightened her bow. "I want you to stay on the case. Find out who sent this. What they want."

Veenie pointed at the note. "Says there they want twenty thousand dollars."

"I can read, Lavinia. I meant what they *really* want. If they want to embarrass my family, this won't stop here, and I'm not paying hush money. Furthermore I won't be humiliated by some hill jack because the men in my family scattered a few wild seeds. Men are like that. Sleeping around. It's the way they're made. It's been happening since God hung the sun in the sky. My goal is to put a stop to this. Make sure whoever's doing this gets his rightful due."

I eyed Avonelle. "You sure you want to know? You could just ignore this."

That suggestion made her squirm. "I am an Apple. We don't run and hide. We face our troubles." Her nose flared. The little tendons in her neck tightened up, pushing out her Buster Brown bow. She stood up and handed the invoice and blackmail note back to me. "Find out who sent this note." She sat down, bowed her apricot head, and started in on a second set of paperwork.

Realizing we'd been dismissed, I rose and motioned for Veenie to follow me out of the office.

Veenie was chattering like a rattlebrained chipmunk by the time we reached the Impala. "I tell you, them Apples are hiding big piles of poo-doo. Didn't I tell you Bert was skulking behind the curtains, acting odd? And here Avonelle is, wanting to spend more money. Avonelle spending *more* money on us, *with no questions asked*. That alone ought to tell you we've stumbled into something. Somebody knows something about them Apples all righty, and Avonelle aims to hush them up for good."

"Lavinia, maybe being blackmailed don't sit right with her. You know how people are. Everybody's got a skeleton or two in the family closet. And she's right, if you pay blackmail, it's like handing a boozer a bottle. They'll be back for more. Suck you dry. Avonelle is trying to make the best of a bad situation. What would you do if someone was blackmailing you?"

"Wish them luck. I ain't got nothing."

"Oh for Pete's sake, it would make you madder than a wet hen. You'd scratch their eyes out. This is Avonelle's way of scratching back."

"We got two other cases now. We got to find out who sent Fussy to see Saint Peter, and we got to get Sassy out of jail. Also, Joyce is expecting us over at her place in Bloomington."

"Maybe Harry could pitch in."

We both laughed at that.

As if on cue, my cell phone exploded. Joyce. She wanted to know where we were. When would we be at her place? Were we on the way? Her texts were loaded with tiny pictures of life savers, SOS signals, and cracked hearts.

I used my words and texted back, "On our way." On our way out of town, we whizzed past Shap Reynolds driving fast down Main Street with a pickup load of seed corn. He had a new gun rack mounted in the back window of the pickup. It was sagging with shotguns.

Veenie tossed Shap a big wave.

He waved back.

"Boy, oh boy, too bad we got to leave town." Veenie craned her neck around as Shap braked and pulled his pickup onto the sidewalk in front of Pokey's Tavern and Pool Hall. "I wouldn't mind seeing Harry pick buckshot out of his ass just one time."

I kind of agreed with her, but reckoned the way Harry was going, we'd get to witness that and a whole lot more before spring fever tuckered everybody out.

CHAPTER EIGHTEEN

Joyce greeted us at the front door. She ushered us into her fancy house like we were poor relations she didn't want anyone to see visiting her in broad daylight, probably because we were.

She looked a lot better than she had the night before. She'd had her hair blown-out. Her makeup was perfectly smooth, like vanilla pudding. She was wearing sparkly heels that looked to be new and a flowing flowered blouse with a scoop neck. Her skirt was full and fit her nicely. A purple paisley silk scarf drew attention away from her little double chin.

Joyce was a good kid, but she'd always been uppity. She'd gone off to college at IU and married an educated man. She had a whole new backstory that conveniently left her real kin out of the picture. Last I heard the story from a college friend of hers at a casual county meet up, Joyce's daddy was a doctor who'd died working to save the poor in Africa. I was a singer who'd been killed in a plane crash on the way to his funeral. Eddie, her little brother, didn't even exist. I reckoned he was such an embarrassment she decided there was no use trying to salvage him for public consumption. I kind of knew where she was going with that one. I supposed Joyce's fibbing was my fault. Veenie let on like it might be. I let Joyce watch *Dynasty* and all that trash TV in the seventies because I couldn't afford a babysitter. Her upbringing hadn't been all that glamorous. Couldn't blame the kid for fairy-dusting up a better backstory for herself.

Veenie strolled around the three-stories-high entryway. A white staircase swirled down from the upper stories like a cork screw. It looked a lot like the entryway in *The Beverly Hillbillies*.

"Boy, oh boy, this place ought to have come with its own Rhett Butler," Veenie said.

Joyce beamed. She figured that was a compliment. I wasn't so sure. "This whole development has a theme of Tara, like in *Gone with the Wind*. It shows, doesn't it?"

"Uh huh," I said. Joyce's husband, Russell Krotch, the polecat we were there to spy on, was from Atlanta. He shared Joyce's love of glitz. He loved dressing up in costumes and doing local TV commercials for his insurance business. The two of them together sparkled like a pair of cheap pasties once they got going.

Veenie plopped down on a red-and-gray silk divan. "Where's old Rusty Krotch?"

Joyce cringed. Her shoulders pulled back a bit like a pigeon. "Lavinia, you know he wants to be called Russell. *Russell*, not Rusty."

"Rusty Krotch makes him a whole lot more memorable. I bet he'd sell a heck of a lot more insurance. Ain't nobody going to forget a name like that."

"I'm not sure his clientele would appreciate that. They're educated people, for the most part." Joyce looked at me for assistance reigning in Veenie.

I walked around the room pretending not to see the pleading in her eyes. "Rusty at work?"

"Said he was going there this morning. He doesn't normally get home until after six. Lately, it's been more like nine o'clock. That's part of what's got me worried."

"He give any reason why he's coming home so late?"

"Says it's the busy time of year, but we've been together twenty years. He's never come home late every night like this before." Joyce played nervously with a diamond tennis bracelet on her wrist.

"You know the passwords to his home computer? His cell phone?"

"He never uses the computer in the den. He has a laptop. Takes it with him everywhere. Uses it to write up policies. I never use it, so I never asked him for passwords. We've always trusted each other."

Veenie piped up. "That there is your first mistake. You got to assume a man is vulnerable when it comes to his giggle stick. He's got all these shiny things." Veenie tossed her hand around the room. "Bimbos love shiny things. At his age, with all this stuff, he's big time skank bait." Veenie snooped around in a glass box on the mantle. She yanked out a cigar. "Didn't know Rusty smoked."

"He don't. I mean, he doesn't. Those are from Cuba. They're just for looks, meant to impress people." Joyce took the glass box from Veenie and set it carefully back on the marble mantle.

While her back was turned, Veenie pocketed the cigar. I could hear Rusty, who'd never been a big fan of our family, bellyaching now. "Why'd you let them in? Now we have to count the silverware."

In Rusty's defense, there had been that one incident with my older brother, Basil Lee. The Christmas Joyce and Rusty first bought Tara, they invited the whole dang family over, hoping to wow us. Well, we were wowed, Basil Lee more than anybody. She knew Basil liked to take a few mementos from the places he visited. Heck, we all knew that. We all put the shiny things away when he visited. And, in Basil's defense, those living room lamps had been real sparkly.

The whole thing would have blown over, but Rusty made things worse by confronting my brother. He stomped out to Basil's pickup and lugged the lamps back in. Everybody knew you waited a day or two, then went over to see Basil's wife, Nancy Jane. She'd have the things ready for you to tote back home. No one in the family ever spoke about Basil's sticky fingers, certainly not out loud. That would have been downright rude.

Veenie asked Joyce if she could write down all the places Rusty might go during the day, constructing a kind of time table of how his daily routine went. Joyce pulled a paper out of her skirt pocket. "Did that this the morning. He goes out sometimes to see clients in their homes. The big ones. He always works the big accounts himself. He has some corporate clients. That's where the gold is, in corporate insurance."

Veenie and I studied the paper. It listed a thorough break-down of Rusty's favorite lunch and dinner hangouts, along with a detailed list of his largest insurance clients. I was impressed at how well-organized and thorough Joyce had been. But then she always had been a cracker-jack student. It was her nerves that were jumpy, not her mind.

Veenie asked if Joyce had a list of possible suspects in terms of who Rusty might be stepping out with.

Joyce nodded and handed us another piece of paper. This one had photos and write-ups on three women. It also listed the women's addresses, car models, license plate numbers, phone numbers, email addresses, and Facebook pages. Joyce was clearly serious about getting to the bottom of her husband's peculiar behavior.

"All three of these women are skanks, near as I can tell. They all gush over Russell like he's was the Lord All Mighty." She fiddled with her tennis bracelet again. "You going to follow him? I think you should follow him. Tonight, when he gets off work. That's only an hour from now." Joyce was pacing now, her heels clicking on the stone floor.

"Stop fussing and fretting," I said. "We'll get to the bottom of this."

Veenie piped up. "We'll get it done, all righty. If some skank's yanking Rusty's wonder worm me and your mama will nail her in no time."

I might have put that differently, but hey, the sentiment was dead on.

CHAPTER NINETEEN

Half an hour later, Veenie and I were parked across the street from the Krotch Insurance Agency. Veenie was munching on a family-sized bag of Cheetos. Her mouth was ringed in orange, and her fingertips were stained orange too. She was slurping on a striped straw that bobbed around in a NASCAR emblazoned plastic Big Gulp cup of Big Red pop.

Veenie stared at the lighted sign that dominated the front of the office building that Rusty owned. "Boy I don't envy ol' Rusty Krotch. If he's cheating on Joyce, he better hope *his* crotch is fully insured. Hate to think what that girl might do to him once she gets going."

Veenie had a point. Once Joyce got knocked off center, it was like watching a tornado slam a trailer park. Everything splintered. Once, she got mad at her little brother, Eddie, for calling her a "fatso" on the school bus. I came home to find him stuffed in the clothes dryer with his mouth duct taped shut. Joyce was up on her tiptoes on a stool ready to flip on the dryer. She aimed to send her brother for an hour-long, seventy degree tumble. She'd had this glazed look in her eyes, like she might have been possessed by a demon.

Eddie never teased Joyce after that. He always got one of his friends to do the dirty work. Joyce didn't get just a little bit mad. She went full demon. All her screws popped. It didn't last long, but Lord, when it hit, that girl destroyed everything in her path.

I was watching the Krotch Insurance Agency with a pair of binoculars. Luckily, it was in an old two-story limestone building with a glass front, just around the corner from the Bloomington courthouse square. I could see all the employees scurrying around like ants, answering phones, printing out paperwork, and guzzling coffee from one of those fancy Italian coffee machines.

Joyce had been right. Rusty worked in a sea of young women. He was about the only man in the place. His desk was in the back, in a separate office with a huge glass window. I could see most, but not all, of what went on inside his office. It was closing time. People were starting to put on their jackets, grab their purses, and spill out the door. Rusty didn't move though. He was hunched over a pile of papers on his desk. He was dressed in a blue pin-striped dress shirt and a right nice maroon tie with his sleeves neatly rolled up. A navy jacket hung on a coat rack behind him. He wasn't the world's most handsome man, pretty darn average when it came to looks, but Veenie was right: women didn't marry men for their looks so much as for their ability to provide, and he'd done right by Joyce in that regard.

Veenie complained. "My calves are cramping. I think I might be getting one of those deep vein blood balls that kill people. I got a heart condition, you know." She made a show of kicking out her stubby little legs. "He still in there?" She had her nose pressed to the Impala's window now. "That him in the back office?"

I swept the binoculars away from my eyes and handed them to Veenie. "Yeah. He's just sitting there, working, near as I can tell."

Veenie whipped off her glasses and slapped the binoculars tight to her eyes. Her vision was going in spots, but she could still see fairly well in bright daylight or with telescopic assistance. "Who's the high-class doll in his office?"

I squinted. Someone had scooted into his office and was standing in front of Rusty's desk with her arms crossed. Rusty was looking up at her. Everyone else had left the office now. I pulled the paper Joyce had given me out of the glove compartment and studied the photos of the three women she considered the most likely suspects. "Looks to be Kayleigh Burton."

Veenie put down the binoculars and studied the photo. "Yeah, that's her. How old is she?"

"Says here she's twenty-one. Just graduated IU. Real estate major. An intern."

I picked up the binoculars and studied the action in the office. Kayleigh was a petite trim woman, but stacked. She had short, dark raven hair with a little natural curl. She was dressed professionally in a shirt-waist silk jacket and skirt with a tight-fitting blouse. She was dripping in gold bling. Definitely attractive. Her hands were off her hips now, and she was pacing back and forth in front of Rusty's desk. Every now and then she threw her hands up in disgust. Rusty was standing up behind the desk now. He was running his hands through his hair. Then he placed his hands on his hips. His little pooch belly strained against his dress shirt. Kayleigh started shaking her fist at him. He shook his fist at her in return. Rusty's face turned brick red. Kayleigh ran over to the window in Rusty's office. Next thing I knew, a forest green venetian blind rolled down and I couldn't see a dang thing.

Veenie made a sucking sound with her dentures. "Looks like a lover's spat to me."

I hated to admit it, for Joyce's sake, but I had to agree with Veenie. Rusty and Kayleigh were definitely arguing about something. And they'd waited until everyone left the office to light into one other. It was killing me that I couldn't see anything. Lordy, what I'd have given to hear the conversation inside that office.

Veenie and I waited and watched for an entire hour. It took that long for the lights to go off in Rusty's private office. As soon as the lights snapped off, Kayleigh strolled out into the main office, grabbed her purse off a desk, and strutted out the main door. Walking briskly, she headed south toward the courthouse square.

Rusty popped out next. He had his jacket on. His tie was snug to his neck. He was all neat, every thin little graying hair in place. He locked the door on his private office then flipped off the outer lights. He strolled out and climbed into his black BMW, the only car left in the gravel lot at the side of his building. He peeled out of the lot and headed toward the main road out of town that led to the subdivision where he and Joyce lived.

Meanwhile, my cell phone was exploding.

Veenie peered at the screen of the phone, laying on the seat between us. "It's Joyce."

"I figured as much."

"You going to answer that?"

I looked down at the messages. A lot of broken hearts. A crying face or two. A sizzling bomb. A woman with a dagger in her back. "Nope." Right at the moment, things weren't looking so good for Joyce's marriage. Knowing how crazy Joyce could get, I wasn't going off half-cocked. I needed proof, something solid, before I got her all whipped up.

I texted Joyce that everything "seems normal, so far," and told her that Rusty had been working late at the office but was now headed home.

She texted back praying hands and a dozen happy faces.

Veenie eyed me. "Why you keeping this from her?"

"I'm not keeping anything from that child."

"What exactly you think they were doing in that office for an hour with the blinds yanked down?"

I chewed my cheek. "I'm not getting Joyce riled up unless we got something solid."

"Ruby Jane, you know as well as I do that men don't lock themselves in a room with a hot young piece of chicken and pull the blinds down except for one gosh darn reason."

"Dang it, Lavinia, we need proof. You know how Joyce gets. We need to tell her the whole story, and we need to get it right. We can't be going off half-cocked. If she gets riled up, she could end up wiping out half of Monroe County."

"Reckon you're right, but how we going to catch ol' Rusty in the act?"

"I dunno yet. We'll think of something. Maybe that tracking device will give us some clues. Let's watch it for a day or two."

When we'd first arrived, Veenie had gone to the parking lot and slapped a GPS tracker under Rusty's back bumper. We could now track every move he made in his BMW. If he was sleazing around town bumping uglies with his interns, he almost certainly had a private love nest somewhere. Once we found that love nest, we could close in and get some photos. Joyce would need evidence if she hoped to get a decent divorce settlement. Dang it, she'd invested so much in keeping up her appearance, her marriage, her kids. I just hated to see her little fairy-dusted heart smashed to pieces like this.

"Let's head home," I sighed as I keyed the Impala. It was growing dark, and the back roads from Bloomington to Knobby Waters were windy and hilly, not all that well-lit. The old Chevy had coughed and puffed a good bit crawling around the hills on the way to Bloomington. It could get temperamental, and I didn't want to get stranded out in the countryside.

"Fine by me," said Veenie. "Can we cruise through the drive-in window at the Bedford Frosty Top? They got a chili dog special on Tuesdays, ten percent off for seniors." Veenie pulled a coupon out of her bra.

"I thought them chili dogs barked back at you."

"They do, but so does everything I eat."

She had a point. Besides, the whole Rusty thing had me depressed, and eating always helped. I cheered up at the thought of a double chili dog with extra mustard barking my name.

CHAPTER TWENTY

T he next morning over breakfast, Veenie checked with the bank online to confirm that Sassy's thousand dollar retainer had cleared the agency's account. "Lookie there," she said to me between slurps of corn flakes. She was pointing to her cell phone screen. "Sassy's check cleared. Reckon we'll have to spring her now." She sounded kind of disappointed.

Sassy herself was fuming by the time we got to the jail and picked her up. The judge had voted her an unlikely flight risk and signed her release. She'd have to appear in court for an arraignment, but that was a few days away. And frankly, given what I knew, I didn't think there'd be enough evidence to indict her. But then again, what did I know? Pretty much zippo.

Sassy slid into the backseat of the Impala and hunkered down low. Glancing in the rearview, I could practically see steam rolling off her hay pile of hair. Her mascara was dripping down her eyes like one of them "Kiss" band guys my son Eddie had idolized since the seventies. Her lips were chapped and cracked like big, dry pawpaw leaves. "Get me home," she croaked, "before someone sees me looking all natural like this." She slid down in the backseat and stayed that way until we reached our house.

I felt sorry for her.

Even Veenie softened toward her.

Heck, both of us knew full well that Sassy, for all her faults, was not a murderer.

I fixed her a hot breakfast of eggs and bacon and some home-squeezed OJ once we got home. She wolfed it down, along with a couple of cups of hot coffee sludged up with diet sweetener and powdered cream. I retrieved my notebook from my messenger bag and began asking Sassy questions. I was hoping she had some idea who might have gigged Fussy. She kept shaking her head. "No, no, no."

"I barely knew the man," she complained as she blew on her coffee cup, cooling it down. "He was taking me out to steak dinners and promising me cruises on his yacht over at Lake Monroe. Why on earth would I murder the guy?" She'd washed her hair and had it trussed up in a flowered towel turban. Her face was slathered with pink cream. She'd swaddled herself in a red silk robe and was wearing her faux diamond stud earrings. Another two hours in front of the mirror, and she'd look like the pert old Sassy again.

"We believe you," I said. "But it looks kind of bad from the outside, you being the last one to see him and all."

"Yeah," said Veenie. "What we need is another suspect. A plan B. We need someone to pin this on, so Grape Nuts will leave you alone."

"Well," said Sassy, "I don't have one iota of an idea who'd want to kill Fussy. We hadn't even made it to second base yet. I mean, sure, I was upset about the lingerie thing and all, but Lordie, no one kills someone over that. Do they?"

Veenie shrugged. "I might."

"What about your ex?" I asked. "Boots said he's out of prison."

Sassy's eyes grew big as blue moons. She bit her bottom lip. "Doogie? Doogie Duval? Why, he's not supposed to be released for another ten years."

"He wasn't released. He escaped." Since talking to Boots, I'd looked up the news online in Terre Haute, where the state prison was. I'd discovered that Doogie had hidden in a laundry cart. He'd left the prison in a wad of dirty bedsheets the week before. They had a statewide APB out on him.

Sassy sucked in a load of air. "He's out of jail?"

Veenie eyed Sassy. "He dangerous? The jealous type?"

"Lord, he is a bit jealous, but he'd never murder anyone."

Veenie seemed dubious. "He's a thief, ain't he?"

"He's a con artist," she objected. "Gentle as a kitten. He don't kill people. He's not that kind of man."

I'd never met the fellow, but Sassy seemed pretty sure of that last point. "You think he'd come looking for you?"

Sassy clutched at her robe and squirmed in her seat. "Maybe. He might."

"Why's that?" asked Veenie.

Sassy hemmed and hawed. "Well, truth be told, I might have a wee bit of his money stashed away."

Veenie clicked her teeth. "That money he stole from all those dim-witted investors with his real estate scheme?"

"Look, I don't know for sure where that money came from, but it's mine, fair and square. California is a joint property state." Sassy was pouting now. She'd finished her coffee and was rinsing the pot in the sink. "If you ladies will excuse me, I got to get my face on. I need to get out and about. Don't want people talking."

Veenie snorted. "You're about sixty years too late for that."

Sassy stuck out her tongue.

Veenie did the same.

"Oh for Pete's sake, stop it. Both of you. This here is serious. Sassy could go to prison." I stared Veenie down. "Also, she's our client now."

Veenie made a face but mumbled an apology.

"Before you go, Sassy, is this pretty much what Doogie looks like?" I showed her a couple of photos on my phone that I'd found online in the local news reports. One was his mug shot. In the mug shot he looked like a short, runty, crazy-eyed little guy with a flattop. He looked suave in the other, taken before his prison days at some California fundraiser for his real estate development, Sun City. In that photo, Doogie had his hair combed up on top of his head like a woodpecker. The top was jet-black—obviously a dye job—and the sides were white, all slicked back. He wore overly large, thick-rimmed black glasses, the stylish kind I'd seen movie directors wearing on TV. He wasn't very tall, but he was all puffed up in an expensive wide-lapel gangster suit.

Sassy pointed to the suave photo. "That's what he looked like when I was married to him. He didn't need the glasses, except to read, but he read somewhere that people trusted people who wore glasses, and he wanted people to trust him. Said it was easier to fleece them that way."

Veenie studied the photo. "Not bad looking. You know he was a crook when you hitched your wagon to him?"

"Lord no, Lavinia. I thought he was rich. Successful. He told me he was from Terre Haute, descended from French royalty. Terre Haute, that's French you know. In restaurants he always ordered in French. And boy, could that man French kiss." Sassy got a kind of dreamy look in her wide blue eyes.

I pointed to a news article I'd read on him. "Says here he was born in Terre Haute on the wrong side of the tracks. Says he spent time in the Indiana Boy's Home for petty crimes." As far as I could see, the only French Doogie might have been wise to was french fries.

"I don't know anything about that. Besides we all make mistakes when we're young. We met at a real estate open house in Canoga Park, California. He looked like a man ought to look to me. I was coasting on a big alimony payout from hubs number three. We hit it off when I offered to pay cash up front for a four-bedroom raised ranch he was showing. He got a kick out of the fact that we were both corn-fed Hoosiers living it up in the big city."

Veenie wrinkled her nose. "Nothing seemed suspicious about him?"

Sassy shrugged. "Everybody has rough spots. He looked successful to me. And he was a gentleman. He never once modeled my underwear."

I studied my notes. "So, you reckon he might come looking for you? He might have been watching you? Saw you and Fussy getting all intimate? Got mad? Took a pop at Fussy?"

"He might have. Sure. I mean, he might have challenged Fussy to a fight, but he sure as all heck wouldn't have killed him."

Veenie chimed in. "You got his money. I imagine that might have riled him up. If there's anything a thief hates it's having his stash stolen."

I thanked Sassy for all the information. "I'll see if I can't talk to Boots, get him thinking more about Doogie being the prime suspect here. We got to give them someone to go after so they leave you alone."

Sassy slid over and gave me a big hug, then another. I could feel her warm tears mingling with the cold cream on her cheek. She went for Veenie too, but Veenie, who hated to be squeezed on, dashed out onto the porch, out of Sassy's reach.

"You go on," I said to Sassy, motioning her down the hallway. "Shoo! Put your face on. Me and Veenie will snoop around. Take care of this thing for you."

Sassy gave me a final hug before sashaying down the hallway in her silk robe and disappearing into the bathroom.

CHAPTER TWENTY-ONE

Later that morning, I checked the online dashboard for the GPS tracker Veenie and I had stuck on Rusty's BMW bumper, only to find that he'd gone nowhere but straight home last night, then straight back to the office this morning. Nothing more we could do to help Joyce until Rusty did something suspicious or stupid.

Veenie texted me that she'd be down at the VFW gathering intelligence for most of the day, so I fired up the Impala and headed downtown by myself to check in with Harry at the office.

Veenie and I were now juggling three open cases. There was Sassy's murder case, my daughter Joyce's cheating-heart husband, and Avonelle's mysterious blackmail case. Might even say we had four cases because I still didn't believe that Bromley Apple had died of natural causes. I reckoned whatever had happened to him was connected to that blackmail note Avonelle had given us. Until she got another note with more instructions about the twenty thousand, there wasn't a whole lot more Veenie and I could do to move forward. Still, we were juggling a lot of balls. Truth be told, Veenie and I could have used an extra pair of eyes and hands. I was hoping the boss might see it the same way.

Harry was in the office all dolled up in his three piece suit when I arrived on Monday. His hair was slicked back, fresh out of the shower. His mustache was neatly waxed, and his tie was impeccably tied. Obviously, he'd not done the tying. He always got it a bit cattywampus.

Dottie Reynolds was still hanging out with him, or more accurately, on him. She jumped off his lap when I came in and starting scurrying around the office all pigeon-toed in her pink sparkly hot pants and midriff top. She was wearing dangly, purple feather earrings that hung down to her bony shoulders. She'd made Harry a pot of coffee. It looked like she'd also fetched him some morning donuts from the Roadkill Café down the street. He was sitting with his feet up on his desk, sucking on a chocolate sprinkle donut when I shouldered in with the morning mail, mostly bills, but there was a yellow circular for half-off on a gallon of rope bologna at the Hoosier Feedbag. I saved that for Veenie because her daddy, Pappy Tuttle, was a rope bologna fiend.

"You're late," Harry whined, gesturing wildly at his wrist watch. Donut crumbs danced on his mustache.

Dottie rushed over and wiped the crumbs away for him. Besides being pigeon-toed, she was also a bit knock-kneed. I don't know how she ran without tripping all over herself.

I reckoned her husband, Shap, must have been out of town on errands again. I made a mental note not to hang too long at the office. I didn't want to die in what Veenie referred to as, "an incident of testicular manslaughter" because Harry couldn't control his Mr. Happy.

"I'm not late," I insisted as I slapped the mail down on Harry's desk. "Veenie and I worked late yesterday. We were down at the jail, springing Sassy. Her retainer check cleared the bank. We interviewed her at home. She's all shook up."

Harry grunted. "She shouldn't have gigged ol' Fussy."

"I'm pretty sure she's innocent."

Harry popped the last of the donut into his mouth and licked his fingertips. "That's what they all say."

I explained to Harry that I thought the more likely suspect in Fussy's murder was Sassy's ex, Doogie Duval.

Harry tweaked his mustache. "You got any proof he's even in town?"

"Working on it." I fired up my computer. I wanted to check the phone databases to see if Doogie had any living relatives close by. Most people relied on family and old friends when it came to hiding out from the law.

Harry sauntered over, hands on hips. He stared at my computer screen. "Where's Lavinia?"

"She texted me she's over at the VFW snooping for clues on our cases." Veenie's favorite part of detecting was digging for gossip down at the VFW. She usually managed to dig up some mighty helpful stuff. Most people who hung at the VFW were retired or disabled or both. All of them were bored silly. Veenie had recruited a gang of them to be her snitches. They were a motley lot, but Lord they knew the scuttlebutt on who was sleeping with whom and who had money problems. Veenie always came back from the VFW hall dripping in gooey gossip. We only used what we uncovered for professional reasons, of course.

Harry asked why Avonelle was keeping her case open now that Bromley's death had been ruled natural.

I slid the blackmail note out of my top desk drawer and showed it to him. I had it in plastic so it wouldn't get messed up if we needed it for evidence. I'd dusted it for prints, but it was pretty much clean as a whistle. The cut-out letters used, near as I could tell, came from the *Pawpaw County Banner* and some Hoosier Feedbag circulars.

Harry read the note and handed it back to me. "Why is she being blackmailed?"

"Dunno. Claims she don't know either."

"You believe her?"

"Not right sure. How about you?"

"Seems to me if she was innocent and had nothing to hide, she'd have ignored this here note."

"Veenie said the same. I'm inclined to agree."

Dottie came over and nosed in over Harry's shoulder, trying to get a peek at the note. "Who's being blackmailed?"

Harry flipped the note over so Dottie couldn't see it. "Nothing to worry your sweet head about, honey buns. It's detective stuff. A case we're trying to crack."

Dottie "ooed" and "awed" and petted Harry's tie. She started hoovering his neck again.

Oh boy. I was getting ready to gather my things and vamoose—I was never going to get any work done there at Harry's House of Ho's—when my cell phone danced. I picked it up. I was expecting more hearts and hieroglyphics from Joyce, but instead it was a text from Avonelle. "Meet me. My house. Now."

I thumbed back, "Okay. Fifteen minutes."

I clicked off the computer and grabbed the keys to the Impala.

"Where you going?" Harry asked.

Dottie was busy climbing him like a tree. He had to stick his head out and look around her to yell at me.

"To work," I said as I scurried out the door.

CHAPTER TWENTY-TWO

A vonelle was waiting with the front door wide open when I pulled up in her driveway. She stepped onto the porch. She shot glances up and down the street before ushering me inside. After we were safely inside, she lifted the curtains and peered up and down the street. Then she yanked a cord and pulled the drapes shut tighter than a clam. She looked pale. She was dressed in one of her smart little peach-colored knit suits, but her Buster Brown bow was all loose and floppy. I'd never seen her so discombobulated. One of her apricot eyebrows was drawn on crooked. She was definitely stressed.

She asked me if anyone followed me, or if I saw anything suspicious outside around her house when I drove up. I said, "Nope."

We sat next to each other on a burgundy-and-gold striped divan in the living room. She handed me another piece of lined yellow paper. It had a message spelled out in cut-out news letters in the same style as the first blackmail note. It read, "$20,000. Skaggs's barn loft. Hound Holler. 9 PM tomorrow."

Avonelle sat up stiffly, hands on knees. "This was taped to my door when I came home from the bank."

"What do you want me to do?"

"Do??? What do I want you to *do*??? I want you to find out who's sending these ridiculous notes." Steam was close to escaping out of her ears.

"Would help me if you told me what in the name of Sam Hill this is all about."

She stood and paced the carpet. "Bromley had a few debts."

"I've discovered as much."

She sat down next to me. "His debtors want paid. That's all."

"Why don't they file a claim in court against the estate?"

Avonelle put her hand to her throat and laughed nervously. "Estate? He wasn't very good with money. He might have fallen in with some men who weren't all that reputable. It wasn't his fault. He never had much of a head for business. Like his father that way." She sighed.

"You know who these people are?"

"I have my suspicions."

"But you're not telling?"

"Wouldn't make much difference." She stood up and strolled to the gilded mirror that hung above the limestone fireplace. "Lord, I look a fright." She fixed her tie and messed with her hair. When she came back, she was composed, very cool. Her eyes were chips of blue ice again. "I'll not pay the money until I know who I'm dealing with. I need you to show up for this meeting Friday, see who's trying to milk me. Keep me, Bert, and the bank out of this in the meantime. Can you manage that?"

I was about to say yes when the house phone rang.

Avonelle froze. She got up, took me by the elbow and rushed me to the door. I was booted out the door before I could say much more.

Avonelle got in the last word. "I'll text you. Tomorrow." The door slammed in my face. I heard two clicks as she double bolted the door shut behind me.

Avonelle wasn't fooling me. She was spooked, and it wasn't me that had her shaking in her hundred-dollar shoes. Bromley had been in some kind of deep doo-doo before he died, and she wasn't about to let the family name, or her considerable assets, be dragged through the mud.

Still stunned by Avonelle's sudden dismissal, I drove over to the VFW to update Veenie. It was bingo night, still early, but the gravel parking lot was already brimming with cars and trucks. I parked across the street in the IGA lot and loped over to the VFW building.

The VFW was housed in a red brick building that used to be the Farm Bureau, nothing fancy. Outside, a flagpole was hoisted with the Stars and Stripes, a POW flag, and the Indiana State flag. The front door was a screen job set in a battered aluminum frame. I stepped straight in onto a chipped yellow-and-white checkered linoleum floor. Card tables were scattered around. A long, yellow pine counter lined the back, with a kitchen. There was a bar with two beers on tap behind the counter. The building was used for bean suppers, bake sales, and memorial services. Tonight was countywide bingo, so vodka well drinks and chicken wings were half-price. Cold beer came in two flavors: PBR or Bud. Blue oil cloths draped the tables.

Bingo at the VFW went on for hours. It was serious business. The jackpot was up to two thousand dollars. People put on their Sunday clothes and drove over from Jackson County, Lawrence County, Washington County, and Jennings County hoping to get in on the wild action.

Over to one side, Veenie's son, Fergie Junior, and my son, Eddie, were busy setting up their band, The Lonely Lip Lizards. Junior was the lead vocal and guitarist. My son Eddie was the drum man. They had a standing gig to play a few country-rock songs before bingo and during the break. They played at Pokey's Tavern several nights a week and raked in some extra bucks with sets over at the Stumble On Inn in Ewing.

Eddie sauntered over and asked me if he could bend my ear for a minute. I said, "Sure," and waved at Veenie, who sat over at the bar holding court with her snitches. I made some hand motions to let Veenie know that Eddie and I were going over to have a private family chat in the back.

Veenie gave me two thumbs up and went back to chatting with the boys at the bar.

Eddie was tall, like me, and so skinny his bones practically rattled when he walked. All the Reynolds men were like that, not an ounce of fat on any of them no matter what they ate. All his life he'd had to wear a belt with two extra punches in it to keep his jeans from falling off his washboard ass. As a kid, he'd been all elbows and knees, with his bony white ankles pushing out of his pants, and as an adult, there wasn't a spit more to him. His hair had been the same style since the seventies, long and thin, bleached and streaked blond, but now that he was pushing fifty, his hairline had gone gray and receded into a widow's peak like my daddy in his senior years. It was band night, so Eddie wore his usual stage outfit of white denim bell bottom jeans, a red bell-sleeved shirt with an open throat, and a fringed brown leather vest that I'd made for him in high school. He wore overly large, gold wire-framed glasses, which made his brown eyes look bug-eyed, too large for his long skinny face. His Adam's apple bobbed up and down as he rubbed a couple of fingers under his nose, where he had a whisper of a mustache. He looked sad.

"What's up?" I asked.

"Need a couple of bucks."

"Trouble?" I asked.

He looked down at his feet, which were encased in red Converse high-top sneakers. He shuffled his feet a bit and wiggled his hands, which were shoved flat in the front pockets of his jeans. "Nah. I'm groovy. Got a big mowing job this weekend out at the Proctor Cemetery. Just a little short on buying the gas I need to get the work done."

We'd had this conversation before, a few hundred times. Eddie never had cared much for money. He liked poetry and songwriting a whole heap better. For pocket money, he did his music, and for bigger stuff, like groceries, he mowed yards all around the county, small commercial accounts for the town and the county mostly. He did okay for the most part. He'd even sold a song or two to some music producers down in Nashville, but every now and then he ran low. He had the heart of a poet and a bank account pretty much the same. He'd been married once, but that didn't take. These days he lived in an old Bunny Bread truck that he'd converted to a mobile bachelor's pad. I was all right with that once he stopped parking it in my driveway.

"I got twenty," I said, as I opened the flap of my messenger bag and pulled out my little zip purse. I didn't add any kind of lecture because Eddie was Eddie, and well, I reckoned there was a reason God made him this way—all soft and dreamy like an ice cream cone that was forever melting under the heat lamp of life. He seemed happy enough with his lot in life, and I knew darn well that he was good for the twenty. It might take a week or two, but that twenty would meander its way back into my purse. He mowed my yard right regular, for free, weekly, and that was a sight more than most moms got in the way of a thank you these days. Plus, he'd never once been inmate of the month at the Pawpaw County Jail.

His face brightened a little. "Thanks, Mama. I'll get this back to you come Monday."

I nodded as he loped away toward the stage, a little more bounce in his step.

When I got back out front, Veenie was still busy holding court at the bar. She was perched on a bar stool with a frosty cold PBR in front of her, her chubby little legs dangling free. To her right sat Twinkles Tatlock, the beauty technician at Reddy's Funeral Home and a decorated Vietnam vet. He was a notorious bingo addict when his husband, Daddy Dewey, a short-haul Tennessee truck driver, was out of town on a run.

Twinkles offered me a seat at the bar next to Veenie. "Been saving this here seat just for you," he said.

"Thanks a heap," I said. It was hard to get a good seat at the VFW on bingo night. I fiddled with the red leather barstool, which was near as old and tattered around the edges as me, until I had it screwed up high enough for my giraffe legs. Sitting on a low stool made my knees ache. Luckily the stool Twinkles had saved for me still had some spin in it.

I ordered a Bud from the barkeep and complimented Twinkles on his outfit. He wore a cute little red blouse with a peek-a-boo chest piece and a matching pair of palazzo pants with white piping trim. His red leather ankle boots sparkled like they were covered in a mess of yellow fireflies. He'd let his dark hair down but had it curled in finger waves like Veronica Lake.

I had to admire the man. He was clearly born to accessorize. Veenie and he got along swell on account of their shared fashion sense. They sometimes went shopping together down at the Goodwill and the Pawpaw County Second Chance Charity Store that the Methodists ran to make money for their weekly free chili supper for the poor and the downtrodden. Twinkles was a kick-ass seamstress. He owned a professional sewing machine the size of a John Deere riding lawn mower. He'd bought it at auction years ago when the Excello Shirt Factory went out of business up in Seymour. Veenie and he were forever dragging home vintage fabric finds and gabbing fashion while they whipped their Goodwill wardrobes into shape.

"You put battery lights in them shoes?" I asked Twinkles.

"Sure did," he said, as he stuck a size thirteen ankle boot out and made it blink a bit. "I'm test driving these for the big chicken dance competition next month at the Chickenlandia Festival. "Veenie helped me rig them up. I can make them flash in time with the music if I want." He flashed his toes again, just to show off.

I was impressed, and said so.

That made Twinkles beam. "Thanks. Veenie and I work right nice together. We're plotting a new business. Aiming to start a new fashion trend for men. Lord knows most men could use a little spit and shine." He rolled his eyes as he took a sip of his vodka well drink.

Veenie reached down and pulled something out of an orange Hoosier Feedbag grocery bag that laid at her feet. It wasn't groceries through. She stretched a sparkly blue piece of cloth over one of each of her pointing fingers and made the thing snap. "Whaddaya think?" she asked.

Twinkles giggled.

"What in tarnation?" I asked. I adjusted my bifocals so I could see better and fingered the thing. "Are those panties?" I asked. They looked a little like a thong or a G-string that had been fattened up.

"Sorta," said Veenie. She danced her fingers around the fabric a bit. "Me and Twinkles call it a ding-a-ling sling. It's fancy summer wear for men."

"I dunno," I said, eying the thing that did look sort of like a skinny hammock. "I don't think many Hoosier fellows would wear that sort of thing."

Twinkles shot his head around Veenie's shoulder. "Too sissy?" he asked.

"Too sparkly. They comfortable?"

Twinkles took another straw sip of his drink. "Scratchy. We're still working on the details. It's comfy other than that. Once you get into it, you hardly feel like you're wearing anything at all."

I wasn't all that up to date on men's underwear. I reckoned Twinkles and Veenie knew that end of life a whole heap better than me. I went for comfort and durability in my underpants but realized a whole lot of folks liked more sparkle and sass in that department. "Who's your market?"

Twinkles fielded that one. "Anybody who wants a little more excitement in their downstairs."

"Well," I said, as Veenie flung the ding-a-ling sling back into the bag, "those ought to do the trick."

Veenie nodded. "We figure we can sell them to the Millennials down at the community college. Like a sexy nature boy thing. Those Millennials don't think there are two sexes. They like to mess things up a whole heap more than we did back in the sixties."

Twinkles nodded. "That's true. I was born way ahead of my time. Ain't nothing these days for a fellow to wear a bit of makeup and a man bun. I'm practically a plain Jane." He looked a little sad at that declaration.

"Well," I said, draining my beer and motioning for the barkeep to bring me another mug, "ding-a-ling sling, that name sure is catchy. Maybe you can get Devon Hattabaugh to test drive a pair." Devon was the junior law officer for the Pawpaw County Sherriff. He had side whiskers, wore a beret, and fancied himself worldly. I could sort of see him wearing a ding-a-ling sling, though Lord I didn't want to hold that image in my mind's eye for too long, afraid I might burn out my retinas.

After sipping at my second cold Bud, I asked Veenie if she'd uncovered any new gossip related to our cases.

"Loads," she said. "We ought to hang out here more often, Ruby Jane. These folks got more good gossip than the *Squealer*."

Twinkles chuckled. "You hang, you hear."

I asked Twinkles if he was the source of Veenie's intelligence.

He shook his head. "Nope. I do enjoy a fresh meaty piece of gossip, but my clients don't tend to bend my ear all that often." He giggled.

Pooter Johnson, a pre-teen snitch who cruised Knobby Waters scouting for things he could sell on the side, including newsy tidbits for the *Squealer*, broke out of the crowd at my elbow. Pooter was too young to drink, only about eleven, but he had his lips pressed to a straw stuck in a bottle of Big Red pop. "I'm your source," he proclaimed proudly. His eyes were shielded with his customary dark aviator sunglasses, which boasted fat chrome rims. His hair, the color of a field mouse, was home buzzed. The blue, wide-lapel jacket he wore was new and too long in the sleeves. He had the sleeves cuffed up. His scabby knees poked out from a pair of blue knee-knocker seersucker shorts. He looked *Miami Vice*, in a Hoosier sort of way.

I was about to ask Pooter for an official briefing when the lights went low in the VFW hall and the announcer informed us that the Lip Lizards were about to do a set of songs to get us in the mood for the big bingo jackpot, which he reminded everyone was now worth over two thousand dollars.

Everybody hooted and clapped and whistled. The crowd got so worked up the floorboards rattled and jumped.

I signaled Pooter that we'd gab later. Asked him to meet us out in the Chevy when all the bingo and hooting and hollering was done.

He gave me two thumbs up and disappeared into the crowd.

Veenie's son, Fergie Junior, stepped into the spotlight at the mic in the front of the room. He was wearing a ripped-sleeve, wife-beater T-shirt with fatigue-style capri pants and his little round John Lennon glasses. He stomped his booted foot a couple times and howled out Kenny Roger's hit song, "The Gambler." "You gotta know when to hold them …" while my son, Eddie, banged drums to perfection in the background. The noise was too loud in the VFW hall now to talk about much of anything, so we leaned back and let the music get us in the mood for a mad night of gambling away our Dairy Queen money.

It was after midnight before Veenie, me, and Pooter convened in the quiet of the Impala in the IGA parking lot. I was all ears as Veenie and Pooter filled me full of hot gossip, most of which surprised the holy heck out of me.

Chapter Twenty-Three

"Y ou're sure about this?" I asked Pooter. We sat facing each other in the front seat of the Impala with Pooter sitting between me and Veenie, chewing his fingernails. The pole light in the IGA parking lot sprayed a cone of light into Veenie's side of the car. The light bounced off Pooter's sunglasses and chrome frames, making him look like a large-eyed insect. He had a pack of cigarettes stuck in the breast pocket of his wide-lapel jacket. I'd seen him working the backdoor at the VFW, selling the cigarettes at a quarter a pop to folks who snuck out the back door into the parking lot to steal a smoke during the bingo showdown. Folks rarely carried pocket change, and most of the crowd at the VFW drank too much. All this meant that Pooter often raked in a paper dollar for each cigarette. Not a bad gig for a kid his age.

I asked him where he got his new suit jacket and seersucker shorts, and he hitched a thumb toward Veenie. "Granny Goens."

Veenie shrugged. "Plucked it up at the Goodwill. Thought it would look mighty good on the little fart." Veenie had a soft spot for Pooter, whose dad had a perpetual time-share over at the state prison, but she wasn't about to admit it. Most days the two of them pretended to tolerate each other, but they didn't fool me. Pooter made the best snitch because he roamed around town on his sister's banana-seat bicycle, sticking his sun-crisped nose into everybody's business. He could be found every Monday morning in the back parking lot of the Hoosier Feedbag, selling past-its-prime produce the Feedbag had tossed in the dumpster or that he'd bogarted from the gleaned fields. He called himself an "entrepreneur," though when he said it, it sounded more like "enter-manure."

I asked him again if he was sure about the news he'd reported to me and Veenie.

"Course I'm sure. I seen it with my own two little eyes." He jabbed two fingers toward his insect eyes. "Down by the river at the Moon Glo Motor Lodge."

What Pooter claimed to have seen was Bromley meeting up in a motel room with a man who was, as he described it, "a right fancy dresser."

"And you didn't recognize that man?"

"Nah, ain't from around here. I'd never seen him before he showed up out at the Moon Glo."

The Moon Glo was an old motor lodge out by the covered bridge that passed out of its prime about the same time Veenie and I did: the early seventies. Its neon sign had lost its fizzle. About the only guests who stayed there long term these days was a family of turkey buzzards who nested in the fizzled-out neon sign. Back in the day its air-conditioned rooms and Magic Finger beds had attracted tourists, who came for the catfishing. These days, the clientele were mostly cheating-heart Romeos who needed someplace to do the dirty that was a bit more romantic than the rusted-out bed of a pickup truck. These days, the rooms were rented out by the hour. Even the air conditioning was busted.

Veenie piped up. "I bet you a dollar to a donut Bromley was gay. Bet that's what Avonelle and everybody has been hiding from the town. He probably took up with some party boy with sparkle panties from Louisville, got himself into some deep doo-doo."

I shook my head. "That doesn't sound right to me. Everybody knows Bromley couldn't keep his hammy hands off the ladies."

"Bet that was a cover," suggested Veenie. "Used to, nobody wanted you to know if they was a poofter. And you know how sourpuss Avonelle is about appearances."

"Nah," I said. "Even if Bromley were gay, nobody cares about that. It's downright fashionable to be gay these days."

Pooter squeaked up. "I ain't saying he was gay. I said he was meeting up with some strange man who dressed in some pretty fancy duds. But, heh, it is a motel. There's nothing to the place but a rented room with a bed. What's a decent fella to think?"

"Describe the man for me," I said.

Pooter wiggled around in the Impala seat and pulled a tiny notebook out of his back pocket. "I keep my snitch notes in this here notebook Granny Goens gave me."

Veenie beamed with pride. "I want the little fart to be accurate when he fingers perps. Got him in training as a PI."

Pooter cleared his throat and read aloud from his notebook. "The fella is right short, with hair sticking up on top like a rooster. His hair is all black. His face is grandpappy old. All wrinkled up like a raisin."

Pooter slipped his sunglasses down on his nose and stared at me with a look in his beady, little brown eyes that asked if I wanted to hear more.

I nodded. "Yeah, sure. Go on."

"Suspect is wearing a big gangster suit and thick black glasses. Looks like a Hollywood movie guy." Pooter flipped shut his notebook.

I asked how the man got to the motor lodge out by the river. "Did he have a car?"

"Nah," said Pooter. "Bromley always drove him out in his big-ass Lincoln. They came out together. Went into a room together. Then came back out together about an hour later."

Veenie asked Pooter if he ever saw them squeeze each other's butts or anything untoward like that.

"Nah," said Pooter. "They weren't doing any of that stuff, but they did argue some."

"What about?"

"I couldn't hear much of what they said all that clearly, but the Hollywood guy yacked a good bit about condiments … stuff like that, and when he talked about that stuff, the other guy, the dentist, well, he would swell up big and red, like his head was a pimple that might pop off."

"Condiments? You mean condos?" I asked Pooter.

His face screwed up a little. "Yeah, could have been that."

Lightbulbs popped on in my head. I pulled my cell phone out of my messenger bag and flipped on the dome light in the Impala. I flicked through my cell until I found the photo I was looking for. I held the photo up to the light so Pooter could see it too. "This the Hollywood guy Bromley was with, out at the Moon Glo?"

Pooter sniffled and wiped at his nose with the heel of his hand. "Yeah, might be. Maybe."

Veenie rubbernecked around Pooter until she could see the picture on my cell phone. "Ain't that Doogie Duvall, Sassy's felon husband?"

"One and the same," I said. I hadn't a clue what this meant, but I reckoned either Sassy or Avonelle, or the both of them, knew a good bit more about these cases we were working than they'd been letting on. And come Monday morning I intended to twist both their tails until one of them hollered and came clean.

I kept the promise to myself. On Monday morning, over a pot of coffee and a bowl of Cheerios, I drilled into Sassy about her husband and Bromley.

"I got no notion what you're talking about," she claimed as she clutched at the buttons on her housecoat. "Doogie and Bromley? That's plain silly. How could they possibly know each other?"

Veenie eyed Sassy. "You want a free trip to the big house?"

"Course I don't," Sassy croaked.

"Then you better come clean."

"Gosh darn, Lavinia, why you got to stick your big nose into all this?"

"Cause, gash darn, Sassy, you hired me."

Sassy looked distraught. "Guess I did, didn't I?" She took another big gulp from her coffee. "God's truth, I don't know why Doogie would be hanging out at that fleabag river motel with Bromley. I suppose he might have been looking for me, trying to get some information on where I was, what I was up to."

I refilled my coffee mug. "Why would he ask Bromley about you?"

"How should I know? I hired you all to get to the bottom of this. If I knew any of this, would I have hired you all?"

"Doogie and Bromley never met, far as you know?"

Sassy clutched at her housecoat again. "Not that I know. I mean, obviously Doogie kept secrets from me. I guess this was just another one of his big ol' secrets. Boy, you think you know someone ..." Sassy reached up and fussed at the lines in her forehead with her fingertips.

I was about to ask more questions when my cell phone, which sat on the kitchen table, started to jump and hum. I flicked it open to a batch of texts. Some were from Avonelle. Some were from Joyce (those were punctuated with dagger hearts). I decided to deal with Avonelle first and hit the reply button to let her know that Veenie and I were headed over to the bank to see her as soon as we finished our morning coffee.

"Sooner," Avonelle texted back.

CHAPTER TWENTY-FOUR

Things were hopping at the First National Bank by the time Veenie and I arrived. Dode Schneider, a farmer we knew from a previous case, stood at the barred deposit window in the limestone lobby. He was fussing up a storm at the teller, a young guy with thick glasses and a scraggly red goatee, wearing a dark blue suit and skinny tie. The teller didn't look happy. His face was scrunched up in frustration.

Dode, who was dressed in worn overalls and a plaid, long-sleeved flannel shirt, kept pointing at a bank statement that he had pushed into the copper sliding area under the bars in the deposit window. "It ain't right. It's all wrong," he kept repeating as he shoved the statement at the teller. "Wrong. Wrong. Wrong."

"Mr. Schneider," said the teller with a huff of exasperation, "I'm pretty sure that statement is correct." He gently pushed the paper back toward Dode's side of the window.

"No it ain't, boy. I been paying on this tractor loan every month. That there amount due ain't what it should be."

The teller bit his lip. "What should it be?"

"Three cents less."

"Three cents?" the teller's eyebrows shot up and then he snorted.

"Yep. And that's my three cents, so I want it back. Right there. I want to see it right *there*. Darn it." Dode poked a bony finger at the paper statement. "And lookie here," Dode hitched to the left on account of his busted right hip and pulled some rolled up papers out of the back pocket of his overalls. "You all been cheating me for months now. Stealing three cents every month, right regular. Thought I was too addled to notice, didn't ya?"

"Sir," the teller began, "if we were going to cheat you, wouldn't we steal more than three cents?"

Dode's face reddened. "I said you was thieves. Nobody said you was smart thieves."

Avonelle came down the hallway while Dode and the teller were still going at it. She walked straight up to Dode and promised him she'd personally look into his problem if he'd give her a day or so.

Dode cocked his head. "A day?"

"Or two." Avonelle had her hands on her bowling-pin hips.

"Well, okay, missy. I guess I can wait another day. But I want interest on my stolen money. Will you give me interest?"

The teller objected, "On three cents?"

Dode glared at him.

"Yes," said Avonelle. "If there is an error on your account, the bank will make good, *with interest.*"

"Well, all righty then," said Dode. He rolled the statements and slipped them back into his hip pocket. "I'll be back then," he said triumphantly to the teller, who was already busy with the next customer, a boy too short to reach the window who'd brought in his passbook to make a deposit into his Christmas Club account.

"Fine," said Avonelle. "We appreciate your business and your patience, Mr. Schneider."

Avonelle turned to us. "This way," she said. She hurried us down the hallway to her back private office.

Avonelle wasted no time drilling into us. "You have a plan for tomorrow?"

I bit my lip. "You asked us to go out to Barbara's barn at nine p.m. and meet whoever shows up and report back to you."

"Yes, I did. I was hoping you'd uncovered the identity of my blackmailer in the meantime."

Veenie spoke up. "Last night was jackpot bingo over at the VFW. Our minds was busy working on that. We got us some hunches. It's setting up solid in our minds now, like Jell-O. Thinking takes time."

"Hunches?" Avonelle leaned forward and eyed us both. "All right, then. Tell me your hunches, ladies. Who's on your suspect list?"

"Hold your horses," said Veenie. "Suppose you tell us who has reason to be blackmailing you. You done something real bad, didn't you?"

Avonelle flinched. She sat up in her chair and yanked down on the lapels of her jacket. "I have done nothing. I told you, Bromley wasn't good with money. He had debts. I imagine this blackmailer is one of his debtors wanting to be paid off, or some kin of that Skaggs woman thinking I'll pay to keep the fact that William had kids with Barbara out of the public domain."

I asked Avonelle if she was willing to pay for either of these things.

She sighed so deeply I thought she'd blow us right out of her office. "I don't know. I won't know until I know who we're dealing with, and what they imagine might be worth twenty thousand dollars." I could see her face reddening, the patience draining out of her.

I decided to go at Avonelle a bit more while she was off kilter. I was willing to meet up with her blackmailer, but I wasn't buying the fact that this whole blackmail thing was a big mystery to her. "You know a fellow named Doogie Duval?"

"No."

"Bromley never talked about anyone of that name?"

"Not that I recall. You think he's the blackmailer? Who is he?"

Avonelle's face was smooth and calm. She didn't blink an eye. If she was lying now, she was gosh darn good at it.

Veenie spoke up. "He's a felon. Sassy's ex-husband. He was doing time in the big house over in Terre Haute, but he busted loose last week. He was seen with Bromley out at the Moon Glo."

"And who told you this?" asked Avonelle, her arms crossed against her chest.

"Pooter Johnson. He's one of our snitches."

"Pooter Johnson is a boy. A juvenile delinquent. And not a very smart one either, if what I've heard of him is correct," said Avonelle.

Veenie sat on the edge of her seat ready to defend her source. "That boy saw what he saw."

Avonelle shook her head. "So why would Bromley meet with a felon at a second-rate motel?"

"Didn't we just ask you that?" Veenie said.

I jumped in. "Doogie was in jail for running a real estate scam out in California. Did Bromley own any California real estate?"

Avonelle shrugged. "Not that I know of. He didn't even own the house he lived in. I hold the mortgage on that. Fussy was kind enough to let me assume the payments when Bromley started defaulting last year. Fussy did very well for himself when he built Camelot Court and Leisure Hills. Came to see me about Bromley's loan default, let me assume Bromley's payments as a professional courtesy."

I remembered Gretal, Bromley's wife, confirming that same fact about Bromley's house as she blew out of town.

The buzzer on the intercom on Avonelle's desk rang. She leaned over and flipped on the speaker. "Yes?"

"Your ten o'clock appointment, Mr. Peesley, from the Office of the Comptroller of the Currency up in Chicago, is here," said the voice on the other end.

"Send him back, please," said Avonelle as she rose from her chair and smoothed out her skirt. "You two," she eyed us. "Go out to that barn tonight. Meet whoever shows up. Find out what they know. Report back to me when you have some facts. *Facts* not rumors. Not speculation. *Facts.*"

Veenie and I brushed past a middle-aged man in a blue banker's suit as we exited the hallway back into the lobby of the bank. He carried an expensive thick, black leather briefcase in one hand and an equally expensive blue hat in the other. He wore heavy black-framed glasses, like the type Clark Kent wore. He bumped full into Veenie but said nothing and kept right on moving.

Veenie called out over her shoulder, "Hey, you always beat up on old ladies in hallways like that?"

The man glanced at Veenie but hurried on toward Avonelle's office, not bothering to give her a reply.

"Big city folks. Got no manners," Veenie muttered under her breath.

CHAPTER TWENTY-FIVE

"**W**ell," Veenie said, "now what?" as we climbed into the Impala.

I felt as frustrated as a hen brooding on a nest of eggs that refused to hatch. I let the keys dangle in the ignition of the Impala before turning over the engine. "Wish we could talk to Bromley. Looks like he took a heap of secrets to the grave with him."

Veenie popped open the glove compartment and rummaged around. "We got something better than talking to him." She pulled Bromley's cell phone out of the glove compartment and held it up to the sunlight. It glinted silver.

I'd forgotten about the phone. Gretal Apple had tossed it to us when we'd asked about Bromley's girlfriends and his little black book. We'd tried to snoop through his phone log and text messages when we'd first gotten it, but Bromley's fingerprints were required to unlock the device. "We can't crack that doohickey," I reminded Veenie. "It's locked up tight."

Veenie eyed me, her little blue eyes twinkling with mischief. "I got us a plan," she said. She turned the glinting phone around in her hand and mashed at it with her thumbs. The phone lit up, then a giant blue fingerprint splashed across the screen. Veenie mashed at the fingerprint pattern with her thumbs but the phone just blinked "unauthorized" and flashed off.

"You know how to hack a fingerprint lock?" I asked.

"Nope, but I know where Bromley's fingers are."

I stared at Veenie. Bromley's funeral showing was this afternoon, right after lunch. He was being buried the old-fashioned way: stuffed and dolled up with an open casket.

"Dead people still got fingerprints," said Veenie. "We just got to mash his fingers to this here screen and his whole life will spill wide open."

I thought about that idea for a moment and then keyed the Impala and roared toward the funeral home. I aimed to make us first in line to pay our respects to the dearly departed.

When we got to the funeral parlor the front door was locked tight. There was no sign of a hearse or any another vehicle in the parking lot. The lawn sign confirmed that Bromley's service was at one o'clock, with burial to follow in the White River Cemetery. My wristwatch said it was ten in the morning.

"Bet the back door is open," said Veenie. "That's where they roll in the bodies. They got to keep that door open 24-7. People die all hours. They can't be leaving them out on the front porch. Coyote might get to them. They got to refrigerate them right away."

Veenie bounced around back to the striped green awning that shaded the service door, and I followed. She pushed with both hands at the big silver button at the side of the doorway, and the two doors swung open slowly. Bodies were delivered through this entrance, so they'd installed a hands-free feature for people wheeling gurneys and caskets in and out.

It was cold and quiet inside the funeral parlor. The air conditioning sent a soothing hum through the place. We were in the hallway in the back, the hall that led to the body prep lab. "I bet Bromley is already laid out nice for his viewing party. Twinkles does that, and he's real efficient," said Veenie.

I heard a rustle, and another door popped opened at the far end of the hallway. Twinkles poked his head out the door. His hair was tossed up in a bun. He had a blue hair net stretched over the bun and a pair of plastic splatter glasses on his face. He wore a stained blue work smock over what looked to be a pink sweater with a white pearl design across the chest. "Oh, hi there, gals," he said. "You're early. Funeral isn't until one. I'm working on Juanita Gomez right now, trying to get her eyebrows drawn on right."

"Juanita died?" I asked. Juanita had been the clerk at the water department for as long as I could remember. I'd seen her Wednesday when I'd paid our water bill. She'd been grumpy, per usual, but she'd looked healthy enough.

"Honey, I hope she's dead, or else she's gonna be real mad she wakes up and finds me messing around with her makeup." Twinkles giggled.

Veenie explained why we'd come.

Twinkles listened and shook his head. "That's real creative of you, coming up with that idea. He's still got his fingers, sure enough. They're a little stiff, but I don't see why we can't limber them up. Put them to work. We'd not be breaking any laws or anything like that. I mean, his widow gave you the cell phone, and she's his legal next of kin. We'll be respectful and all. Let me strip off my gloves," he held up his hands, clad in blue plastic, "and I'll be right with you gals."

Bromley was laid out in his Sunday best suit, a baby-blue linen ensemble. He had prime billing in the Eternal Slumber Chamber, the largest and fanciest viewing room at the Reddy Funeral Parlor. A mess of flowers had already been delivered. His casket was heaped so high with flowers that he looked like he was taking a nap on a float on his way to the Rose Bowl Parade. Twinkles had artfully arranged the flowers, per usual.

"Lookie there," said Veenie, tapping at the wooden casket. "Avonelle sprang for the Supreme Slumber Rest Walnut 3000. That's top of the line."

Like I said, Veenie had booked her funeral with Beryl Reddy last spring on the layaway plan, so she was up to date on the most fashionable caskets and accessories. "That model," she continued, "has extra eggcrate foam in the mattress so you get a nice extra-comfy send away. You know I got a cranky lower back, so I ordered from the three thousand line for my send away."

I wasn't sure what to say about that. Getting a kink in my back from a poorly padded casket had never been a prime concern of mine. I reckoned if I ever woke up in a casket I'd have a heap of other worries to keep me occupied.

Veenie peered into the casket. "Gotta hand it to you, Twinkles. He looks a whole heap better dead than he ever did living."

"Thanks," said Twinkles. "Those new face paints from Louisville have a little more color and sparkle to them than the old line. You know when your time comes, we have to turn you upside down, drain all the blood out the wrists, so the body stays fresh. It's mighty hard to get color into a body when it's got nothing in the veins but formaldehyde."

Veenie nodded. "That's a dandy suit too."

"Smart as a whistle. Nice and cool for a spring layout. Avonelle brought it on over. This whole party is on her dime, and I gotta say she didn't scrimp, not one cent. She even ordered the full French manicure. Look at how his nails shine."

Veenie nodded. "Wish I could get mine to shine up like that. Got nails like a raccoon, all split and dry." She held her hands next to Bromley's and spread her fingers wide for emphasis. They were a bit cracked.

After snorting at her nails, Veenie pulled Bromley's cell phone out of her pocket and flicked it on. "You lift his hands," she said, nudging me in the ribs, "I'll smash his fingers to the phone until we find one that works."

I was considering this when Twinkles, probably sensing my hesitation, said he'd get the fingers up and moving. "Fingers don't move so well after they sit for a spell. And his have some makeup on them. I'll brush that off a bit, so you can get a good print going." Twinkles pulled a hankie out of his pocket and rubbed gently at Bromley's hand. I could see the makeup crumble off his hairy knuckles. "There," he said. "I'll work his fingers back into shape when you all get done. Won't take me but a minute or two."

Veenie slid the phone around under Bromley's manicured fingertips while Twinkles pressed the fingers into the screen. They tried every finger, but the cell phone didn't spring to life. "What the dickens," mumbled Veenie, frustrated. "Mash them fingers harder."

Twinkles tried, but the phone, like Bromley, was dead to the world.

Meanwhile, I'd been googling. "Gosh darn it," I said. "Says here cell phones have a heat sensing thingamabob on the fingerprint lock. If the thingamabob don't feel the heat of a body, it won't register a fingerprint. Says here if the body has been dead more than an hour or two, the unlock command won't work."

Veenie twisted her lips. "You reckon we could heat up his fingers? Like on a hot plate, like they was hot dogs."

Twinkles shook his head no. "That would be disrespectful. Also might burn his fingers."

Veenie grabbed Bromley's hand. "He feels all cold and rubbery."

"That's pretty much normal," said Twinkles.

"Can't you warm him up from the inside?"

"Don't think so," said Twinkles. "Not without messing him up."

Something clacked over by the front door, and a man wearing a blue chef's hat came into the front foyer wheeling a serving cart.

"Caterer," said Twinkles. "Avonelle ordered the full spread. Twinkles nodded to the man and pointed at a serving table that was set up in the reception room, which fed into the Eternal Slumber Chamber. "Set it up there," he instructed the caterer. The man got busy transferring silver serving dishes off his cart onto the table.

Twinkles consulted his watch. "You gals gotta go now. Folks will be arriving soon—the organist, the singer, the preacher too. And Avonelle. Don't want her throwing a hissy fit because we messed up Bromley's big to-do."

Veenie didn't look happy as we sauntered toward the front door, but she brightened a bit when she saw giant shrimp and a whooper-sized Velveeta cheeseball on the serving table. She popped a few shrimp into her mouth and poked at the cheeseball. "I bet they used a whole loaf of Velveeta on that cheese ball. And lookie, they rolled it in some fancy nuts." I had to shoo Veenie's little hand away to keep her from picking all the nuts off the outside of the cheeseball. Thanking Twinkles for his help, I steered Veenie on out to the Impala before we ended up in some sort of funeral parlor cheeseball fiasco.

CHAPTER TWENTY-SIX

While Veenie had been busy stealing party shrimp from the dearly departed, my daughter Joyce had flooded my phone with hieroglyphics. I'd gotten so sucked in by our morning meeting with Avonelle and the possibility of cracking Bromley's cell phone, that I'd forgotten that Joyce had sent me a string of distress texts at the crack of dawn. Her messages to me were growing more frantic. "He came home at 3 AM. 3 AM!!!" Dagger hearts. Cracked hearts. A whole row of crying faces. "You tracking him??? Where was he???"

I showed the phone screen to Veenie while I gunned the Impala to get it going. It didn't like to run after it had set cold for more than half an hour, and it was clear now we needed to race up to Bloomington to check in on Joyce and her hanky-panky pants husband, Rusty.

I asked Veenie to check the online dashboard for the GPS doohickey we'd stuck on the bumper of Rusty's BMW. "Thing ought to tell us where he was last night and where he's headed now."

Veenie flipped off her glasses and stuck her nose to the phone screen as we rolled up Highway 50 toward the cutoff to Lake Monroe and over to Bloomington. She punched and grunted at her cell phone.

We were flying along the edge of Lake Monroe by the time Veenie had Rusty's whereabouts pinpointed. "Uh-oh," she murmured.

"What?" I asked as I swerved to miss a pair of gray squirrels who scurried across the asphalt in front of us. "That don't sound good to me. What's up with that uh-oh?"

"This doohickey says Rusty was over at Kayleigh Burton's house last night until the wee hours." Veenie turned the screen my way, and I got an eyeful of an address that didn't mean much to me. "That Kayleigh's address?"

"Yep. That's the address Joyce gave us for Kayleigh. Some apartments on the south side of Bloomington."

"What time he leave there?"

"This here says he left at 2:46 a.m."

"He drive straight home from there?"

"Yep."

I gnawed my lower lip. This was not good news for Joyce's marriage. Kayleigh was young and a real looker. No way Joyce, who was pushing fifty and had a body like a busted can of biscuits, could compete with that. "Where is Rusty now?"

"His office."

I checked my Timex. "Bromley's daughter, Kimmy Apple, lives up in Bloomington. Goes to college there, right?"

"That's what she told us."

"See if you can find her using that that phone whatchamacallit Harry got us a subscription to."

Veenie fiddled around with her cell for a bit and pulled up the phone bank. It only took a couple of minutes for her to locate a cell number and street address in Bloomington for Kimmy. "What you want with this?" she asked.

"Figure maybe Kimmy knows the password to her dad's cell. Her cell phone is probably on his account. I reckon maybe she can get in, unlock his phone from inside the account, maybe take the fingerprint lock off the phone. Give us an account code to crack open his cell."

Veenie's eyes brightened. "Smart thinking. You want me to give her a call?"

I nodded as I prepared to shoot off the back roads and onto the connecting highway into Bloomington. "Call her," I said as I swung the Impala into the thick stream of traffic and headed toward Rusty's downtown office. Bloomington had a lot of one-way streets and a mess of spring pothole repair underway, so driving took both my hands and all my wits. Thick traffic always made me a little nervous, and the dang blasted college kids that attended IU were forever weaving in and out recklessly. I felt like I was playing bumper cars with kindergartners at the county fair.

I could hear Veenie's phone trying to ring up Kimmy. She had it on speakerphone so I could hear, and so she'd not have to repeat the whole dang conversation once she got Kimmy on the line. But Kimmy didn't pick up. An answering system picked up, and a woman's robo voice said to leave a message for Kimmy. Veenie squawked into the phone, explained what we wanted, and left her own cell phone number for a text or callback.

I found a parking space around the corner from the Krotch Insurance Agency and pulled in. The meter for the space was on empty, its red flag flipped up. Veenie and I dug through the ashtray in the Impala until we had enough loose change to feed the meter. I popped quarters into the meter while Veenie checked the online doohickey to make sure Rusty was still parked at the agency.

"Rusty's still at the office," she announced as we hit the sidewalk and ambled toward his building. I could see his black BMW coming into view, parked in a reserved spot in the agency lot. I reckoned we'd mosey on in, pretend we'd come to town shopping for the day, ask if we could use the restroom, see if we could catch him off guard, get him talking. I could feel my blood boiling at the thought of him hurting Joyce. It didn't help that Kayleigh greeted us at the door as we entered and asked if she could be of assistance. She was flipping her hair and acting sassy.

"Rusty here?" I asked.

"Mr. Krotch is very busy with a client. Might I help you ladies?"

Veenie was sniffing around Kayleigh like she was an unwelcome stray.

Kayleigh stepped back and asked me if Veenie was all right.

I looked at Veenie. "Right as she ever was. I'm Rusty's mother-in-law, Ruby Jane Waskom. She's my friend, Veenie Goens."

"Oh," said Kayleigh. She backed up and slid behind her desk, where she took a seat and folded her hands in front of her on the desk, like grade school kids are taught to do when it's quiet time. She wore a mint green suit ensemble with a beige silk shirt that left nothing much to the imagination in regards to her bosom. "Oh," she said again. "Is Mr. Krotch expecting you?"

"No," I said, telling the truth. "We were in town shopping. Thought we'd drop in and say hello. Maybe use the restroom."

Kayleigh's face relaxed a bit. "Oh sure, bathroom's in the back." She pointed down a narrow hallway, past the glass office where we'd seen her and Rusty arguing a few nights before. The green venetian blinds were rolled down on Rusty's office window, so I couldn't see who was with him in the office, if anyone.

Veenie shot down the hallway like a Super Ball.

"She's got a fussy bladder," I explained to Kayleigh.

"I can see that," she said, her lips tight. "Well, have a seat. I don't want to interrupt Mr. Krotch while he's in with a client, but if you'll wait a few minutes, he ought to be done soon." She checked her fancy wrist watch. "He has another appointment, a phone call that's supposed to come in any minute."

I thanked her and took a seat outside Rusty's office. A stack of beauty and health magazines were piled high on the reception table, so I busied myself catching up on how to keep my lips moist. I was barely through the first article (magazines are mostly pictures these days), when Rusty popped out of his office. An elderly man in tennis whites was with him. He wore thick glasses and had a neatly trimmed silver goatee, probably a college professor. Rusty was shaking his hand, congratulating him on how tidy a sum he could draw now in retirement because of that annuity he'd bought a few years back.

Maybe it was my imagination, but I thought Rusty's face fell into a panic when he caught sight of me. I smiled and shot him a little wave. He lifted a pair of fingers my way as a sort of halfhearted acknowledgment as he walked past me. He kept chatting with the goatee man, escorting him all the way to the door. He took his time walking back to greet me. "Ruby Jane, what a delight to see you." He smiled, but I could tell it was fake. His eyes didn't crinkle, and his lips were as stiff as Bromley's.

Kayleigh spoke up. "They were in town shopping, so they stopped to borrow the bathroom, say hello."

"They?" Rusty asked. His eyes darted all around the room.

"Veenie's with me," I said. "She's in the little girl's room."

His face relaxed. "Well, come on in. Always glad to see you. Did you stop by the house? Say hello to Joyce?"

"Don't have time today," I said as I followed Rusty into his office. "We got to be back in Knobby Waters by nine tonight."

"Oh? Your bedtime?" He closed the office door and slid into the seat behind his desk.

"No, we're on a blackmail case, and we got to meet someone."

"Exciting," Rusty said, punctuating it with another fake smile. He was playing with a pencil holder now, twirling it around in his hands. His little chicken hawk face was drawn up in an unpleasant way, like maybe he was constipated. He loosened his tie a tad.

I was fixing to ask him right out if he was cheating on Joyce when Veenie burst through the door.

Rusty's face fell when Veenie swooped in and took a seat next to me. "Lavinia, nice to see you again," he said through gritted teeth.

"Can't really say the same," grunted Veenie.

Ignoring that comment, Rusty offered Veenie some mints from a candy dish on his desk.

She declined. "Mints make me toot." She pinned Rusty to his seat with her tiny blue, dagger eyes.

Oh boy, I had a feeling I knew what was coming next.

"Why you cheating on Joyce?" she blurted out.

And there it was.

Rusty blushed. "I ... well ... I am not cheating on Joyce. Jesus, who told you that?"

"Joyce."

"She did not!" Rusty looked like he'd been kicked in the head. His little mouth drew up in a pout. "She didn't say that about me, did she?"

Oh geez, now he looked like he might cry.

"Afraid she did," I said.

"Why would she say something silly like that?"

Veenie hitched a thumb toward the office door. "That little jezebel you got riding reception might have something to do with it."

"Kayleigh?" Rusty's eyes widened. "My wife thinks I'm cheating on her with a woman young enough to be our daughter?"

"She's pretty much convinced of it," I said.

Rusty bent down and flipped on his intercom. "Kayleigh?"

"Yes, Mr. Krotch."

"Could you come in here for a moment, please?"

"Certainly, sir."

Kayleigh came into the office carrying a pen and her notebook, like she expected to take dictation.

Rusty eyed her. "Kayleigh, are we having a love affair?"

Kayleigh slid her eyes over me, then rested them on Veenie. "Not that I know of, sir."

Rusty raised both his palms up. "See?"

They both looked innocent enough.

Veenie was not convinced. "Why were you over at Kayleigh's last night at all hours if she's not battering your old corn dog?"

"Veenie," said Rusty, his face puckered in disapproval, "I'm going to do us both a favor and pretend you didn't just say that."

"Suit yourself," said Veenie, "but that don't answer my question."

Rusty eyed us. "Have you two been tailing me?" He stood up and placed his hands on his hips. He brushed back the tails of his jacket. The muscles in his jaw twitched. He was clearly unhappy.

"No," I said, which wasn't all that much of a lie because the little electronic gizmo on his bumper had done all the tailing.

Rusty paced in front of us. "I do not have to account for my behavior to you. You have no earthly right to be accusing me of anything."

"Me either," said Kayleigh. "I'll have you know that I have a fiancé, and he's a lot younger than Mr. Krotch, and ... well ... much better looking too." Her face fell into a pout.

Rusty looked a little hurt at that comment. "Thank you, Kayleigh. You can go now. See if you can get the paperwork completed on the IU police union's disability policy and their new workman's comp before you close out tonight."

She murmured something under her breath and backed out of the office, practically slamming the door behind her.

Once the door was shut, Rusty let us have it with both barrels. "Jesus Christ Almighty, I can't believe Joyce called you and told you that I was having an affair. Of all the harebrained notions. You sure Joyce is the one who told you all this?" He squinted his eyes.

Veenie said, "She didn't call. She texted. And if you could keep your wiggle worm in its zipper cage, she wouldn't need to be hiring us to look into your private pokings."

"Hire? She *hired* you?" That seemed to make him madder.

"We're professionals," said Veenie.

"Oh for God's sake," bellyached Rusty. "Well, how about if I hire you to stop snooping on me." He pulled a checkbook out of his top desk drawer. "What's your fee? Name your price."

Veenie looked like she was considering the offer, so I jumped back in. "Keep your money," I said. "Joyce is my daughter. If you aren't running around on her, what were you doing at Kayleigh's apartment in the middle of the night?"

Rusty heaved a sigh. "I can't tell you that, at least not now. I'm having some issues with the business. Little things. Some cash flow problems. But I am *not* cheating on my wife."

"Can you tell us more?" I asked.

"No, I cannot."

Veenie tossed in her two cents. "You better come clean, or we'll have to tell Joyce you're playing ride the bologna pony with Kayleigh."

Rusty shot Veenie a dirty look, which she returned, along with sticking her dentures out at him by way of punctuation.

Rusty huffed. "Lavinia, just so you know, that was uncalled for and very—very—immature of you. I mean honestly, at your age …"

"Hold your wild horses, both of you," I said, breaking into what looked to be a free-for-all brewing between the pair of them. "Veenie, hush up. Give Rusty a chance to tell his side of the story."

Veenie murmured something that sounded suspiciously like "Jackass," under her breath but settled back in her chair, her arms crossed tightly against her chest, signaling that she was willing to shut her pie hole long enough to hear Rusty's side of the story.

Rusty sank down in his chair and loosened his tie. Not able to get it loose enough, he yanked it off and bunched it into his fist a time or two. "You two can't breathe a word of this to Joyce. Understood? I have some financial problems with the business, but I'm ironing those out as we speak. I don't want Joyce or the kids worrying their heads over this. I'll have it all sorted out in a few days. A week tops. Joyce doesn't need to know about any of this. Understood?"

I shook my head. "Joyce hired us to get to the bottom of your odd behavior. What do you suggest we tell her? You're coming and going at all hours. She's going to need some explanation."

He rubbed his lips. "Stall her."

"I don't know," I said. "Joyce is like a tornado. Once she gets wound up, God himself can't hold her back."

Veenie said, "Ain't that the truth. What are we supposed to tell that child? She's all certain that you're up to no good, staying out all hours, sneaking around like a crazed polecat."

"I'm asking that you tell her nothing. Tell her you're still investigating. Stall her until I get this thing sorted out, for Christ's sake. Once I've got this thing under control, I'll tell her everything. Scout's honor." He gave us a little two-finger salute. "Just give me a few days," he pleaded, his eyes earnest.

I looked at Veenie, and she made a little face that suggested we didn't really have much of a choice.

"All righty," I said as I rose from the chair. "We'll give you three days. Three days. That enough time?"

Rusty nodded. "I'll make that work." He looked grateful. His face was more relaxed than when we'd arrived. If he were telling the truth, he was probably mortified that he'd had to admit he had money problems to me, his poor-as-dirt mother-in-law, of all people. Rusty didn't have a whole lot going for him, but he'd always been an ace provider for Joyce and the kids, and mighty proud of it. My heart melted a bit for him.

It wouldn't be easy keeping Joyce in the dark for a few more days, given how all fired up she was, but I reckoned Veenie and I could keep our clappers shut a few days. I knew I could. Veenie was less predictable, but she knew as well as I did that we didn't have any solid proof that Rusty was up to no good. And we still had that tracking doohickey on Rusty's bumper, so we could keep right on snooping, and he'd never be the wiser. In the meantime, we could look into his financials, see if things there supported his story.

I texted Joyce as we left Rusty's office, let her know that we were on the case but didn't have anything solid to report back yet. I wasn't about to stop by the house and look her in the eye, even though she was text bombing me to do just that.

She texted back, "You telling God's truth?"

"Course I am," I shot back, feeling guilty.

I tossed my phone to Veenie, asked her to shoot some comforting words and pictures Joyce's way as I wound around the pothole repair teams and navigated us out of downtown Bloomington. I headed toward the country roads, where all I had to keep an eye out for were deer. This time of year the deer, like Harry, went crazy trying to mate. They'd hump anything that moved. Hop right into your headlights. I didn't want to end up with a big ol' buck as a hood ornament on the Impala.

I stomped the accelerator as soon as we were free of city traffic. We'd have to fly down the back roads if we hoped to make it back in time to meet with Avonelle's blackmailer down in Hound Holler at nine p.m. The Impala coughed a bit, but when I didn't let up on the accelerator, it revved into Indy mode. We were shooting up and down the roller coaster hills toward home in record time.

CHAPTER TWENTY-SEVEN

We were about ten minutes late pulling into the tractor turnoff at the creek across from Barbara's house. We would have been on time, but when we hit town, the Impala threw a hissy fit and started shaking and quaking like a Holy Roller at a revival. We had to park it and let it cool off. It'd be fine in an hour or so, but we needed to get some new wheels under us fast.

Harry, who was hanging out at Pokey's Tavern down the block from the office was kind enough to loan us his Toyota so we could make it to the blackmail meeting at the barn. "Don't be letting Veenie drive," he ordered me, pulling a duplicate car key off his Ball State keyring and plunking it into the palm of my hand.

"You know Veenie doesn't drive anymore."

"Only because you keep an eye on her. I've seen her driving around town from time to time." He dangled a bottle of Schlitz between his fingers before taking a big gulp. "She's like a demon, murdering parking meters and trash cans right and left."

I eyed Veenie, but she just shrugged and made a "he's loco" swirling motion around her right ear.

While I was squaring everything with Harry, updating him on our cases, Veenie scored a bag of cheesy mystery meat sandwiches and a side of onion rings from Pokey. No one knew what kind of meat Pokey and his mama Dolly used in the sandwiches, but they were always hot and greasy and slathered in melted cheese and onions, so no one much cared about the true ingredients, least of all Veenie, who would eat pretty much any meat that didn't bite back.

With a new set of wheels and a hot dinner on the seat between us, we made record time climbing up the knobs and down the other side into Hound Holler. As I pulled the Toyota onto the shoulder, Veenie was busy piling up a stack of crunchy golden onion rings on the pointing finger of her left hand. She'd slathered the onion rings in ketchup and was trying to eat them off her finger without messing herself or the seats of Harry's Toyota. She certainly was enjoying herself.

It was dark but we could see the ramshackle barn across the road, leaning in the direction of Barbara's house. Barbara's car wasn't in the gavel driveway. No lights were on in her house. I reckoned Barbara was at work, maybe had taken the kids to a babysitter. A haze of humidity rose up from the creek bed, which was low because we hadn't had much rain. We had the windows rolled down on the car. Once I flipped the engine off, the mosquitoes swarmed in. I reached over and got some bug juice from the glove compartment where Harry, who was afraid of dying of some hillbilly bug disease, kept an arsenal of sprays. I squirted my neck and chest. That seemed to drive the mosquitoes away. I wasn't about to squirt Veenie while she was eating. I knew from experience that she didn't take kindly to anyone getting between her and her cheesy meat.

Satisfied no one had arrived to meet us yet, I pulled a sandwich out of the greasy white bag on the seat between me and Veenie. I peeled down the paper until I could take a good-sized bite. Veenie stuck a finger my way, offering me an onion ring, which I yanked off and snacked on between sandwich bites. It didn't take us any time to finish dinner. Still no sign of anyone around the barn or the house, other than the mosquitoes. Veenie grabbed the bug juice and sprayed herself. We sat quietly for a few minutes.

Veenie spoke first. "You reckon we should go into the barn?"

I checked my Timex. "Note said we were to meet up in the barn loft." We'd been late arriving, so I supposed it was possible that our mystery blackmailer was already hiding up in the loft waiting for us.

Veenie asked who I thought sent the blackmail note.

I shrugged. "Hard to say. Avonelle said Bromley had a lot of debts. She seemed to think the blackmailer is somebody Bromley owes money to. Can't get the money legally, so he's squeezing her."

"Well," said Veenie, "we better be prepared." She reached under her seat and pulled out her BB pistol from where she'd stashed it when we traded cars. She rattled it a couple of times for good measure. Not satisfied with the sound, she pulled a plastic tube of BBs out from under the seat compartment, sprung open the reservoir, and poured in more little silver pellets.

"You reckon we'll need that?"

"Blackmailers ain't nice people, Ruby Jane."

She had a point there.

I checked my watch again. It was half past nine. "Okeydokey," I said. "Let's see who our blackmailer is."

It was dark, so I picked up a sycamore stick alongside the creek bed and beat at the weeds, mashing a path from the road to the barn. No one had mowed around the barn for a coon's age. The mosquitoes hovered over us like a giant cigar-shaped blimp, held off by the bug juice. I looked for a light up in the hay window on the barn loft, but the place was dark. I gripped a flashlight in one hand. Veenie trailed along after me, griping about the chiggers, which were after her ankles.

The barn had a small side door, so we headed in that direction. Whippoorwills sang out, and I heard something clucking, probably chickens. Tree frogs croaked all around us.

I flipped on the flashlight but held the stream of light low to the ground because I didn't want to spook anyone who might be waiting inside. The barn door had a handmade latch—just a flap of wood attached to the board door with a loose rusty nail. Once I shoved the wooden latch down, the barn door creaked open. A cool blast of what smelled like hay, moldy wood, and cow piss smacked us in the face. Veenie shot into the barn under my arm, not seeming to notice the smell. Her pistol was raised.

It was quiet inside the barn, the dirt floor damp and slick under our feet. I twirled my light up and spied a homemade ladder on the far side of the barn. The rickety ladder leaned up against the edge of a second-story loft. My right knee, which was fussy from driving all day, ached at the sight of the ladder. The weathered board steps were nailed wide apart. It would take a two-handed scramble to get up the ladder into the loft. I peered up at the loft, hoping someone might come on down, but no such luck. I stuck my flashlight in my back pocket. Veenie stuck her pistol in the stretch waistband of her capri pants. I helped boost Veenie up on the ladder, mindful of the location of the BB pistol, so it didn't slip and discharge accidently, shooting off some vital part of her anatomy.

I followed Veenie up the ladder, my head butting up into her posterior, urging her upward. A cloud of mosquitoes had followed us into the barn. Between the mosquitoes, the cow piss smell, and my aching knees, I was thinking maybe, just maybe, being a PI wasn't as glamorous as I'd imagined.

Veenie reached the top. She grunted and rolled across a hay-covered floor, making room for me to roll up and do the same. We lay there in the hay, looking up at the stars through a hole in the tin roof. It was kind of romantic, except for the smell of cow piss and Veenie's snorting and panting. I didn't hear anyone and couldn't see anything, so I pulled out my flashlight and bounced the beam around the loft. No one there except for Veenie. A rusted-out milk pail sat in one corner. A blue tarp that was pretty beat up was stretched across a couple of busted bales of hay.

Veenie had her BB pistol raised. She swung it around in time with the beam of light from my flashlight. "Ain't nothing up here but bad smells," said Veenie.

It was now almost ten p.m., so I reckoned we'd been stood up. And I was ticked off that I'd climbed that ladder for nothing. It'd take a case of Bengay to get my knees moving again.

Veenie sniffled. Then she sneezed, her allergies kicking in. "You reckon he stood us up?"

I gave the loft another go over with my flashlight. All I saw were a pair of deer mice as they dove into a hole in the hay bale. "Gosh darn it," I mumbled.

But then we heard the barn door creak open below. Through the floorboards, I saw a thin beam of light swing into the barn and move toward the loft ladder. Veenie and I held our breath. We heard a scuffle. Then a gun went off, a shotgun from the sound of it. The tin roof above us rattled as pellets scattered holes in the metal. Debris scattered down from the rafters, into our eyes and hair. Veenie sneezed. Another shot went off. Something whizzed past my ear.

"Hit the hay!" I called to Veenie, who dove in front of me into the hay pile. She bounced over onto her belly, her pistol raised.

I heard the BB pistol go off. *Puff. Puff. Puff.* Then I heard more ear-splintering racket as the BBs ricocheted off metal. Down below, I heard the barn door creak again, and the dull thud of footsteps running away. By the time I made my way over to the wall and got my eyes pressed to a crack in the wallboards, all I could see was a shadowy figure disappearing through the tall weeds, headed out into the overgrown field. A beam of light from the runaway's flashlight bounced around, cutting a yellow path through the weed field.

I went back and offered Veenie a hand up. "You okay?" I asked.

She sounded winded as she stood up. "Yep, ain't bleeding that I can tell. Who was that? You see anyone?"

I turned the flashlight on and shone it Veenie's way. Veenie's round face was red, like a piece of fireball candy with white Kewpie doll hair. Her glasses sat sideways on her nose. The knees of her capris were smeared in dirt.

"Dag nabbit! He got away," I whined. "Didn't see a gosh darn thing. Just a shadow scurrying off across the field."

"Avonelle ain't gonna be happy about this," Veenie said as she brushed hay off her legs before brushing some hay off my ass. "You reckon them shots were meant for her?"

"Pretty much," I said.

If there was any doubt in me about Bromley's death being from natural causes or about Avonelle hiding something big, that doubt had now drained away, along with a good bit of my courage. I felt my dander rising. Someone had just tried to kill us, and that didn't sit right with me.

CHAPTER TWENTY-EIGHT

"Someone shot at you two?" Sherriff Gibson asked. His blue eyes squinted up like he didn't believe me or Veenie.

We were in the police station bright and early the next morning, and he was taking our statements. Normally, I tried not to drag Boots into our cases, but he had guns—real guns and real bullets—and right about now, I figured we needed some manly fire power.

"They sure did," I said.

"Sounded like a shotgun to me," said Veenie. "It sound like a shotgun to you, Ruby Jane?"

I nodded.

Boots tipped his sheriff's hat back on his head far enough so we could see where the sunburn on his forehead stopped and the snow white of his receding hairline began. "How you know they were shooting at you?"

"I reckon the bullets that whizzed past my head gave me that notion."

"Smartass," said Boots. "You said it was dark. You were out in the barn loft at Barbara Skaggs's place?"

"Yes."

"And why was that?"

Veenie piped up. "We was meeting someone for a hot case we're on."

"This have to do with Bromley Apple's death?"

I crossed my arms. "That would be confidential."

"I see." Boots leaned back in his roller chair until it squeaked. "Ruby Jane, I can't file a report if you won't tell me what all this is about. Gosh darn, woman, why you got to be so difficult?"

"We don't need you to file a report."

"Why you here then?" Boots eyed me. I could tell he was flustered by the way he rubbed at his lips. He glanced down at the paperwork on his desk, then back up to me. He eyed Veenie.

Veenie said, "Don't give me the hairy Hoosier eyeball. She's your gal."

I was about to object to that comment when Devon Hattabaugh, Pawpaw County's junior deputy, sauntered in from the back room. He was squawking into the little radio he had clipped to his shoulder. "Location?" he asked the squawk box. "Location?"

A woman, Bitsy Gorbett, whose voice I recognized because she was about my age and had been the county police dispatcher since Richard Nixon got booted from office, said, "Leisure Hills."

"Affirmative. Roger that," said Devon. Devon wore khaki knee-knocker shorts and a crisply ironed matching shirt. Probably his mama did the ironing because he still lived with her, having just recently graduated from community college. He didn't have an official pointy hat like Boots. His hair, which he was letting grow out, was tightly pulled back in a tiny ponytail. His muttonchop sideburns were bushed out like squirrel tails. He wore a navy beret, which was his usual headgear. "We got a call out to Leisure Hills," he said to Boots as he drew his aviator sunglasses out of his pocket and slipped them down over his eyes.

"It serious?" Boots asked.

"Nah. Don't think so. Sally Sneed wants to file a complaint."

"Again?" said Boots.

"Yep," said Devon.

Veenie was all ears now. "Who she complaining about?"

"Your pappy," said Devon.

"What'd he do?"

"She claims he bit her."

"She got any proof?"

"She has his dentures. Claims he left them in her right butt cheek. Bit her clean on the ass in the dining hall during breakfast."

No surprise there. We all knew Pappy Tuttle could get a little boisterous, especially when it came to the ladies. He'd been barred from most of the nudie bars in the tri-county area back in the day when he was young and running free.

Knowing Sally Sneed, I imagined whatever had been going on between her and Pappy might have been consensual. Sally was pretty well established as the head jezebel of Leisure Hills. Ever since she had her second stroke, she just loved making whoopee, and she wasn't all that discrete about when or where, or with what either. She and Pappy had an on-again, off-again kind of romance. Sally liked to go off her mood meds when things got boring out at Leisure Hills. And when she did that, she flew around flirting with everything. The orderlies had to pry her off a sawhorse out in the rec barn more than once.

Boots rolled his eyes. "If no firearms were discharged, and no one was killed, I don't see why we need to make an official call."

Devon fiddled with his sunglasses. "I was going out that way, anyway. Got a complaint this morning about some out-of-towners from Seymour setting up a fishing camp on state property, down by the covered bridge. Thought I'd drop in at Leisure Hills, check with the oldsters while I was looking into the illegal camping and fishing complaint."

Devon looked at us. "You two ladies want to tag along? I was thinking Pappy might settle down if you gave him a good talking to. Was hoping we could nip this thing in the bud without paperwork. Nurse Pruitt said he usually pays attention to Veenie." Devon peeked over the top of his sunglass frames at Veenie.

"Reckon we better," said Veenie. "Pappy enjoys it out there. Hate to see him get kicked out because of some fool thing. We told him to leave the ladies alone, but he don't always remember our conversations."

"Or the year," I added.

Boots stood up and waved us toward the door. "Might as well go on out there. You won't tell me what you were doing down in Hound Holler at that barn, so there's no use my opening a case file on it." He eyed me and Veenie like he expected us to object or come clean.

We did neither. We followed Devon out to his patrol car. I gunned the Impala, and we rode his bumper all the way out Poor Farm Road to Leisure Hills.

Devon waved at us and honked and hollered out the cruiser window that he was going on to check on the illegals down by the river as we turned into the driveway to Leisure Hills. "You ladies need firepower, give me a call! I'll be down by the covered bridge all morning," he yelled as he roared away down the gravel road in a cloud of dust.

Inside Leisure Hills, Pappy did not seem happy to see us. "Dang it, she begged me to bite her," he brayed. He slumped in his motorized chair, sulking, his red IU sock cap pulled down to his wiry gray eyebrows.

The tiny black-and-white TV that set on a shelf in the corner of his room blared Fox News. The announcer was going on about some ninety-year-old politician in Georgia with a neck like a turkey who'd been caught trying to diddle a teenage campaign worker.

Veenie took hold of the TV twanger and powered down the sound. "Pappy, you can't bite the ladies. That's illegal now. Nobody finds that romantic no more, at least not in public."

"Humph. She begged me," said Pappy, sticking to his story, defending his own innocence. "I was being polite." He took a reach stick out of his lap and fiddled with the handle grip, trying to grab hold of the TV twanger and pull it back over his way. "I can't hear the TV when it's that low," he grumbled. "That old coot on the TV has been getting some serious whoopee. I wanna hear how he does it."

Veenie stepped between Pappy and the TV. "Sally Sneed told the cops you bit her on the rump without asking permission first. She filed a complaint."

"Sally is a fatso and a big liar," grumped Pappy. "All them Sneeds lie. Bunch of liars and thieves. You know that. Also," he leaned over close to Veenie and motioned for her to bend down, which she did. He then whispered to her, "Just between me and you, Sally is cuckoo. Don't always know what's going on inside her own head." He tapped his own noggin by way of emphasis.

"It don't matter," said Veenie. "I told you not to be messing with her. She gets you all riled up. You get that riled up, the doctor says your heart could bust wide open."

"I like being riled up," Pappy snarled. "Besides, I didn't start nothing. It's those old ladies. They won't leave a fella alone. I'm plum exhausted trying to keep them happy." He sniffled and tried to straighten up in his chair, only to slide back down like a lumpy pile of mashed taters.

Actually what Pappy said was pretty much true. There were ten women for every man out at Leisure Hills. Things could get pretty competitive. It was worse than junior high, what with everyone dating everyone else, and going steady then breaking up and getting hysterical. TV soap operas had nothing on the Knobby Waters' senior set at Leisure Hills.

Nurse Ada Pruitt brought in Pappy's lunch. She wore her customary peach-colored nursing smock and pants and marshmallow shoes. She flipped up the tray on his motorized chair, so he could eat sitting up, without shifting to the dining table chair. He'd been quarantined to his room until he settled down and apologized. So far, he was refusing to do both.

Nurse Pruitt fussed in a circle until she got Pappy and his lunch tray settled. "Thanks for coming out, Veenie," she said. "He was an awful handful this morning. He bit Sally right in the breakfast line. She threw a bottle of maple syrup at him. Then she threw some steak knives, a gallon of grape jelly, and a basket of boiled eggs. The place was a sticky mess. It's been crazy as a kindergarten out here all week."

"Why so crazy?" I asked.

"Spring fever, I reckon," said Nurse Pruitt. "That and we got a new dapper gentleman moved into the Petunia Suite. All the ladies are after him. I think Pappy here is afraid he'll lose his harem."

"I could take that fella if you didn't keep me strapped in this here chair," whined Pappy. "I got to defend my territory, or that old rooster will have the whole henhouse waving their tail feathers at him." His face scrunched up as he sucked in a spoonful of red Jell-O. "Dang blasted Romeo."

I was curious. "Who moved in?"

Nurse Pruitt cut up Pappy's pork chop for him. "Don't rightly know much about him. From out of town. Says he has family over in Terre Haute. He's a looker though. Uses a cane, but he can still strut and drive. He's in a deluxe suite, so he must be fixed with a dandy pension. Got all the ladies in a swoon."

Pappy snorted. "He ain't so special. He uses black shoe polish to dye his hair and mustache. His hair was running down his face in the rain when he checked in. He don't fool me. And he's got real short legs. Looks like a skinny one of them dwarfs on that TV show, *Game of Gnomes*. He's nearsighted too. A runt. Nothing special."

I asked Nurse Pruitt what the new fellow's name was.

"Smith," she said. "Jack Smith."

"Ha!" said Pappy. "An alias if ever I heard one. I'm calling him Pee Wee Ding Dong. Suits him better."

"Why would anyone check into a retirement home under an alias?" I asked.

"Probably hiding from his wife," snorted Pappy, hooking a finger in the corner of his mouth and adjusting his dentures, hoping to get a better grip on the last of his pork chop. "Came here to get nookie. Stealing my nookie, right out from under my nose. Now you see why I had to bite Sally? Trying to keep the ladies happy." He leaned toward me and whispered, "They like it wild."

Someone ding-donged at Pappy's door, and Nurse Pruitt pushed the entry button. All the doors had auto-open features so none of the residents had to walk to the door or worry about accessibility. Also, it made it easier for the emergency gurneys to come and go at all hours, without causing so much mess and fuss.

The door swung open to reveal Sally Sneed sitting in a purple scooter. She wore a red wig and a gauzy fire engine red ensemble with enough bling on her wrists and neck to blind a herd of blackbirds. She was pretty hefty. The skin on her neck hung down in wrinkles, like her neck was made of layers of wet crepe paper. "I was only fooling," she squawked as she power-rolled into Pappy's suite, almost running over my foot. "He's okay. He didn't do nothing I didn't ask him to do. I think I might have missed my meds a time or two. Makes me crazy. Didn't mean to cause no trouble."

Pappy wrinkled his nose, folded his hands on his tray, and looked away like he wasn't quite ready to forgive Sally. "See," he said to Veenie. "That's what I been telling you. We was playing."

Sally revved her scooter over to Pappy's side. She gave him a smack up the side of his cheek, leaving behind red lip prints as big as turkey vulture wings.

Pappy reddened a little.

Nurse Pruitt eyed them both. "You two keep your clothes on. Don't be broadcasting your sinful adventures. And don't come begging to me for meds when you give each other the crotch cooties. We got enough problems out here without you two starting a senior plague." She took Pappy's blood pressure and told him it was too high.

"Course it is," said Pappy. He looked down at his own crotch. "I'm getting a chubby."

I decided it was probably time for us to leave the love birds alone. The door to Pappy's suite remained open. We were saying our good-byes when I spied a short man with a tall black crop of rooster-like hair sneak past the door. He was practically running, leaning into his cane, using it to catapult himself forward. I think he'd been eavesdropping at Pappy's door. By the time we got to the door and into the hallway, the man had vanished.

"Who was that fellow?" I asked Nurse Pruitt as she logged her visit "in" and then "out" on the chart on the wall outside Pappy's door.

"What did he look like?" she asked as she erased a mistake on the little whiteboard with the wet tip of her finger before attacking the chart again.

I described the little black-haired guy with the cane.

"Must have been Jack Smith. The gals call him Smithy. Pappy's arch rival. He's about the only guy in this wing who doesn't use a chair to get around."

Veenie and I headed through the lobby, where a wild game of euchre had a table of women wearing Purdue sun visor hats in an uproar. As soon as we were alone in the foyer, I confessed my suspicions to Veenie. "I think Doogie Duval is hiding out here."

Veenie craned her head and scanned the lobby. "Sassy's husband? Where?"

"Jack Smith," I said. "I saw him, just a glimpse, but everything—the way Pappy and Nurse Pruitt described him, right down to the dyed black hair—matches how Pooter described seeing him slinking around at the Moon Glo with Bromley. From what I saw, old Smithy looks a heck of a lot like the photos we have of Doogie Duval from that online booking database."

Instead of heading out to the Impala, Veenie and I decided to head back inside Leisure Hills in search of more information about the mysterious, dark-haired Romeo, Smithy. If Smithy were Doogie, I doubted his being at Leisure Hills was a coincidence. And I, for one, was dying to question him about Fussy's untimely gigging and why he'd been keeping company with Bromley down at the Moon Glo. Whoever had killed Fussy was still at large, and Doogie Duval, retirement home Romeo and jailbird on the fly, was the only darn suspect we had.

CHAPTER TWENTY-NINE

N urse Pruitt seemed surprised to see me and Veenie back
on her wing. She was at the charge desk, typing notes
into a computer. "Forget something?" she asked. She wore a set
of white-and-yellow striped dime store reading glasses. She'd
not been wearing them before, so I assumed they were for
computer work.

I asked which suite Smithy was holed up in.

She slid off her glasses and chewed an earpiece. "Why you
asking?"

"Just curious."

She twisted her lips. "We're not supposed to give out that
sort of information. Confidential."

Veenie jumped in. "How long you known us?"

"All my life."

"We ain't identity thieves or nothing peculiar like that,"
said Veenie. "You know that."

"Reckon I do." She slipped her glasses back on and
punched a few keys on her terminal. "He's at the end of the
hall, suite 125. Can't miss it. But if anybody asks, we never had
this conversation. *Never.*"

"Course not," said Veenie. "This here is a confidential
matter, and we never talk about our cases."

"A case?" Nurse Pruitt sat up in her chair. She lowered her
voice and leaned toward us. "This related to all those questions
you asked me earlier this week about Bromley Apple?"

I remembered Veenie telling me that Nurse Pruitt had told her that Bromley had gone into Doc Scarborough's office in town for a prescription for gonorrhea, then bribed his way out of filling out the information sheet as required by the state health department. Veenie had said that Nurse Pruitt filed the VD report in her trash can after Bromley had offered her two free porcelain crowns as hush money. Nurse Pruitt's teeth confirmed that. She had a shiny new white bicuspid and molar on the right side. Seemed to me those two teeth had been dark silver amalgams last time I paid any attention.

I told Nurse Pruitt that yes, all this was related to Bromley's death.

Her eyes slid up and down the hallway. "I might know something. Been meaning to give you a call."

Veenie piped up. "You remembered something?"

"Don't know if it's important or not. And I wouldn't be telling you this, mind you, if you weren't agents of the law. You being law officers on a case, I figure it's my civic duty to report suspicious items."

Nurse Pruitt was sitting up high now, busting at the seams to gossip.

"That's right," said Veenie. "Harry has a badge and a diploma and all that stuff. And we've been deputized."

I decided to let that last comment slide. If Nurse Pruitt knew something about Bromley's death, I'd take any tidbits she tossed our way. "What did you remember?" I asked.

"Well, like I told Veenie, Bromley wouldn't name names, and well, I could sort of understand that. I mean, it is a private thing. Not the kind of thing you want typed up and stored in a government database for all eternity. I mean, that's why I took his offer for some free dental work. I'd helped him out of a jam, and the way I saw it, he was reciprocating because the nurse's union here don't offer any dental coverage. Not a dime. You believe that?"

I nodded my head in sympathy and Veenie did likewise.

Nurse Pruitt looked relieved, like she was satisfied that she was doing the right thing, and that anything she blabbed would be safe with us. "Well, Bromley was a real gentleman, not naming names and all, but that same week a lady came in, all itchy, and she had the same thing going on downstairs."

"Gonorrhea?"

The nurse nodded. "Yeah, we see more of that than you might imagine. It's worse with the oldsters. None of these old farts want to put a glove on it. You know how they can be."

Veenie nodded vigorously. "What lady was this?" she asked.

Nurse Pruitt put her hand to her throat. "Well, this won't surprise you none, probably. It was Dottie Reynolds."

"Shap's wife?" My voice went up an octave or two. Harry was not going to be happy to hear this about his little springtime lust bunny.

"One and the same," said Nurse Pruitt with a knowing nod. "One and the same."

A young candy striper rolled a med table over to the central station, and she and Nurse Pruitt had a chat about afternoon meds. The candy striper, a brunette with a ponytail who chewed gum, asked Nurse Pruitt if she wanted to oversee the cardiologist who was making his weekly visit that afternoon. After checking her wristwatch, she said yes. "Nice chatting with you gals, but I got to get back to work now." She and her young charge took off down a side hall, the med cart squeaking in front of them.

Veenie eyed me. "Don't surprise me none. Dottie's been with everybody and everything. I think she's one of them nimrod maniacs."

"You mean nymphomaniacs?"

"You know what I mean."

Whatever one called it, Bromley and Dottie neither one could keep their clothes on. They were sort of made for each other.

"Think we ought to tell Harry?" Veenie asked.

"I suspect his crotch will be telling him soon enough."

I shrugged, and we headed down the hall toward the suite where Nurse Pruitt had told us Doogie—aka Smithy—was hold up. His exterior door was decorated with a lot of hand-scribbled notes from ladies wanting to know if he was coming to dance class, the Hawaiian luau, or the rose gardening class on Saturday. Several ladies had scribbled hearts after their messages.

"He sure is popular," I said.

Veenie mashed his doorbell.

We heard it ring, but after several minutes of button mashing, no one came to the door.

Veenie tried to tiptoe up to see in the peep hole. "I bet he's in there, hiding."

"We can't make him answer the door," I said.

"We could bust the door in." Veenie eyed the door.

"No," I said. "We've had enough excitement for one day. I think we ought to drop by later, see if Pappy has calmed down. Maybe we can catch Doogie at one of his social events."

Veenie moped. I could tell she wanted to have a go at the door, but those doors were steel reinforced. Her leg would splinter up like peanut brittle if she kicked that door.

Veenie's cell rang, dragging her out of her mope. She answered and flipped it on speakerphone as we walked down the hall toward the front exit. It was Kimmy Apple, calling to tell us she had received Veenie's voice mail and had access to her dad's cell phone account. She'd turned off the fingerprint lock on his phone. "His new access code is 111111," she said. "That ought to get you into all his contacts and phone records."

Kimmy was right. As soon as we got to the Impala, Veenie successfully unlocked the phone. Bromley's personal life tumbled out across the screen. It was easy to see based on his texts, videos, and voicemails, why a whole heap of people might have wished him dead.

CHAPTER THIRTY

H aving struck gold with Bromley's cell phone, Veenie and I scooted back to the office to make sense of the mess of information and figure out our next course of action. Harry was in the office, on the phone. He appeared to be working, trying to collect a past due bill from a client in Oolitic who'd skipped out on his bill after hiring Harry to get the goods on his partner, who'd been bilking him on a stone quarry deal. He was talking tough on the phone, trying to shake a credit card number out of the ne'er-do-well. I had to hand it to Harry. He was darn good at collections.

Dottie Reynolds was still in the office. She was busy filing paperwork for Harry. "Howdy gals," she said. She wore a pair of bedazzled denim hot pants and a midriff top with short ruffled puffy sleeves and a generous display of cleavage. She had one yellow pencil clenched between her teeth, another stuck in her hair bun.

Veenie admired the trim on her blouse.

"Thanks," she said. "Got it at Goodies. Thought the little daisies were darn cute." She fingered the bottom band of the sleeves, which were dotted with tiny embroidered daisies.

"You moved in here?" Veenie asked.

"Heck no," she said. "Shap's mad at me again. Thought I'd hang out here a bit until his temper fizzles out and he calms down."

"Don't think your being here is going to calm him down much," said Veenie.

180

"Yeah, well, if he wasn't so darn mean, I might stay home more often." She sat down in an office chair and chomped on the rubber end of her pencil. She had a row of files stuck in an alphabetizer on Harry's desk.

I'm old enough to know people have all sorts of marriages. I don't understand being married and running around like you aren't hitched all at the same time. When I was married, I'd been too tuckered out to get juiced up over some other fellow. But nowadays everybody seemed to think there was something wrong with you if you didn't have a special friend or two on the side. Dottie and Shap didn't have kids, so I reckoned maybe they had extra energy to spread around. And as Veenie and I now knew, extra energy wasn't the only thing Dottie had been spreading around Pawpaw County.

Harry put his hand over the phone receiver and motioned wildly for us to be quiet. "Trying to scare up your next paycheck," he barked. "Zip it, okay?"

I picked up the outgoing mail and asked Veenie if she wanted to tag along to mail the bills and grab a bite of late lunch at the Roadkill Café. I didn't have to ask twice. I asked Dottie if she wanted to tag along too. She said, "Oh, heck, why not?"

I figured this was as good a time as any to get Dottie alone, ask her about her affair with Bromley. I didn't want to bring it up in front of Harry and have him go all mopey on us. Seemed it might be better to have a girl chat in private about the whole thing. As unfaithful a hound dog as Harry was, he always took it hard when a woman cheated on him.

We were in luck at the Roadkill Café. They had a late lunch special on double-decker BLT's. I ordered one on toast, and Veenie ordered one on toast, hold the lettuce and the tomato. Dottie ordered an extra-large iced tea, lemon, no sugar. "Watching my figure," she said as she patted her waist.

Veenie eyed her cleavage. "You and most of the rest of the county."

Dottie shrugged. "Guess you don't approve of me?"

"Marriage is marriage," she said. "Why you run around on Shap like that?"

Dottie picked up a straw and blew off the paper wrapping. "Bored, I reckon."

Veenie suggested a divorce.

"Nah," said Dottie. "I'd have to move into a trailer. All I can afford. I hate trailers. Like living inside a pop can. Besides, I love old Shap." She got a dreamy look in her eyes like that might be true.

The BLTs arrived, so Veenie and I hushed up while we devoured our lunch. While we ate, Dottie chatted on. She asked us if we were still working on Bromley's case.

I found that an interesting question. "You know him?" I asked, washing down a bite of my sandwich with a gulp of Mountain Dew.

She rolled her eyes. "Sort of. He was my dentist and all."

Veenie piped up. "We heard you and him were an item."

"Who told you that?" Dottie sucked at her iced tea, her eyes cast downward.

Veenie held up Bromley's cell phone. "You did, in your sexy messages to him."

Dottie paled. She bit her bottom lip. "Hey, things like that are private. He know you have that?"

Veenie shrugged. "He don't know much of anything these days. His wife gave us his phone. Told us to dial up his girlfriends if we had questions about his death."

Dottie's eyes darted back and forth, taking us both in. She seemed to be trying to decide how much we knew before yapping.

Veenie spared her the pondering. "This here phone pretty much says you and him were a hot item."

Having drained her ice tea, Dottie sucked up an ice cube and crunched on that. When she was done, she looked Veenie dead in the eye. "So?"

"So," said Veenie, "according to this phone, you were the last person to send him a text message."

"Less than half an hour before he was found dead on Barbara Skaggs's porch glider," I added.

Dottie straightened in her seat. "Now wait just a gosh darn minute. I don't like the sound of that. I sure as heck didn't kill him."

I said, "But you were in Hound Holler in that barn with him, right before he died?"

"You got no proof of that," she said, folding her arms across her bosom and locking them there.

Veenie clicked on the phone and read aloud the last text message in Bromley's cell register. "Dorothy will be right there, you horny little scarecrow." The message had been sent in response to a selfie photo Bromley had sent to Dottie of himself grinning ear to ear. He was dressed in Barbara Skaggs's scarecrow attire.

One mystery solved.

Dottie squirmed in her seat. She flagged down the waitress, who was making the rounds with the water and tea pitchers, and asked for a refill. Once her glass was filled, and the waitress was out of earshot, she snarled at Veenie. "Okay, so maybe he texted me. Said he wanted me to meet him out at that barn. Have a little fun. My legal name is Dorothy. He thought it would be cute if we did this *Wizard of Oz* thing. What? Don't look at me like that. It was his idea, not mine. He had a huge crush on that Dorothy girl when he was younger. He thought I kind of looked like her. A blonde version of her." She patted her bun a little.

I didn't see the resemblance, but then again, I wasn't a fifty-year-old horn toad of a dentist. And after reading

Bromley's sexts, I was beginning to see that my sex life had been pretty darn dull—get-it-done-in-the-dark procreation, pretty much like the Lord Almighty meant it to be. Apparently a lot of other people in Knobby Waters were writing their own scripts and letting the cameras roll. The video bank on Bromley's cell phone pretty much attested to that.

Dottie gulped at her tea. Then she stuck the straw in and had another go at the glass. "That's it," she said. "Nothing more to tell."

"You had sex with Bromley?"

"Course I did. I mean, we weren't in love or anything. It was all good fun. He said his wife didn't care. He was my dentist. Knew I wasn't rich. Never charged me a cent. He even whitened my teeth for free." She smiled widely. I had to admit she had a nice set of teeth for a woman her age. I was beginning to think maybe every woman in Knobby Waters but me had been getting free dental work all these years. I felt a little cheated.

Veenie picked up the questioning. "Who killed Bromley?"

"I dunno," she shrugged, "certainly not me. I mean, we did the dirty. Then I left him there, happy as a puppy with two peckers. I swear on the baby Jesus's halo that man was alive and feeling mighty good when I left him. Besides, the paper said he died of a natural heart thing. Maybe I got him riled up and he couldn't take it. All I know is that when I left him, he was breathing. Pretty hard, in fact." That last sentence made her pause and think a bit.

Veenie looked suspicious. "Why was he out at Barbara Skaggs's?"

Dottie shrugged again. "Said he had business with her. Said his dad had kids by her and she was about to embarrass the whole family. I wasn't all that interested in his personal life. He'd been whining lately about money problems, bad investments. I didn't pay him much mind. I mean, who don't have money problems?" She sucked her tea dry again. "Anyway, he wasn't like Harry. Harry and I share something special."

Veenie asked Dottie if Bromley gave her the clap. "Well, honestly, Lavinia Goens, don't you think that's a rude thing to ask a lady?"

Dottie checked the clock on the wall and gathered up her purse. She laid a quarter on the table for the tip and said she had to run. She said one last thing as she rose. "Don't be telling Harry I got the clap," she said. "That was cleared up before we took up. Don't want word getting around town that I'm a loose woman."

"You might be a couple of decades too late there," Veenie called after Dottie.

"We don't talk about our cases," I promised Dottie, who looked relieved as she exited the café.

CHAPTER THIRTY-ONE

B efore Veenie and I left the café, we checked our cells. Avonelle had left both of us voicemails and texts. She demanded we report to her at the bank as soon as we got her messages. She'd starting sending them late last night, asking about our botched meeting at the barn with her blackmailer. Veenie and I were still puzzling how to handle that situation. We compared Avonelle's string of messages.

"Reckon we ought to mosey on over and update her," Veenie said as she laid down the money to cover her half of the lunch check.

I matched Veenie's payment. "I still think Avonelle knows darn good and well who's blackmailing her."

Veenie nodded. "I bet it's that Money Boy. He sounded like a no good hound dog."

Money Boy was the most frequent texter on Bromley's phone the last week before his death, even more frequent than Dottie. Veenie and I had scrolled through his messages enough to know that whoever he was, he'd been pressing Bromley to wire large cash payments. We'd tried to trace down his cell number to get an ID, but all the cell numbers associated with his texts proved to be dead ends. He'd used disposable burner phones. Whoever Money Boy was, he didn't want his identity revealed, and he'd been milking Bromley for hefty cash payments.

"Maybe we can rattle ol' Avonelle enough to get the truth," I said as I shouldered my messenger bag. Full of bacon sandwiches and senior sass, we ambled to our meeting with Avonelle, two blocks down the street at the First National Bank.

Despite all her frantic texts and messages, Avonelle was in a meeting when we arrived at the bank. We took a seat on a waiting bench and enjoyed the air conditioning. Veenie busied herself poking at the lobby ATM. She checked the cash slot in case anyone had accidently left money behind. Then she poked at the machine some more. "That's not a slot machine," I said.

"I know that, but I found a twenty dollar bill stuck in this one once. I figure it's always worth a finger poke or two. Our cookie jar fund is getting low. We need us some more fun money."

While Veenie was fiddling with the machine, Dode Schneider ambled in. He wore his customary bibbed overalls, long-sleeved flannel shirt, and clodhopper work boots. He had a few spots of white tissue paper stuck to his chin where he'd nicked himself shaving. "Howdy, missy," he said as he scrambled over my way. "Bank been cheating you too?"

"Not that I noticed," I said. "You get that missing three cents credited back to your account?"

"Sure enough did. They'd been cheating me for darn near a year."

"Computer error?"

"Don't rightly know." Dode sniffled. "But I was over at Pokey's last night, and him and his mama, Dolly, had the same sort of peculiar thing going on with their accounts."

"Three cents missing?"

"A bit more than that."

"What did Avonelle say about all this?"

"Said it was the dang blasted computers. Anyway, I came in to thank her. She fixed me right up."

"We're waiting for her now," I said, "but she's in a meeting."

"Guess I'll wait here with you then."

Veenie, tired of poking at the ATM and checking for loose change around the deposit table, came to sit next to me. She nodded at Dode. "Everything all right out at the farm?" she asked.

"Oh, sure. Yeah, boy, putting in watermelons this year. Got a sunny patch cleared. My pappy used to grow them in the exact same spot."

Veenie nodded. "I remember them watermelons. Juicy. Best I ever had."

"Oh sure, they was. Pappy was a dandy melon farmer. Grew cantaloupes in the Sand Lane river bottoms, over by Vallonia, near the old Shelton homestead, but I rent all that acreage out now. Don't have the get-up-and-go I used to for big crops. A couple of young fellas, the Daulton brothers, big strapping boys, farm most of my bottomland."

I asked if those boys were related to Bull Daulton, who'd been a year ahead of me in school and had a physique worthy of his nickname.

"Oh sure. Grandsons. Good boys. Hard workers."

I heard Avonelle's voice as she strolled down the hall toward the lobby. She was walking alongside the fellow with the expensive briefcase and blue banker's suit who had rough bumped Veenie in the hallway last time we'd visited. They were talking, but not loud enough so that I could make out the words. In fact, they seemed to be speaking in deliberately hushed tones. I could only decipher the last few words. The blue-suited fellow said something about letting the men in Chicago know and clearing out the banking system. When they reached the end of the hallway, the fellow slid his hat onto his head and shook Avonelle's hand. "We'll be in touch," he said as he strode toward the front exit.

Veenie, who'd seen him and apparently recognized him, bounced in front of him at the revolving doorway.

He tried to slide around her, but her being round as a beach ball and a fast bouncer, she slid over and successfully blocked his exit.

He stopped in his tracks and eyed her suspiciously. "Can I help you, ma'am?"

"Last time we met you was awful rude."

"We've met?" The man, who clutched his briefcase, sounded perplexed.

Avonelle entered the conversation. "Veenie, don't be pestering Mr. Peesley. He's from Chicago. He certainly doesn't have time for you."

"Chicago?" Veenie eyed him. "Why you here? You lost?"

The man did not look amused. "Bank business," he said.

"Good-bye, Mr. Peesley," Avonelle said, taking Veenie gently by the shoulders and guiding her out of the man's way. "Come back to my office," she barked at Veenie. She turned on her heels and headed that way with authority.

Veenie and I fell into step, eager to hear what she had to say.

CHAPTER THIRTY-TWO

I was surprised, when we got inside Avonelle's office, to find Bert sitting in a black leather captain's chair next to his mother's seat.

She scooted around him and motioned his way. "My son, Bert, you know, of course."

We nodded.

"You may speak freely in front of him," she said.

Bert threw us a weak smile. He looked a little peaked, but his hair was immaculately combed down. He wore his dentist's jacket over a nice pale-blue striped shirt. I wasn't sure why he was there but figured Avonelle was paying us, so she had the right to invite the whole darn town to her briefings if it so pleased her.

I decided it was time to stop beating around the bush. I told her we had cracked Bromley's cell phone with Kimmy's help. I told her that it appeared Bromley had dressed like a scarecrow as part of some roll-in-the-hay sex play he had going on with Dottie.

"Dottie? Dottie Reynolds?"

"Yep," I confirmed.

"Dear Lord, I had no idea, I mean, that things had gotten that bad with his, well his ... sexual problems." She threw a glance at Bert, who simply nodded.

"You knew he played around?" I asked.

BABY DADDY MYSTERY

"Whole county knew that," said Avonelle. "But really? Dottie? Dottie Reynolds?" She made a sour face. I reckoned Dottie wasn't her idea of a daughter-in-law.

I shrugged. From the messages on Bromley's cell phone, I'd have to say he wasn't ever all that discriminating. "Did you know he was treated for VD?"

Avonelle tightened her lips. "I'd gathered as much. Bert, unfortunately, had informed me of this. This will all stay confidential. Yes?"

We glanced at Veenie, who sat perched on the edge of her chair next to me. "What?" cried Veenie. "Why is everybody staring at me? I didn't do nothing."

Avonelle spoke up. "And let's keep it that way, shall we."

Avonelle asked if we were satisfied that Bromley's death was of natural causes. She said she and Bert now believed it to be a natural death.

I said we had no reason to believe otherwise, given what Dottie told us and the nature of Bromley's cell messages. "Barbara told us Bromley had been to visit her, tried to pay her off to take the kids and move out to California. We reckon maybe he was down in Hound Holler hoping to have another try at her, made it as far as the front porch, and his heart gave out on him after all that rolling in the hay with Dottie. You know anything different about why he might have been in Hound Holler?"

Avonelle drew in a sigh and fussed with her Buster Brown bow. "He did know that Barbara had sent me that letter asking for child support. He begged me to let him handle that, told me it was all a scam, but let's say I'd lost faith in his judgment by then. I decided to handle it straight on myself. That's why I hired your firm. I figured it'd be best to handle this whole affair professionally."

"He thought Barbara was pulling a scam?"

"Convinced of it."

"Did he give you any evidence in that regard?"

"No, and frankly, I wasn't sure. I'd always felt maybe William had been keeping someone on the side, but well, he was a decent husband. That's just how men were. As long as he was discrete and it didn't threaten our marriage, I'd made my peace with the whole affair, until Ms. Skaggs sent me that child support letter. And the DNA test was conclusive? Yes?"

"Pretty much," I said. "I mean, we saw Billy Junior spit in that tube, and we mailed in that sample."

Veenie jumped in. "Plus them kids have the Apple ears. You can't fake something God awful like that."

Avonelle winced a bit and adjusted her jacket. "Fine, but if Bromley's death was natural, who's sending me these blackmail notices? And who shot at you in that barn?"

That last question was certainly one I wanted answered.

Avonelle plucked a small key from a chain from her purse and flicked open the top drawer on her desk. She pulled out a sheet of lined yellow paper and slid it across the desk to me. I took the paper and read, "Stupid move at barn. Will now cost you fifty thousand dollars to keep me quiet. Will send delivery notice soon."

I eyed Avonelle. "Why are you being blackmailed?"

She squirmed. "I told you, I don't know."

I glanced at Bert, whose face looked pained, like he might throw up. "You know who the blackmailer is?" I asked him.

"Certainly not," he said as he fiddled with his tie. "Of course not. Why would I?"

Veenie, who'd been uncharacteristically quiet, jumped in. "Who's Money Boy?" she asked.

Silence.

Avonelle and her son exchanged nervous glances.

"I saw them glances," Veenie said.

Avonelle asked how we knew about Money Boy.

I said, "He's all over your son's cell phone. Near as we can tell, he was milking him for blackmail payments, but we don't know why. You two know?"

Avonelle bit her lip.

Bert leaned forward in his chair and opened his mouth.

Seeing Bert move, Avonelle motioned for him to sit back and keep quiet.

He complied.

She straightened in her chair. "You think this Money Boy is the one sending me blackmail notes?"

"Seems logical," I said. "He was blackmailing Bromley. Bromley died. Can't get milk out of a dead cow, so it makes sense he'd turn to you. Everybody knows you got money."

Bert spoke up this time. "Mom, I think it's time we filled in some of the blanks for the ladies. This is all confidential and frankly, dog-gone-it, we could use some help." His words tumbled out like he was afraid he'd be shut down before he could complete his thoughts aloud.

Avonelle considered her son's comment. "Fine." She motioned with one hand for Bert to continue talking.

"Money Boy," began Bert, "has been stealing from the bank."

"I didn't know the bank had been robbed."

"No one knows," said Bert. "And it wasn't really robbed. Someone installed software on our central system, and that software has been skimming small amounts out of people's accounts and depositing them into an overseas account in the Cayman Islands."

I pondered that. "Small amounts, like three cents at a time?" I thought of Dode Schneider and his complaints about the missing three cents on his monthly bank statement.

Avonelle said, "Precisely. Tiny amounts like that. And the virus, which started here, has spread through all the banks in southern Indiana. It's called salami slicing."

"Salami?" I asked.

"That's what con artists call it. It's ingeniously simple. They get someone inside the bank to install a virus that visits all the bank's accounts and skims a few cents off each as a fee credit or miscellaneous charge. The software does that thousands of times and rakes the pennies into a central off-shore bank account. It's like taking tiny slices off a big salami. It takes a while, but millions can be siphoned off and stolen this way without a single soul noticing. Most people don't look at, let alone reconcile, their bank statements. And if they do, they see a charge for a few cents coming from the bank, and they figure it must be legitimate. Not many people would take the time to dispute a three-cent error."

"Except for Dode Schneider," I said.

Avonelle nodded. "Yes, he was one of our customers who complained, but not the only one. Turns out people in Pawpaw County still read their bank statements and are willing to fight for their pennies."

I pondered this information. "You know who Money Boy is?"

Bert opened his mouth, but Avonelle shook her fingers at him, motioning him to be quiet.

He shut his mouth but didn't look happy about it.

Avonelle spoke. "We suspect he's the one sending those blackmail demands."

"What does he know that's worth money?"

"That the bank had been embezzled. Frankly that all the banks in southern Indiana have been embezzled."

"Why would you hide that?"

Avonelle shrugged. "We're not hiding it going forward. I reported it to the Office of the Comptroller of the Currency. They operate out of the United States Department of the Treasury, Chicago regional offices. Mr. Peesley," she nodded Veenie's way, "you met him, Lavinia, is here investigating.

We reported it last week, soon as we discovered the problem. I suppose Money Boy wants me to pay him to keep the embezzlement out of the papers, but at this point we've cleaned the system and repaired the breach. We'll be announcing it soon ourselves." She tugged at her lapels, looking smug and satisfied.

Veenie spoke up. "You want us to do anything more about that blackmail note?"

"I want you to find out who is sending these notes and why. I need a solid answer. If we can flush Money Boy out into the open, the Treasury agents can arrest him. Right now, they have no suspects."

I wasn't sure I favored that idea. "You want to use me and Veenie as bait?" I asked.

"Well, I wouldn't put it quite that way."

Veenie squeaked. "Well, I gosh darn would. You already got us shot at. We only make minimum wage, just so you know."

Veenie loved a good crime-cracking case, but I could understand why she wasn't all that keen on taking a bullet for Avonelle. I was with her on that one.

I stood up. "Let us think about this some more," I said. "Not sure we can help you out all that much. Might be best to let the Feds handle this from here on in."

Avonelle didn't object or say anything in reply. She simply stood up and showed us briskly to the door. Bert followed, looking peevish, but he didn't say a word until we were well outside the bank, standing next to the Chevy. With his mother gone, words rushed out of him like penny candy out of a fat piñata.

CHAPTER THIRTY-THREE

I hurried Bert off the sidewalk and ushered him into the back of the Impala, which was parked in front of the detective agency. I knew Avonelle wouldn't want him spilling the family secrets to us, so I figured it was best if we talked to him in private. Bert apparently knew more than his mother let him reveal to us in her presence. Veenie and I had been shot at once. I wasn't in any hurry to duck and dive through another shower of shotgun shells. My knees still ached from the big shootout at the barn. If I had to scramble like that again, there'd not be enough Bengay in all of Indiana to get me upright and ambling.

And I wasn't about to get one of them bum knee replacements at the Pawpaw County Hospital. Last person I knew who did that, Johnny Bill Guthrie, walked like a duck after they were done with him. They left him with one leg shorter than the other, God's truth.

Having nowhere in particular to go, and wanting to chat with Bert outside the range of prying eyes and ears, I gunned the Chevy and we headed out of town toward the knobs. My stomach was unsettled. I felt I needed a piece of pie—or two. Heck, maybe even a whole pie. Ma Horton, who ran a free range chicken farm on top of the knobs, Chickenlandia, also ran Pawpaw County's emergency pie shed. It was an old tool shed that she kept stocked with homemade pies. Anybody could roll up the knobs and pick one up anytime. I was fairly near in love with her coconut cream pies.

Veenie squeaked with excitement when she noticed I was headed up the knobs. "Pie?" she asked, her little blue eyes twinkling with hope.

Bert stuck his head up between me and Veenie and rested his chin on the top of the front seat like a dog. "Where are we going?"

"Emergency pie shed," I said.

"They have chocolate cream?" he asked.

"Yes."

"Count me in," he said.

It was late afternoon, and there wasn't any traffic going up the knobs, which was good because the road was narrow and twisty, and the Impala wasn't always up to the climb. It was really a one-way road. You couldn't see around the hair-pin curves until you were halfway around the bends. The gears ground on the Impala as we climbed the steep hills, but the poor old gal held steady all the way to the top.

Veenie turned her head and studied Bert, who sat quietly in the backseat like a kindergartener, his dental coat a wee bit too short for him in the sleeves. "You got any money?"

He sprung open his wallet and pulled out several twenties, which he fanned over the edge of the seat. "That do?" he asked as I shot down a gravel road toward Ma Horton's farm.

Veenie snatched the money out of Bert's hand and tucked it into her bra. "That'll get us started."

I pulled in tight, under the shade maples, next to the pie shed. Veenie sprung open the car door and sprinted up to the shed like she was a twenty-year-old with no heart problems. Pie had that kind of magical effect on her. Ma Horton wasn't around, neither was Peepaw, but the door to the pie shed was open. Veenie darted in.

While Veenie was inside the shed gathering up a selection of ten-dollar pies, I asked Bert to start telling me everything he knew.

His face filled up with relief. Leaning forward, taking a deep breath, he started yacking at me like a schoolgirl.

By the time Veenie came back to the car with the pies—she had four of them balanced in a tower against her body, one hand on top of the tower and one on the bottom—I was beginning to get a good idea of who Money Boy might be, and some of what Avonelle might have been hiding from us all along.

Bert stopped yakking when he saw the pies. Veenie handed him a chocolate cream pie across the seat, along with wad of napkins from the glove compartment and a white plastic fork.

"My own pie?" Bert asked. He looked like he might cry.

"Course you get your own pie," Veenie said. "You paid. Plus we don't share pie, do we RJ?"

I really couldn't answer that because my cheeks were busting with coconut cream pie.

It was late in the afternoon, so we decided to just eat the pie right then and there in the shade of the maples. We opened all four doors on the Impala to let in some breeze. It was a nice day. Chickens clucked in the background. Ma and Peepaw Horton had fifty hens and one cocky old rooster named Dewey. I enjoyed my pie while I watched Dewey's antics with the ladies. He was pestering one fat, old speckled hen, trying to mount her, but she was having none of that. She pecked and squawked until he flew off and perched atop a fence post to nurse his pride.

Chickenlandia wasn't an ordinary kind of chicken house, but then Ma and Peepaw weren't ordinary folks. Peepaw Horton was an energetic fellow, and Ma loved her chickens. It showed in the fancy housing they built for their fowl. They'd used scrap lumber to fashion replicas of the White House, the Supreme Court, and the Senate building. The buildings were connected with two-by-fours and chicken-wire catwalks. It wasn't a chicken house, more like an entire Chickenlandia, which was how the place got its name.

Veenie finished her apple pie and made a sound like it might all come back up. Thankfully, it didn't.

"You ate that whole pie?' I asked. I'd only made it through two pieces of mine, which was about right. The rest I'd chill up for supper once we got home.

Veenie belched. "Course I did. I only had that bacon sandwich for lunch. No lettuce. No tomato. I had extra room in me for pie."

Dewey flew our way and perched, claws out, on top of my open door frame. He balanced there, swaying back and forth like a drunken ballet dancer. He cocked his head at me and cawed.

I dipped my finger in coconut cream and held it out for him.

He pecked the pie neatly off my finger like it was a fat wet grub.

Veenie stiffened. "You know I don't like chickens," she said. She rummaged in the glove compartment and pulled out her BB pistol.

"That's not a chicken," I said. "That's a rooster."

Veenie pointed the pistol at Dewey. "Don't care. If he comes my way, he's gonna be supper."

I was about to tell Veenie to put her gun away when Dewey flew off, back to the Senate to see what the chickens were squawking about.

Bert, who'd been devouring his chocolate cream pie, spoke up from the back seat. "I just love to bake. Should have gone to pastry school, but Mother had other plans. Then I got married, and my wife never would let me bake or eat pie."

Veenie looked shocked. "Why not?"

"Oh something about how only sissies bake. She never let me eat sweets. Said they hung on my hips. She always thought I was too fat." He leaned back in the seat and patted his pooch belly.

Veenie eyed him. "Fat looks good on you. Don't fat look good on him, Ruby Jane?" she asked me.

I wasn't sure how to answer that, so I just nodded.

"Thanks," said Bert, as he closed the lid on his pie box and set it aside. "I gain weight in my hips. I have Mother's body." He dabbed at his lips to wipe away the chocolate. He nodded at the pie on the seat next to him. "I never knew Ma Horton sold her pies like this, right out of the shed, all hours."

Veenie nodded. "Course she does. We come up here all hours. Pie fixes everything," she said. "If you're ever down in the dumps and fixing to kill yourself, try pie. It'll fix you right up. It's a big part of what's kept me alive all these years." Veenie belched again.

Bert nodded, his eyes sad. "It's been a really rough year," he said. "Never been so blue and troubled in my whole life."

Veenie nodded back. "You miss your brother?"

"A bit," he said. "But he caused me and Mother a whole lot of grief. Always did cause trouble." He sighed and looked up, toward heaven.

"You mean like embarrassment? With the women and all?" I asked.

"Oh sure, that. But he also ran up a lot of debt. Made it hard for me keep the business afloat. And heck, I never even wanted to be a dentist. It was him and Mother who wanted the whole dentistry thing. Money, prestige, that sort of thing. I would have been happy opening up a bakery."

I asked Bert if he knew who Money Boy was. I'd formed an idea, but I wanted to know straight out if Avonelle knew too.

He twisted his lips, then rubbed them. "Some con artist Bromley got messed up with."

"How so?" I asked.

"Oh well, look, like I told you when Veenie was getting the pies, Mother wouldn't want me to tell you two this, but heck,

I'm tired of covering up for Bromley. He darn near ruined me, our family, and the business. And he's dead now. Mother wants to keep the family name out of scandal, but it's not right, her letting you get shot at and all."

Veenie and I nodded in vigorous agreement.

I asked Bert to tell Veenie what he'd told me about the California real estate scam Bromley had fallen into.

"Well, it was pretty simple," he said. "And pretty stupid too," he added as he brushed some fallen hair out of one eye. "He saw this ad on Facebook for a seminar about investing in time-share condos out in California. The ad made the place sound like a Playboy paradise. Like a place a fellow could go to with his mistress or whatever and never be bothered. Or a fellow could go there, and they had ladies on payroll who'd do pretty much anything you asked them to do. They had a whole setup where if you invested and paid extra, you'd get this whole cover-up package that would make it look like you'd been out in California on some business trip. They gave fake receipts for conferences and seminars and hotel stays. They even gave a fake eight-hundred number for verification so that you could give it to your wife or business partners if they got suspicious."

"Sneaky," said Veenie. "I bet they made a lot of money from horned toad men."

"Well," mused Bert, "they pretty much cleaned Bromley out. I mean, he bought into the thing hook, line, and sinker."

Veenie nodded. "Bromley had women out in California too?"

"He thought he was going to, but the whole thing turned out to be a scam. There were no time-share condos. No women. Nothing but a giant sandlot, empty promises, and high monthly charges on our company credit cards for dental conventions and seminars that never happened."

Veenie clicked her teeth. "This place have a name?" she asked.

Bert nodded. "Oh sure. It was called Sun City."

Veenie looked at me, her eyes wide. "Ain't that the name of the scam Sassy's husband was running?"

"One and the same." I turned to Bert. "Tell Veenie who Money Boy is."

"Near as we can tell it's this fellow Doogie Duval. He was running the ads, targeting them to doctors and professional men, insurance agents, dentists, and engineers in rural Indiana, using Facebook. That's how they snagged Bromley."

"Bromley couldn't see through that sort of thing?" Veenie asked.

"Oh please, he thought with his scrotum when it came to things like that. He was the perfect target. Besides, they did a good job looking legitimate. Once they found a fellow, they invited him to a local investment seminar and lured him to a rented auditorium on the IU campus up in Bloomington with an invite to a free steak dinner. They had some fellow they called a "professor" who gave the investment pitch. I mean, when he first showed me the brochures and all, I thought it might be a legit real estate investment, but I nixed it, because frankly, we were already cash poor at the practice."

Veenie eyed Bert. "If you're so poor, how'd Bromley ever get the money to invest in the first place?"

Bert scrunched up his face. He looked pained. "This is the part Mother hasn't been telling you."

It seemed to me Avonelle hadn't been telling us a lot, but I kept my clapper shut and motioned for Bert to keep spilling the beans.

Bert sucked in a deep breath and continued. "Bromley blew all the cash and credit he had trying to buy into Sun City. Once he'd exhausted that, his agreement called for him to lose all his investment if he couldn't keep up with the monthly payments. Apparently, even though the place was a scam, the contract he signed for installment payments was legit."

Veenie piped up. "Avonelle gave him the money to keep up payments?"

"No, she flat out refused. Saw through the con."

"Where'd the money come from?" Veenie asked, her eyes wide.

"Doogie made a deal with Bromley. Told him he'd reduce the direct payments and keep his name out of the whole scheme. Not implicate him to the Feds as a partner and co-owner if he did him this one favor."

"What favor?" Veenie asked.

"He gave Bromley special software."

"Software?" Veenie asked.

"Yes, a virus that Bromley put on Mother's laptop at work."

"Uh-oh!" cried Veenie. "You mean?"

Bert nodded. "It was Bromley who got the slicing software onto the bank's computer system by infecting Mother's laptop. He set up Mother as an embezzler."

CHAPTER THIRTY-FOUR

When we arrived home that night it was already dark. Sassy was sitting on the porch swing next to Boots, waiting for us. They'd switched on the porch lights. The bug lights I'd screwed into the outdoor light fixtures bathed them both in a wash of yellow. Sassy's face was all puckered up, like she'd been sucking a pickle. Boots looked nonchalant, per usual, his sunburnt face shining like a large red zinnia in the yellow bug light. He had his hat off and was balancing it on his right knee. They weren't facing each other, but staring out toward the street.

Sassy waved and hollered when she saw me and Veenie careen around the corner in the Impala and pull into the driveway.

Veenie jumped out of the Chevy and scrambled up onto the porch while I maneuvered around Boots's cop car and parked in the back of my driveway. I gathered up what was left of the pies and ambled toward the house, eyeing the unhappy pair on the porch swing.

Sassy was on her feet now, one hand to her sternum. She ran to the edge of the porch to greet me as Veenie shot past us and into the house, headed to the bathroom. She'd had her legs crossed since we'd dropped Bert off out at his place in Camelot Court.

"Where in God's name you two been all day?" Sassy croaked. She didn't sound happy.

"On a case." I said. "You two want some pie?" I nodded at the pies in my arms. We had a blueberry crumble and most of my coconut cream leftover after encouraging Bert to take a spare chocolate cream home for himself.

Boots said, "You got any coffee to go with that pie?"

Sassy made another pickle face. "I got to watch my figure." She patted her midriff. "Besides I'm too upset to eat a dang thing. Boots here is trying to arrest me."

I eyed Boots. "That true?"

"Yep."

I rolled my eyes. I was tired and ready to hit the hay, but since Sassy was a paying client, I'd have to perk up enough to cipher out what was going on.

Seeing my hands full, Boots stood and opened the screen door for me. He lumbered after me and the pies into the kitchen while Sassy stayed out on the porch calling out to me, "Talk some sense into your man. I'm paying you and Lavinia good money to clear my name. I'm counting on you, *you hear?*"

Boots asked if I wanted him to put on the coffee pot while I fussed with the pies.

"I'll get it," I said. "I've tasted your coffee."

He snorted a bit.

I asked him why he was on my porch and what had Sassy in such a tailspin as I cut him a generous slice of blueberry pie and warmed it up in the microwave.

"DA isn't too happy with Sassy."

"Why not?" I asked as I dug around in the freezer for some vanilla IGA ice cream. I'd known Boots my whole life, so I knew how he liked his pie.

He shrugged. "All the evidence pretty much shows that Sassy was the last to see Fussy walking and talking. The crime forensics came back from the lab, and there's not a whiff of anyone else on any of the crime scene samples except for Sassy. The gig gun had been wiped clean of all prints but for Fussy's."

The microwave beeped, and I scooped out some ice cream and sat the pie and ice cream on the table in front of Boots before running hot water through the coffee maker.

He thanked me for the pie before digging in.

I mulled over what Boots had said as I rinsed out a pair of coffee cups for the two of us. I considered making a cup for Veenie, but I'd heard her bedroom door slam down the hallway, so I figured she was down for the count, which was where I wanted to be.

I slid the coffee cups onto the kitchen table and sat down across from Boots. "You know full well that Sassy is not a killer."

He stopped shoveling pie and looked up at me, wiping his lips on a napkin. "Do I?"

"She has no motive."

"Some people say she's got a temper, mighty hard to get along with if she don't get her way."

"They say the same thing about you."

His face reddened.

I puffed out a deep sigh. "What about Sassy's ex-husband, Doogie?"

"What about him?" Having finished the pie, Boots swirled the coffee around and took a hot sip. "That's good coffee," he said.

"Doogie Duval is right here in town," I said. "He's likely been here since he slipped out of prison over in Terre Haute."

Boots eyed me. "You seen him?"

"I think so."

"Think so?"

"Darn it. Boots, why you always have to interrogate me? Most people take me at my word."

"They haven't known you as long as I have." He took another shot of coffee and pulled a toothpick out of the little ceramic mule on the table that held them in his saddle bags. "Did you see Doogie or not?"

"Yes, I saw him. Out at Leisure Hills."

"Leisure Hills? What was he doing out there? He's a wanted felon. Seems odd that he'd be hanging out in public with the oldsters, chatting them up."

"He has a suite out there. Registered under the name John Smith. Smithy, they call him."

Boots got up and rinsed his pie plate and cup in the sink. He sat them in the drainer. "That makes no sense at all."

"I didn't say it made sense. I said it was God's truth."

"You just found him there and walked up to him and said howdy, are you the guy who busted out of prison over in Terre Haute awhile back?"

I blushed a little. "No. I saw him scooting down the hallway there, but when Veenie and I went to his suite, he wouldn't answer our knocks. But gosh darn I know it was him." I then told Boots how Pooter had seen a man who answered to Doogie's description out at the Moon Glo Motor Lodge with Bromley right before his death, and how Bert had told me and Veenie that Bromley had been deeply invested in the Sun City real estate scam with Doogie.

Boots rubbed his upper lip and looked around the kitchen like he might be perturbed. "And this is the first you thought to report any of this to me, law enforcement?"

"For Pete's sake, we just learned most of this today. Veenie and I were busy doing our jobs. This is the first I've seen of you since this morning when you brushed us off about getting shot at out at the barn."

Boots stood up, scraping his kitchen chair back with more noise than necessary. "I didn't brush you off. You went all mum-lipped about why you were out at that barn, and then I spent the rest of the day chasing down clues, cause dang it, I care about you, Ruby Jane."

The tips of his ears had gone red, his cheeks too. I felt a little sheepish. I mumbled a "Sorry."

"No matter," he said. "You were out at that barn meeting someone who's trying to blackmail Avonelle. That right?"

I narrowed my eyes. "How'd you know that?"

He pulled his cell phone out of the leather snap case on his holster belt and flicked it on. "Whole town knows that." He showed me the screen, which was open to the front screen of the *Hoosier Squealer* website. Under "Breaking News," I read:

Shades Agency Caught in Lead Shower at Hoosier Barn Shootout

If you were down near Hound Holler lately and thought you heard firecrackers or gunfire, you'd be quite right. It was gunfire, folks. This all happened in the exact same place prominent town dentist Bromley Apple was found dead as a rutabaga dressed like a hobo scarecrow on Ms. Barbara Skaggs's front porch last week.

The shots were coming from the barn on Ms. Skaggs's property. Sounded like a shotgun, not a rifle, to those who heard it. No one knows who fired said shotgun, but everybody knows who it was that had to outrun the buck-shot. Per usual, it was professional snoops Mrs. Lavinia Goens and her longtime friend and business acquaintance, Mrs. Ruby Jane Waskom.

The two senior sleuths were on a case for the Shades Detective Agency. They had been hired by Mrs. William Apple to snoop and determine who might have killed her son, Bromley. Our lovely coroner, Ms. April Trueblood, has since ruled Bromley's death one of natural causes— seems he was born with a bum ticker and just didn't know it—but it's still a big secret why he was perched on Ms. Skaggs's porch in odd attire. Some believe it was a sexual thing (the odd attire, not the death per se.)

Ms. Skaggs says she remains in the dark about the dead dentist and why he decided to expire at her front door.

"I've had a run of bad luck lately," she said. "I figure this is just more of the same."

The real mystery: why were the two lady PIs out at that barn after dark? The local rumor mill says blackmail may be involved. Who's being blackmailed and why? Nobody knows for sure, but Mrs. William Apple, president of our esteemed First National Bank, may be involved. There have been several reports of bank statements with pennies missing here and there. Sounds to us like the world's smallest bank robbery may be afoot, but you never know, so stay tuned to the Squealer for updates.

In any case, Mrs. Lavinia Goens says she does not take being shot at lightly and wishes the offending party to know that when he is caught, she fully intends to, "Kick his sorry butt from here to next Christmas." Those who know Mrs. Goens assure us that she is quite capable of making good on that threat.

Doc Scarborough is sponsoring tonight's special news bulletin and wishes to remind everybody that an annual checkup is a wise investment if you're over fifty and not feeling all that nifty. Head on over and let the doc check your tick-tock. Mention the Hoosier Squealer and get a free oatmeal raisin cookie baked by Mrs. Wilma Scarborough, herself, Pawpaw County's own Cookie Queen.

I wasn't happy to read that report. Veenie had to have been the primary source of the news, and she knew full well we weren't supposed to talk to the press about cases. I was pretty much boiling mad. I reckoned I knew now why she had scurried off to her bedroom and hit the hay early.

"Well?" asked Boots as he clicked off his phone. "That part about blackmail being why you were out at the barn, that right?"

"Maybe. Some of it," I grumbled.

He crossed his arms against his chest. "Which part of it?" He had his heels dug in. He clearly wasn't going anywhere until I told him the whole story, or at least as much of it as I knew and understood.

I sighed and sank down in the kitchen chair.

Boots folded his arms against his chest and let his eyes drill into me.

I told him all about Avonelle and the bank and what Bert had told Veenie and me about Bromley and how he had put the virus on his mom's computer to pay Doogie off and keep him quiet about his investment in the Sun City real estate scam.

"Well," mused Boots as he stroked his closely cropped white beard. "So Doogie probably is in town? And he's the embezzler behind this whole missing pennies scheme?"

"Near as we can tell."

"And Avonelle has reported all this to the bank authorities?"

"Yep, a Mr. Peesley from Chicago. Veenie and I met him."

"Doggone it!" He shook his head as he stood up. "You ought to tell me these things, woman. I'm the law around her." He poked at his own chest. "I ought to know this kind of stuff."

"I just told you," I said in my defense. I stood up and looked him square in the eye. "You going to leave Sassy alone now?"

"Nope," he said as he headed toward the door, one hand on his ring of handcuffs, the other on his pistol.

"No?" I cried, my voice hoarse. "You're taking her back to jail?"

"Course I am. The DA wants her behind bars. Got no other suspects. All the evidence points to her. I can't just up and ignore a court order. I'm sworn to uphold the law. They've set a trial date. She'll get a chance to plead her case in court, same as everybody."

We were out on the porch now, and Sassy had heard that last part. She looked white as a ghost, save for her lips, which were fire engine red, per usual. "You're taking me in?"

"Sorry. Got no choice," said Boots as he pulled the warrant out of his pocket. "You're going to trial. You can call a lawyer soon as we get to the jail. We'll make you as comfortable as we can."

"But what about Doogie?" she screamed loud enough to wake up the whole neighborhood. In fact, across the street I saw the lights go on in Thelma Nierman's living room. Thelma was in her nineties and stayed alive pretty much just to spy on me and Veenie. She loved listing out our sins and indiscretions. She was certainly getting an eyeful and an earful that night.

"What about Doogie?" Sassy cried as Boots cuffed her and led her down the porch stairs. "He must have killed Fussy. He's the jealous type. Real jealous. Once, he hit a guy in the nose just for looking at me for too long."

Boy, I thought, a day ago Sassy was all, "Doogie is a gentleman. Doogie isn't violent. Doogie wouldn't hurt a fly. Doogie's a good Hoosier boy." But now, with Sassy's neck in a noose, the story had changed. By the time Boots had Sassy escorted to his patrol car and had her head lowered to help her into the backseat, she was screaming accusations, like Doogie might be the long-lost Night Stalker.

The one saving grace: Boots didn't flip on his cherry or his siren. He pulled quietly away from the curb. As he passed under the streetlight at the intersection, I saw Sassy with her pasty-white face plastered to the window lipping out a plea for help.

Our only hope now was to find Doogie and bring him to justice.

CHAPTER THIRTY-FIVE

T he next morning, when I went to check on Veenie in her
room, she'd vanished. She must have run off to hide from
me. Probably figured I'd read the *Squealer* by now and figured
out that she'd tattled stuff that she ought to have held in
confidence. And gosh darn, I could have used her help. Sassy
wasn't getting sprung from jail all on her own.

When I arrived at the office, Harry was sitting behind his
computer, his sleeves rolled up. His ashtray was brimming in
cigarette butts, and his eyes were a little bloodshot, like he'd
been working for a while. Before he could bellyache about the
whereabouts of his coffee and donuts, I flung a white bakery
bag of day-olds from the Roadkill Café onto his desk and
headed to the coffee machine to start the morning perk.

"Why you acting like that?" Harry asked as he looked up
from the computer screen.

"Like what?" I asked.

"Like you been sucking on persimmons."

I updated Harry on Sassy's arrest and Veenie's disappearance. I also filled him in on what we'd learned from Bert about
Doogie and the bank scam.

He tugged at one end of his mustache. "Things don't look
so good for Sassy, that's for sure. Maybe you ought to take a
run out to Leisure Hills, see if you can shake Doogie out of his
hidey-hole."

I pondered that idea for a moment and decided it was a
darn good one. Doogie seemed to be the key to a whole lot of

things. Maybe if we could pin him down, we could get him yakking. I was about to ask Harry if he wanted to arm up and ride shotgun with me out to Leisure Hills when Veenie burst in the door. Her face was red as a fireball candy and she was winded like she'd been running from the law or after a fresh-baked pie. The sweat was pouring off her chubby cheeks, and her white hair stood up on top of her head like a Mohawk.

"What's up?" I asked.

"Get your car keys, Ruby Jane. Hurry it up!"

I grabbed the keys off my desk and shot toward the door. Veenie had already turned heel and was halfway out the door. I called after her, but she was headed straight to the Chevy like a fat little BB. She was firmly seated on the passenger's side, rolling down the window by the time I caught up with her. I jumped into the Impala and keyed the ignition, but it just sat there, dead as a tin can. No noise. No rumble.

"Dag nabbit!" I cursed.

"Let's go!" Veenie yelled. "He's getting away! He's running for it!" She was twisted around in the seat, pointing down Main Street behind us. She was kicking her fat little legs against the car seat like it was a horse she could spur into action.

"Who?" I asked. "Gosh darn! Who we chasing?"

"Doogie!" she yelled as she pointed far down Main Street at the figure of a short man with dark hair who was carrying an orange Hoosier Feedbag grocery bag in one hand and a six-pack of Big Red pop in the other. The man was walking fast, tapping his cane as he went, eating up the sidewalk with each brisk little step. He was wearing clip-on sunglasses over his regular black-framed glasses and a hooded, blue windbreaker. He kept looking nervously over his shoulder in the direction of the police station, then the bank. By the time my eyes were focused in the bright daylight, he'd turned down the alley at Pokey's and disappeared from sight.

I jammed the key around in the ignition and hit the accelerator, but the Impala sat there dead as a doornail.

Veenie looked at me, then at the ignition.

"It won't start," I explained.

"You still got the spare key to Harry's Toyota?"

"Sure."

Veenie popped open the door and ran out behind the Impala to Harry's Toyota and yanked on its door. It wasn't locked. She was seated in the shotgun spot by the time I got in and keyed it to life. One click of the key, and we were off. I caught sight of Harry standing at the big front office window, waving his arms and yelling naughty things after us. I spun his car around and headed around the corner to where the alley came out on the other side. I threw Harry a wave and a kiss as I shot after Doogie.

We rounded the corner, squealing rubber, but the alley was empty. I stomped on the brakes. No sign of Doogie or anyone else.

"He had food and pop. Where you reckon he was going?" I asked Veenie.

Her face scrunched up in thought.

Just then, Pooter swooshed around the corner on his banana-seat bicycle. He flipped up his aviator shades and asked us if we were looking for the Hollywood guy.

We both nodded vigorously.

"If you hurry, you can catch him. Saw him squeal out of the bank parking lot in a beat-up old Caddy, black, out-of-state plates."

"Which way did he go?" Veenie asked.

Pooter pointed to the right. "Poor Farm Road."

Veenie tossed Pooter a dollar bill from her bra, and we hung a right to catch Poor Farm Road.

Veenie was sitting on the edge of her seat now. She had the binoculars pressed to her glasses. Sometimes it helped her see a little better in bright light. The binoculars were cracking against her glass lenses as the car sped along, so she gave up after a while.

"Lay rubber, Ruby Jane!" she shouted. The air conditioning was blasting full speed. Veenie also had all the windows powered down in the Toyota. It sounded and felt like a tornado was beating on my ear drums. "There!" she screamed

We were on the gravel road now. Up ahead a cloud of dust swirled. I could make out red brake lights on a black car. The car skidded. The Caddy was traveling fast. It fishtailed in the gravel, wobbling and swaying like a sick possum. Approaching the gate house to Leisure Hills the Caddy didn't slow down. It blew right through the mechanical arm. Metal flew everywhere. I gunned Harry's Toyota and followed suit.

The Caddy squealed into the back lot of Leisure Hills, and Doogie jumped out, holding the orange Hoosier Feedbag bag close to his chest, along with the six-pack of Big Red pop. He scurried up the back walkway and disappeared into the building.

Veenie didn't wait for me to park the Toyota. She jumped out while I was still rolling. Somehow she hit the ground running and shot toward the back door where Doogie had vanished. By the time I had the car parked and made my way to the back door, she was standing with her hands on her knees, wheezing like a hundred-year-old pump organ in need of repair.

I eyed the door. It had a key card unit on it. No way we could bust in.

I looked at Veenie. She looked like a sweaty fireplug.

"Whad'da'ya waiting for?" Veenie wheezed.

"To see if I'm going to have to bury you." I gave her a few seconds to catch her breath while I contemplated the situation. Doogie was inside, so I reckoned we had him cornered now. We could saunter in the front door. If need be, we could call Boots for backup. But from the way Doogie crashed through the mechanical arm on the gate and the sound of the cop car siren I heard wailing not too far away, I reckoned he or Devon would be along shortly.

Nurse Pruitt rolled up next to me and Veenie by the back door. She was wearing her peach-colored uniform and her giant marshmallow shoes. She was riding high-and-mighty in a golf cart. "You gals need some oxygen?" she asked as she pointed to a pair of tanks and a coil of plastic hose with a face mask in the back of the cart.

Veenie rolled onto the backseat of the cart and took a giant hit of air. Then another one. That brightened her up. Her cheeks plumped up like little red apples.

I explained to Nurse Pruitt what was happening, and she gave the cart a stomp, giving us a quick ride up to the main entrance. "You gals sure you don't need a doctor?"

Veenie was up now and raring to go. "Nah, I'm okeydokey, but you better keep a doc nearby for that old hound dog Doogie. Soon as I get a hold of him, he's gonna be needing someone to put the pieces back together again." She'd just finished talking when we both saw Doogie through the wide picture window on the front porch, running through the lobby toward the kitchen, his cane about the only thing keeping him upright. That's all the encouragement Veenie needed. She was off again. And I was after her, bringing up the rear.

Spying us, Doogie ran, slipping and sliding, into the kitchen. By now he'd dropped his groceries and the Big Red pop. The pop cans had burst and rolled across the floor, spitting red and slicking up the linoleum. I slipped in a puddle of Big Red but regained my footing by grabbing hold of the salad bar cart. I heard something rip and hoped like heck it was my pants, not my tendons.

By the time I got into the kitchen, there was a circle of people in white serving hats gathered in the back near the freezers. I elbowed my way through the circle to find Veenie sitting on top of Doogie, who was face down on the checkered linoleum. He was kicking and screaming, but she was giving it right back to him. Weight wise, Veenie had the upper hand. She was sitting on his lower back, yanking at his rooster comb of hair with both her hands. Whether he liked it or not— guessing by the way he was cursing and kicking, he did not—Doogie Duval, senior Romeo, was down for the count.

CHAPTER THIRTY-SIX

B oots stood in the doorway of the holding cell at the jail, his hat in his hands. He had his sunglasses off and clipped to his shirt pocket. "You gals blew right through the front gate out at Leisure Hills. That's a crime, just so you know."

Veenie shook her head. "Doogie did that."

"She's telling God's truth," I offered.

Boots murmured something under his breath.

We weren't in the jail cell, but Doogie was. He was sitting on a cot looking forlorn, his chin cupped in his hands. He was a tiny fellow. Up close, I could see that he was wearing elevator shoes, black ones polished to all get-out. Boots had let him use the restroom to clean up after Veenie had walloped him half to death. His hair was slicked up neat on top of his head again, woodpecker style. It was black as coal, except for the sides, which were white as snow. Definitely a dye job because he was older than me, and his face showed it. Veenie had broken his glasses in the tussle, but Boots had taped the nose bridge together with a strip of silver duct tape. "I'm entitled to a lawyer," he bellyached. "I want a lawyer," he moaned over and over again. He looked like he might cry.

"Course you do," said Boots.

Doogie had clammed up as soon as Boots clinked shut the door on his cell.

I was pondering how to get his lips moving again.

Veenie had gone at him full force, peppering him with questions, but that just made him pout more. He didn't seem all that fond of her.

I asked Boots if he'd bring Sassy in from the back cell.

He eyed me like I was up to something, which I was, but heck, it was a good something, not anything sneaky or dirty handed. I guess he finally decided the same because he left and then came right back, Sassy in tow. She was wearing an orange jumpsuit (not her color) and black cloth slippers. Her wrists were cuffed in front of her with plastic ties.

Doogie's face melted when he saw her. "Honey Bunny!" he cried as he jumped up off the cot.

"Rooster!" she called. I reckoned that was her pet name for him.

They sat on the cot together and just sort of rubbed noses for a bit. It was sort of romantic and cute, except for the handcuffs and all.

Once they were done jail smooching, Doogie gave us a dirty look. "Why you got my little Sassy all tied up in here? She didn't even know I was in town."

And there it was: Doogie's lips were working again.

I explained to him that Sassy was being held for the murder of Fussy Jones.

He looked at her a bit odd. "You killed a man?" he asked, sounding awfully surprised.

"Heck no," she said. "I thought you did."

"Me?" His darkly dyed eyebrows shot up like raven's wings.

"Well, I mean *they* thought you might have killed someone." She threw a hand at us. "I knew you wouldn't hurt a fly, let alone murder some fella." She shot us the evil Hoosier eye.

I was starting to feel like I was watching a reality TV show. It wasn't half bad.

Doogie shook his head. "I'm guilty of a lot of things, Honey Bunny, but not murder."

"Well, I know that. Heck, you didn't even know Fussy Jones."

Doogie's face fell a little. He stared at his elevator shoes. "Well, truth be told, Honey Bunny, I did know Fussy Jones. He's the guy who built Camelot Court and owns controlling interest in Leisure Hills. That fellow, right? Well, I sure enough did know him. He gave me the place out at Leisure Hills to hide out."

Sassy's forehead wrinkled so hard it looked like an accordion. "How in the heck did you know him?"

We all leaned in closer, toward the cell bars, waiting for the rest of the story. Veenie was mashed up against me so tightly I had to poke her in the ribs to get her to back off. She grunted, but complied.

Doogie sighed. "Well, I've already been found guilty of this, so I guess I can tell you all that he was one of the fellows who invested in Sun City. Right nice fellow too. Kind of hated to take his money."

"But how'd you know him?"

"Through that dentist."

"Bromley Apple?" asked Sassy.

"Sure. I paid all my investors a grand each to bring in new investors. I found Bromley through my Facebook ad after you suggested to me that Indiana might be a good place to dig up some new business. Once Bromley was in deep, he organized a big meet up at IU up in Bloomington. He brought in some more fellows. Fussy was one of them. And his own brother, Bert."

I raised my hand. "Wait just a dog gone minute. Bert Apple was invested in Sun City?"

"Oh sure. In fact he threw more into the pot than Bromley."

Sassy seemed puzzled now. "But I read all the court papers, and none of those men were mentioned or called as witnesses."

"That's because they made a special deal with me."

"Special?" asked Sassy.

"Sure. I mean they weren't happy when they found out the condos were, well, sort of not real, and that I'd sort of been arrested. I might have told them that they were all just as liable as me because they were sort of legal partners because they'd recruited investors. And I might have mentioned that I had the paperwork to prove they were involved, and then they might have asked if there was any way that paperwork could get lost. And then I might have said maybe the paperwork might get lost, if they'd do me a favor or two."

I felt I knew where this was going. "So you asked Bromley to put that slicing software on his mother's computer to steal from the bank?"

Doogie stared at me. "Nope."

"No?" We all cried.

"It wasn't Bromley. He didn't want anything to do with embezzlement or hurting his mom. Said it wasn't his style."

"Who was it then that put the slicing software on the bank's system?" I had to ask.

"Why, it was Bromley's brother, Bert."

My head ached now. I could tell by the look on Veenie's face, it was all twisted up, that hers did too.

Sassy spoke up. "Then you didn't kill Fussy?"

"Why would I do that, Honey Bunny?"

"Well, I was sort of dating him."

Doogie's face fell. He looked like a hound dog that had been slapped.

"I'm sorry, Rooster," Sassy said. "I thought you'd be in jail for the rest of our natural lives. And you know how I just hate being alone. It wasn't anything serious with Fussy, but dang it, I have to keep a hand in the game. I'm not made to be single. I'm just not!" Tears welled up in her eyes.

Doogie draped an arm around her shoulders to comfort her.

A number of questions were welling up in me. I asked Doogie why he was blackmailing Avonelle and why he'd shot at me and Veenie when we'd gone out to meet him out at Barbara's barn.

He fiddled with the tape on the bridge of his broken glasses. "I didn't do any of that. I don't even know how to shoot a gun. Guns scare the bejeebers out of me. Heck, *she* scares me." He pointed to Veenie.

Just then Devon rattled in, bringing supper trays for Sassy and Doogie. His eyes were all bright and his step full of spring. He was excited to have a big time felon in custody. He'd made extra copies of Doogie's wanted poster and already had one pinned on the office wall behind his desk.

Boots said we should clear out and let the jailbirds eat in peace. Said we could all come back tomorrow during visiting hours.

Veenie and I walked slowly out to Harry's Toyota. We both felt like we'd been chasing polecats and rolling around in the dirt all day, because well, we had. "We still don't know who killed Fussy," I said with a deep sigh. "Or shot at us. And if we don't solve Fussy's murder, Sassy and Doogie will have matching cells over in Terre Haute. And Indiana has the death penalty for murder."

"You believe that lying little Rooster?" Veenie asked.

"Think I do. I mean, he seemed trustworthy enough."

"What about his claim that Bert was the one who set up his mother as an embezzler?"

"He's got no reason to lie about that." Bert, I was thinking, had pulled the wool over our eyes but good. He had every reason to lie about embezzling. And he knew full well his dead brother could never sit up and defend himself.

While Veenie was puzzling over all this new intelligence, I clicked on my cell. I'd been letting it charge in the jailhouse and hadn't checked it all day because of all the commotion.

As soon as I flicked it on, the thing practically blew up in my hand.

Joyce was back with dagger hearts, saying she'd dropped by the insurance office to take Rusty to a surprise romantic dinner at this new Italian restaurant only to find that he and Kayleigh had both been checked out all day. No one could tell her where they were, only that they'd not be back in the office until tomorrow. "Find him!!!" Joyce texted me.

Joyce had always been bossy, but this time she was paying, so I reckoned she had a right to be ordering me and Veenie around. I asked Veenie to pull up the BMW tracking gizmo on her cell and check on Rusty's whereabouts. We were both stunned when the tracker put Rusty's BMW less than two miles away. He was just outside Knobby Waters. At the Moon Glo Motor Lodge, to be exact. "That's not possible," I said. "Why would he be there?"

Veenie rolled her eyes. "Why does anyone check in at the Moon Glo?"

"That doesn't make sense."

"It sure does if he's diddling Kayleigh. We're onto him. He knows Joyce is onto him. She'd kicked down all the swanky hotel doors in Bloomington to get at him, but you know how she hates coming down here. No way she's going to find him at the Moon Glo. She'd not risk getting poor folk cooties."

"But Rusty seemed so earnest when he swore to us that he wasn't having an affair."

Veenie shook her head and fiddled with the air conditioner knob. We didn't have air in the Impala, so she was hogging it up in Harry's Toyota while she had a chance. "I swear you are as naïve as a puffball kitten, Ruby Jane. Men always lie about their ding-a-lings. You ought to date more. You'd find that out right quick."

"Nobody left to date," I complained as I fired up the Toyota. "You and Sassy have them all tied up."

And in Sassy's case, I meant that literally.

I pulled out of the jailhouse parking lot and headed toward the covered bridge. I really didn't want to go out to the Moon Glo, partly because it was late, and partly because my knees were aching, but mostly because I feared what we'd find out there might snap my daughter's brittle little heart in two.

CHAPTER THIRTY-SEVEN

It was a dark night. The moon had disappeared behind a black fist of clouds. Veenie was freezing me out with the air conditioning, so I powered down my window as I drove. Crickets cried, and turkey buzzards squawked as we bumped down the dirt turnoff to the Moon Glo Motor Lodge. The smell of dampness from the river flooded the car as we neared the motel. The motor lodge sat on a weedy lip of sand not far from White River, just up the bend from the Boat and Gun Club. The big neon sign didn't work, but someone had rigged a string of high-powered aluminum clamp lights to the rotting overhang above the office door, so the path to the little strip of motel rooms was lit. The rigged lights provided a beam of light wide and bright enough so that anyone could find their way to a room with a bed. Even a drunk fellow.

The Moon Glo wasn't romantic, but it was convenient and dirt cheap. Those dual features were enough to keep the place hopping. Rusty's black BMW was parked in front of number ten, the last room on a long row of concrete block rooms. Three other vehicles, a blue dented-up minivan with Missouri plates (probably a legit fisherman), a red Chevrolet Silverado double cab pickup, and an older model silver Honda Odyssey van, were pulled tight to the doors of rooms seven, eight, and nine.

Veenie tapped on the window of Harry's Toyota as I parked close by the office, out of the glare of the utility lights. She pulled off her glasses, then slid them back on and squinted.

"That red Chevy?" she asked. "That belongs to Principal Patsy, don't it?"

I squinted. "Yeah. Maybe."

"And that Honda next to it, don't it belong to Coach McCoy?"

"I think so. What about it? They're grown adults. Married. They're allowed to do what they want," I defended them mostly because we had our hands full, and I wasn't itching for a new case or a bucket of trouble. Veenie had been known to drum up cases when things turned slow. Some folks didn't appreciate that. The way things were going this month, I was feeling like maybe we ought to petition the mayor to change the name of the town from Knobby Waters to Sodom and Gomorrah.

"Sure, they're married," said Veenie, "but not to each other."

I shot Veenie a look. "Let's take care of Rusty and his wandering wiggle worm first," I said as I heaved open the car door and headed heavy-footed toward room number ten.

Veenie followed in my wake. She was humming something. Sounded to me like Hank Williams's, "Your Cheating Heart Will Tell on You."

We stood at the door to room number ten for almost a minute. I couldn't bring myself to lift my hand and knock. I could hear the TV blaring on the other side. It sounded like a news station. The curtains, a moldy plastic pair decorated with blue sunflowers, were drawn tight.

Veenie asked me if I was scared.

"Yeah, but not for me. For Joyce."

"Stop fretting, Ruby Jane. Joyce will be ok. She'll skin him clean for all he's worth and go on to the next fellow. Probably get a better one next time. Admit it, you never did like old Rusty Krotch. I know I didn't. Lots of fish in the river. She's a survivor, like you. You know that."

She had a point there. Joyce's heart might crack, and she might go down over this, but she'd never stay down. It wasn't in her. She was a kicker. A biter. A screamer.

I was working up my courage to knock on the motel door when it swung open. Rusty stood there, his tie off, his sleeves rolled up. He was holding a pink plastic ice bucket in one hand and a cracked plastic scoop in the other. He blinked several times like he thought—hoped?—he might be hallucinating.

"Howdy!" said Veenie as she popped into the room under Rusty's upraised arm. "We was just passing by and thought we'd come in and visit for a spell."

I tossed Rusty a weak smile.

He backed up and ushered me into the room.

Kayleigh was sitting in an overstuffed corner chair flicking through things on her cell phone. She looked startled to see us. Thankfully, she was fully dressed.

She and Rusty exchanged glances.

Both beds were made. Veenie bounced on the one nearest the bathroom. "Getting hot ain't it?" Dust flew everywhere. A pillow flipped off onto the floor. "This place smells like cat upchuck. It smell like that to you guys?"

Rusty ground his lips together. "What are you two doing … here?"

Veenie bounced some more. "This ain't a very good bed. I would have thought you'd be the kind of guy to spend an extra dime or two on the ladies."

Rusty shook his head. "What on earth are you talking about?"

I found my voice. "You told us that you and Kayleigh weren't having an affair, and gosh darn it, I believed you. Wanted to believe you." My voice cracked like peanut brittle. I suddenly felt old and tired.

Kayleigh set aside her phone. She flipped her long hair. "He told you the truth."

I could feel the hair on the back of my neck rising. "Kayleigh, honey, I'm old, but I'm not an idiot. You two are in a motel, where apparently you've been holed up together all day. I think what you two are doing is gosh darn clear at this point."

Rusty slid the empty ice bucket he'd been holding onto on the bedside table. "I'm broke," he said. He sat down on the bed opposite me and buried his face in his hands. "Dead broke."

Kayleigh spoke up. "Rusty made some bad investments. My fault partly."

"Bad investments?" I asked.

Rusty looked up and wiped his face with his palms. He pinched the bridge of his nose and cleared his sinuses. "Real estate. Kayleigh attended a seminar on the IU campus. They'd sent me an invitation, some of the guys from down here that Joyce went to school with. I figured they were legit. They were looking for investors for a condo complex. I invested heavily. It was a scam. I'm busted. Can't make payroll, and I'm too ashamed to tell Joyce."

His shoulders fell. He looked exhausted but relieved. "There," he spat out. "Now you know. I'm humiliated ... and now you know."

Kayleigh confirmed Rusty's story with a nod. "I'm partly to blame. I recommended the investment. And now he can't pay me either. He's a month behind on salaries. We're down here trying to get some of his money back."

"Why here?" I asked. But then it hit me full on, like a cat tossed into a tornado. "Wait, was this real estate in California?"

Rusty nodded.

"Sun City?"

He nodded more vigorously.

"And you're down here to meet up with Doogie Duval?"

Rusty messed with his hair, flipping back the thinning part that had fallen into his eyes. "No. I mean, yes, Doogie Duval was the fellow behind the original scheme, but we're here to meet with Bert Apple."

"Bert?" Veenie screeched.

"Yeah, Bert. He was one of the guys who invited me to the seminar. He got paid to recruit me into the scheme. Now he wants more money to keep my involvement quiet. Stupid me, Kayleigh and I recruited two other guys, IU professors, thinking all this was on the up-and-up. Bert's pressuring now, saying he'll turn me in as a knowing accomplice unless I pay him to keep quiet."

My throat tightened. "Bert has been blackmailing you?"

"Yes. And I've decided not to pay. I've already talked to my lawyers, and they assure me that given the texts and other evidence I have on file from Bert, I'm completely innocent in the eyes of the law. I couldn't tell Joyce *any* of this until I had it cleared with the lawyers. I didn't want to implicate her, in case things took a sour turn for me. I was trying to protect her." He rubbed his forehead and went into the bathroom to draw a glass of water.

Kayleigh piped up. "I've been going along, hoping to get my back salary and clear my name. I'm young. This could ruin me. I'll never get my insurance or financial planner certifications if any of this gets out."

Rusty came out of the bathroom and handed Kayleigh a glass of tap water, which she declined. She looked down her nose at the glass of water, like it contained a shot of the bubonic plague.

I sat down in the chair by the window and let everything sink into my skull, which felt about as thick as a pumpkin. "You said you had evidence that Bert was blackmailing you?"

"Sure, texts mostly."

"From his cell?"

Rusty shrugged. "He always texted from a different cell number. Burner phones most likely, but he always used the same handle. Same name, like he was proud of it."

"Was his handle Money Boy?" I asked.

Rusty looked surprised. "How did you know?"

"You weren't the only fish he hooked," I said. Boy, oh boy, Avonelle was *not* going to be happy to hear any of this. Bert had pulled the wool over all our eyes with his innocent mama's boy sob story and love of chocolate cream pie.

"Holy corn dog!" said Veenie. Her mouth opened so wide in surprise that her dentures almost fell out. The look on her face told me she'd also caught on.

Rusty was in the middle of asking us a question, "How did—" when the window on the motel room shattered. Glass blew into the room like the air outside had exploded. Kayleigh dove to the floor. Rusty fell to his knees. Veenie flattened herself against the bed. And I just sat in the chair, my mouth open.

Chapter Thirty-Eight

"**R**uby Jane!" Veenie screeched. "Belly flop! Get your ass on the floor!"

Veenie rolled down between the two beds and motioned for me to join her.

Shaking myself out of my stupor, I dove down next to her.

"That was definitely a shotgun," she whispered hoarsely to me.

We all lay perfectly still. The only sound I heard was my heart and Veenie's beating in rapid time, like a pair of conga drums.

Veenie spoke again. "Who you reckon is shooting at us?"

I shook my eyes, indicating I had no idea. My mouth was too dry to speak. At this point, Bert Apple seemed the most likely suspect. He sure had been busy lately committing felonies.

Kayleigh croaked from her hidey-hole. "Oh my God. Is someone shooting at us? For real?"

Veenie whispered, more to the carpet than anyone, "Boy, you can tell she's college educated."

We all waited. And waited.

Then came a firm knock on the door.

"Don't answer it," screeched Veenie. "I saw this same trick in a movie once. You answer that door, there's gonna be a crazy guy standing there with a chainsaw. And I got prepaid front row tickets to see Blake Shelton over in Terre Haute next month. Non-refundable. I can't die now."

I heard Kayleigh start to whimper on the other side of the bed.

A series of knocks came again. They were slow and deliberate.

I got up and went to the door, figuring if it was my time to meet the maker, I might as well throw the door open wide and say, "Howdy!"

The door swung open and there stood Shap Reynolds, a shotgun slung over one shoulder. The air smelled like burned gun powder. Shap's face was red. His lips were twitching. He wore a pair of old Levi's and a NASCAR T-shirt and clodhopper farm boots stained with red clay. A tattered straw cowboy hat sat far back on his head. "Where's my wife?" he asked.

Veenie popped up from between the beds. "She ain't here, you ol' fool. Why you shooting at us?"

Shap stepped into the room. He walked the short length of the room and studied Kayleigh and Rusty, who'd come up out of their hidey-holes. "Where's Harry?" he asked as he stepped into the bathroom and raked back the shower curtain with the butt of his shotgun.

"Harry's not here either," I said. "Why you think Harry and your wife are here?"

"That's his car. He tried to hide it." Shap pointed the barrel of his shotgun at Harry's Toyota, which I'd parked in the shadows so we could sneak up on Rusty and Kayleigh.

"Veenie and I borrowed Harry's car. Our Impala is acting up," I explained.

Shap studied me, then Veenie. "Oh, sorry," he said. "I got no beef with you gals. It's Harry I'm after."

He then shouldered his gun and walked out of the motel room and across the lot toward his pickup truck.

"Wait!" I hollered after him. "Did you shoot at us out at Barbara Skaggs's barn down in Hound Holler?"

He had the door to the pickup open and had one foot up on the running board about to swing up into the cab. "That was you?"

"Afraid so."

"Sorry, again," he said. "I followed Harry's car out there. Thought he was meeting my wife. You know lots of menfolk don't much care for Harry. Maybe you ought not to borrow his car so much." Shap hopped into the cab and had his lights on and the engine revving when the Knobby Waters patrol car slid into the parking lot, the red cherry chirping.

Boots stepped out of the car but stayed behind the open door. He had his gun out of the holster. "Got a report of gunshot," he said. "Who's the guilty party?"

I pointed to Shap, who was idling his pickup truck, unable to leave because Boots had blocked the driveway. Beyond Shap, I could see the motel office. The lights were on, shining a bright rectangle of white out the plate glass window. A pale oval face wearing a Red's baseball cap peered out the window. I reckoned whoever was on night duty had called the cops after hearing the gunshot.

Rusty moved into the motel doorway next to me. "Bert out there? I thought it might be Bert. Thought maybe Bert had caught on that I was not paying, going to turn him in to the officials. Bert's not out there, is he?" He shaded his eyes, trying to see through the haze of the glaring lights that streamed in from the sheriff's car.

"Not Bert," I said. "No sign of Bert."

I motioned for Boots to come over, and he sauntered across the lot. I explained the situation to him. He nodded a couple of times. He studied Rusty. "You're Joyce's husband, right?"

"Yes, sir."

"Why you here?"

I explained that Rusty had been an unwitting investor in Sun City and that Bert had been blackmailing him. "He's here to meet Bert. Tell him he isn't paying any hush money."

"Smart move on your part," said Boots. "You can go on home now. Bert won't be bothering you. Won't be bothering anybody no more."

I started to ask what was up with Bert, but Boots held up one hand and cut me short. I could tell he was running short on patience. "We'll get to the details later, Ruby Jane. Rusty there can scoot on home. Bert's not going to be bothering anyone from here on in. Anybody here hurt?" he asked me.

"Nah. Just scared," I said.

"Okay. I'll take care of this. Straighten Shap out. Need you and Veenie to follow me back to the jailhouse." He turned and headed toward Shap.

"Hold your horses!" I called after Boots. "Why we got to go back to the jail? I'm tuckered out."

Boots said a couple of things to Shap, and then Shap followed him over to the patrol car and climbed in the back.

"Why we got to go back to the jail?" I yelled at Boots again as he backed up the patrol car and headed the nose toward town.

He made his red cherry chirp. "Follow me, and you'll find out why," he said as he powered up his window.

CHAPTER THIRTY-NINE

I t was after midnight. Boots sat us down in the booking room. I fussed over a pot of coffee, pretty sure none of us were going to get any shut-eye. Boots made Shap apologize again for shooting at me and Veenie like we were carnival ducks.

Harry was there—Boots had dragged him over from Pokey's—and Boots made him promise that he'd stop messing around with Dottie Reynolds.

Harry was mopey. "She gave me the clap anyway," he whined. "Just found out this morning."

Shap wasn't happy to hear that.

Boots asked us if we wanted to press serious charges against Shap, and Veenie and I both said no, with the condition that Shap not shoot at us or the office again. We all shook on that. Boots said he thought Shap needed a reminder that owning a firearm didn't mean you were licensed to shoot it off at whim. He put Shap in a cell to hold him overnight and charged him with unlawful discharge of a firearm in public and disturbing the peace. He also ordered him to pay the motor lodge for the window damage.

We'd updated Boots on all we'd learned from Rusty about Bert, and how he'd been blackmailing his mom and Rusty, probably Fussy too, under the alias of Money Boy.

"Don't surprise me none," Boots said when he heard about Bert. "It's always the quiet ones. After Doogie told us it was Bert who put the slicing software on his mama's computer, I went on over to his place and rounded him up. He didn't put up any resistance, practically slapped the cuffs on himself and jumped in the backseat of the patrol car. Said the guilt had been killing him. Eating him alive. In fact, he's in the back cell now, and he's got some things to say to you two."

Veenie and I exchanged glances.

Harry said, "Go on, you two. I'm going outside to take a smoke."

Boots scraped back his chair and stood up. "Come on, let's get this wrapped up. I need some sleep. Going fishing tomorrow."

Veenie and I followed Boots to the cell area. Sassy was awake, standing at the bars, looking out of sorts in her orange jumpsuit without her makeup, "Lordie, took you gals long enough. I'm ready to go." She clawed at the cell door lock.

Boots unlocked her cell, and she rushed out and hugged us both, even Veenie, who was caught too much by surprise to side-step the squeezing.

I turned to Boots. "I thought you couldn't let her go. DA said to lock her up."

"I did say that, but new evidence has surfaced. DA changed his mind."

"New evidence?" I said.

A voice piped up from the cell around the corner. It belonged to Bert Apple. We all slid around the corner to see Bert sitting on a cot in an orange jumpsuit, with his knees pulled up. His hair was messed up, but he actually looked happier than last we'd seen him. A good chocolate pie can do that to a fellow. "I confessed," he said.

"To killing Fussy?" I asked.

"Well, sort of. It was an accident. I was blackmailing him. Trying to scrape up enough money to get out of town, start over again. I was going to lose the practice, lose my license to practice because of all the debt and bills. Bromley dug the debt hole, and I thought investing in real estate would help us climb out, but that was just another big swallow hole. Then mother got wise to the software and called the bank auditors. I figured Bromley owed me after all these years covering up for him, so I threw him under the bus. I mean, he was dead, what harm could a felony charge do him?" He shrugged. "Not like I ever wanted to be a dentist, anyway." He sniffled. "It's hard being a dentist. People hate you, you know." I thought he might cry.

Veenie piped up. "Why'd you kill Fussy? He was one of your meal tickets, wasn't he?"

"Hated to do that to him, blackmail him and all, but darn it, he could afford it, and I just had to figure a way out of this. I'd always wanted my own bakery. Everybody seems so happy baking and icing things. I figured once I had enough cash stashed, I could move down south to Florida, start my life all over again. Bake cupcakes. People love it when you give them cupcakes." He got a dreamy look in his eyes, but then his eyes clouded over again. "They don't love you so much when you drill into their teeth."

Given how domineering Avonelle was, I could see why Bert might want to run away and be somebody other than a dentist or her son. But murder? I said as much.

"Told you, it was a full-on accident. Fussy had offered me one big payment if I'd come out and pick up the details on a wire transfer. I had pledged to leave town after that. Leave him alone. He never wanted his name attached to that real estate scheme, him being a contractor and all. He was afraid he'd lose his license, that it would ruin him. That suited me. So I went out to pick up the bank numbers where he was supposed to wire the big payoff. I went to his parked pontoon boat like he'd instructed me. I climbed onto the boat, but no one was there. The sun was down. It was dark out there on the river. The boat was sloshing around in the water. I can't swim, and I don't like the outdoors. All those bugs." He made a face like he's just eaten a heap of raw rhubarb straight up.

"Go on," Veenie encouraged, as eager as I was to hear the whole story.

"Well, I was trying to stay standing up on the boat, and thinking about leaving, thinking maybe I'd been set up. I was getting scared, and the mosquitoes were eating me alive. I grabbed hold of the row of gig guns to steady myself, and one of the guns came out of the holder and I was trying to stay upright and get it put back when all of a sudden Fussy burst out of that little shed on the back of his boat. But it didn't look like Fussy. I mean, the man was wearing women's underwear, for Christ's sake, and a wig and makeup. He spooked me so bad I accidently hit the trigger on the harpoon gun and *zing!* he went down. Hit him dead center. I wiped my prints off the gig gun and ran back home." Bert's face scrunched up like he might throw up.

It all sounded highly unbelievable, except for the fact that Sassy had told us the exact same story. It made perfect sense that Fussy might have heard someone on his boat and hoped against hope that Sassy had come back to give his fantasies a try. He burst out of the shed, all excited, and well …

I was starting to feel a whole lot better about my Amish sex life.

We were all standing around the cell feeling kind of sorry for Bert as he finished his story. He'd got himself into one heck of a mess. Course he'd also messed up a lot of other people's lives. "You were blackmailing your mama too?"

"I needed as much cash as I could carry, so yes. I figured she'd pay to keep the bank embezzlement out of the news."

Veenie shook her head. "But she surprised you?"

"Dug her heels in and sent you two out to uncover my identity." He sighed. "You were late getting to the barn that night, and I got spooked waiting in the dark. I left soon as I saw Shap sneaking around with that shotgun. Figured maybe Mom had hired him to wing me and bring me in."

Bert stretched out on his cot. He looked relaxed, more so than the last time we'd seen him in the bank office with his mama.

Veenie asked him if we ought to call his mama.

He twisted his lips. "I imagine it'll all be in the Squealer come morning. Maybe it's best if she reads about it first. Give her time to mull it over before she has to face the whole town. This is bound to be awfully hard on her. I was the good one, you know." He sighed.

I thought that was awfully sweet of him. It made me a little sad though that his life had gotten so messy. Life could get like that. One minute you're a respectable member of society perched on a front church pew, and the next you're hobbling around with your ankles twisty-tied together, picking up trash along the roadside.

Veenie asked Bert if there was anything we could do to lighten his load.

He sat up and thought about it for a minute. Then his face brightened. "Could you bring me another one of Ma Horton's chocolate cream pies?"

We both nodded.

Boots ushered us all out of the cell room. It was the middle of the night, and outside, the tree frogs were croaking a concert. The sky had cleared, and the moon swung over the trees like a magic ball of light. The air smelled clean and fresh, like life was about to start up all over again, as it did every spring.

Harry was standing by his Toyota, smoking. His fedora was pushed back on his head. He was admiring the moon, which he was trying to lasso with smoke rings.

I was about to join him in admiring the moon when my cell started jumping in my pocket. I pulled it out and flicked it on. There was a text from Joyce. It wasn't a frantic text for a change. "Rusty is home!" read the message. "My love has returned!" It warmed my heart to read a message from Joyce that sounded happy for a change.

I typed back, "He tell you everything?"

"Yes. So relieved!" That was punctuated with a string of smiley faces and a chorus line of dancing Spanish ladies.

"All okay?" I texted in return.

She typed back, "Thank you, Mama. I love you. You're the best."

I held the cell phone to my heart and enjoyed the glow of the words for just a moment, while they were still warm. I knew next time I heard from Joyce she'd probably be back to her uppity self, whining like the gears on the Chevy, but for the moment, I treasured that little spark of all-out love.

Harry ground out his cigarette with the toe on his shoe and offered me and Veenie and Sassy a ride over to the Impala, which remained parked in front of the office. Dog tired, we accepted.

When we climbed into the Impala, it started up lickety-split. No surprise there. The car was fussy like that. I made a mental note to have Dickie look under the hood again when he had some time. As I pulled onto Main Street and steered for home, Sassy started in about how she was going to have to have her hair washed and set professionally just to get the jail cooties out of her head. Then she started in on how she loved Doogie, but gosh darn, they'd never let him out of the big house now. She'd just have to keep auditioning for a new mate.

Veenie started chattering about how upset Avonelle was going to be to find out that her "good" baby boy had caved in so completely under the pressures of life. "Though I got to admit," she mused, "he seemed awfully happy about not having to be a dentist no more."

I thought about Avonelle. "She's got a whole mess of new kids. Two boys and a girl. She could have another run at it." I tried to imagine Avonelle visiting her new family down in Hound Holler. She'd already set up a trust fund for the kids. I was sure she'd spring for their education and dental care, but

Lordie, I had a hard time imagining her cozying up to Barbara Skaggs.

I drove along Main Street, my heart warmed by the knowledge that, at that moment, everybody in Knobby Waters was sleeping peacefully under a blanket of moonlight and a bowl of bright stars, and that up in the big city of Bloomington, my baby girl, Joyce, was sleeping the soundest of all.

Of course, all that peace and quiet didn't last as long as a Slo Poke sucker.

Veenie and I were back to running around, poking our noses into people's private affairs almost as soon as the sun popped up over the horizon. The chaos started with the disappearance of local sourpuss Gertie Wineager, Pawpaw County's BBQ Chicken Queen. It spread across Knobby Waters like the White River bursting its banks, sweeping up everybody, especially the chickens and Ma and Peepaw Horton, in a muddy swirl of feathers, chaos, and confusion …

A free excerpt from the *Chickenlandia Mystery,*
The Shady Hoosier Detective Agency: Book 3.

CHAPTER ONE

"I thought she might of headed on over to her big sister's place. Over in Tunnelton," said Tater Wineager, his gray caterpillar eyebrows knitted together in concern. "But I checked, and her sister ain't seen hide nor hair of her since Easter."

Tater was trying to explain to me and my pal Lavinia Goens—Veenie to most folks— how his wife, Gertie, could have been missing so long—more than a week—without him reporting the incident. We were all ears. This was our first missing person's case in a coon's age, and we were itching to make some pocket money.

Veenie and I were detectives in training at the Shades Detective Agency, the best—okay the only PI agency—in Pawpaw County, Indiana. Our boss, Harry Shades, had been strutting around the office in his cranky pants all morning threatening to off somebody just so we'd have a new case to solve. Tater losing track of his wife Gertie was a godsend to us.

"Anything wrong with Gertie's memory? I asked Tater.

"Nah." Tater gnawed on his tobacco-stained thumb. "She remembers everything, even things that never happened."

Tater glanced around the office. His face was the color of biscuit dough. His eyes were large wet prunes, pressed deep in the wrinkled dough. He was wearing a plaid shirt, Wrangler jeans cuffed up two inches, and worn black Red Wing lace-up boots. He was barely five feet tall. His booted feet dangled from his chair, not quite hitting the ground. He was zipped up in a yellow DeKalb seed corn windbreaker. His hair poked up from his scalp like tiny white scrub brushes.

"A fella allowed to fire up in here?" he asked. His eyes darted around the office in search of something—a "no smoking" sign, matches, an ashtray, something like that. "Used to, a fella could smoke anywhere, but nowadays you got to ask. So I'm asking."

Veenie, who was sitting next to me, slid a glass ashtray that advertised the Moon Glo Motor Lodge over Tater's way. "Fire up," she said. "Me and RJ been around smokers our whole life. We're still kicking."

Tater pulled a Zippo lighter from the pocket of his windbreaker. He torched his Marlboro. When he inhaled, his cheeks blew up like puffball mushrooms. His dark eyes watered up. "Not holed up at her sister's place," he repeated. "Drove over yesterday. Ain't nobody seen her since she lit out of the house last week for her regular color and set."

"Tinky Sue's?" I asked. Most women over fifty in Knobby Waters, the small Indiana river town where we lived, got their hair done at Tinky Sue Knute's Curl Up and Dye. But senior penny-pinchers sometimes frequented Henrietta's House of Hair, the beauty college over in Bedford. If you went to Henrietta's on a Tuesday, you could get a ten-dollar cut from a freshman. A color job was twenty. But then you had to accept whoever was on duty and whatever happened to your hair. And from what I had seen, there was a darn good reason why people referred to the beauty college as Henrietta's House of Hair Horrors.

Tater sucked on his cigarette. "Yep. Never lets anybody but Tinky Sue touch that head of hair. Has this bald patch up top." He fingered his own dome. "Started when she went through the change. Tinky Sue knows how to cover it up right nice."

I made a note of that in the file we'd started on Gertie. "Any reason Gertie might have run away? You have a spat?"

"Not that I noticed, but sometimes we have fights and I don't know it. She has to tell me."

He took another drag on his cigarette and studied the glowing amber. "Long winter. You gals know how it gets. Locked up in a house. We might have said a few things both of us regretted when the river finally thawed. We've been hitched forty years. A body can get pretty testy over that long a stretch."

Veenie said she understood. "Me and Fergus Senior only lasted ten years. He ran around with any hoochie-coochie gal who wiggled his way. You ever hound dog on Gertie? Do something stupid like that that might have ticked her off?"

Tater squeezed his eyes shut against the smoke. "Nah."

Like most men in these parts, he wasn't much for jawing.

"Anywhere else she might have run off to?" I asked. "You can leave us the contact for her sister in Tunnelton. We'll check there, of course. She have any other kin? A friend she might have gone to visit for a spell?"

"Don't think so. She wasn't all that popular. We got a daughter over in Mitchell, but I checked, and she hasn't seen her mama since Christmas. Got two grown sons. Both of them are in the military overseas. I wrote down some of Gertie's vitals so you can trace her. Imagine you use a lot of that fancy computer stuff like on the TV. I wrote down the address for her sister, Lottie. Got a paper on me somewhere. Lottie don't have a phone. Nervous type. Doesn't like all that ringing." He patted at several pockets before pulling a creased Rural Electric envelope out of his shirt pocket. He handed the envelope to me. The back of the envelope had a coffee stain shaped like a half moon and Gertie's vitals: social, date of birth, and a credit card number, all carefully printed in pencil in large block letters. Lottie's address was on the envelope too.

I asked Tater if Gertie had been planning to enter the big BBQ chicken cook-off at the upcoming Chickenlandia Festival. The annual festival started that weekend and was a big to-do for Pawpaw County. "She's the reigning BBQ Queen, right?"

"Oh sure. She's right proud of that. She's taken the crown and sash three years running. Ain't nobody can BBQ a chicken like Gertie." His face beamed with pride. "That's what makes it right peculiar. Her missing, I mean. She'd been hacking chickens to pieces and slathering them in sauce all week. Practicing. Tweaking her secret sauce. I reckon she might run out on me, but she keeps that crown and sash on a special prize shelf above the TV. Shines them up every week when she dusts. No way she'd hand that crown and sash over to some upstart."

The BBQ Cook-Off Queen title was about the most coveted prize in Pawpaw County. The entirety of the Ladies' Farm Bureau contingent throughout southern Indiana spent most of the year cooking up new sauces and trying them out on the Boy Scouts and the old farts down at the VFW. The Knobby Waters Weight Watchers division had to open two new meetings just to help all the folks who'd volunteered to taste test for Gertie. Despite the multi-county competition, Gertie clawed back the title from every new contender.

Tater laid his cigarette in the ashtray and felt around all his pockets. He checked his pants' pockets, his shirt pockets, then both pockets on his windbreaker. "Here's the retainer you said you'd be needing." He handed over a folded check that he'd retracted from his windbreaker.

I wrote him a receipt. He slid the pink receipt into the pocket of his windbreaker, stubbed out his cigarette, and hopped up off the chair. "You'll let me know?" There was a tiny tear in his right eye. He pulled a yellow paisley hankie out of his back pocket and sniffled into it. "Allergies," he said as he blew his nose.

He wasn't fooling me. I could tell he was worried sick. "Don't worry. Me and Veenie are ace at finding lost people."

"And pets," said Veenie. "We found Bet Beesley's wiener dog, Puddles, when he went missing."

Tater looked impressed. "The blind one?"

"Yeah. He ran away. Down to Pokey's. He had a drinking problem. Hard to find a runaway dog. They don't have credit cards or anything traceable like that. They travel pretty light."

Tater seemed reassured by that. "Well, okay. I got forty acres of soybeans to get in now that it's dry. Call me when you got anything." He flipped up the hood on his windbreaker and tottered out of the office. He looked like a sad lemon, his shoulders hunched against the drizzle as he rolled down the sidewalk in the direction of the Roadkill Café.

He was gone a couple of seconds before Veenie piped up. "You ask me, some people are best off left lost."

"You never did care for Gertie."

"It ain't me. Nobody ever cared for Gertie Wineager. You know that, Ruby Jane."

"Tater does."

That gave Veenie pause. "Gertie is a big ol' sourpuss. Maybe she upset someone. Maybe they whacked her. You know as well as I do if you gave Gertie the world with a ribbon tied around it, she'd hurl it back at you, hissing, 'That there is the wrong color ribbon.'"

"Some people are like that."

"Yeah, and them kind of people sometimes accidently trip and fall into the wood chipper."

"You think Tater chipped up his wife?"

"Happens. It was a long, ass-biting winter. They live down there in the old Wineager homestead, down by the river, near the Sparksville railroad crossing, close to the old Temple homestead. That house is so old they have to seal it up in storm plastic just to keep the heat in and the siding from falling off. You know how it gets inside that storm plastic. All thick and foggy. Like living inside a cold jar of Vaseline. Turns people crazy."

"They have new storm plastic nowadays. You can see clear through it."

"Winter still makes people crazy."

"I dunno. I think Tater loves Gertie. They got hitched right out of high school."

"Course he does, but you know well as I do you can love someone one minute and want to hold a pillow over their head the next. Marriage is like that."

I'd been married, so couldn't argue with that. I eyed the file we'd started on Gertie. "Guess the best place to start is over at the Curl Up and Dye. Looks like Tinky Sue may have been the last one to see Gertie."

"Yeah." Veenie peered at me over the top of her Coke bottle glasses. "And you could use a little spit and shine. Ma and Peepaw Horton's Chickenlandia Festival starts this Friday, you know. You're never gonna get a date with that head of hair."

Ma and her husband Peepaw ran a free range chicken farm, Chickenlandia, on top of the knobs. The town had been abuzz all week about the festival, a benefit for the old folk's home. It was a humdinger of a shindig. Anyone who could walk, crawl, or wheel their chair forward went to the annual festival.

There were mule rides and a bouncy castle for the kids, a BBQ chicken cook-off contest for the adults, a hot wings eating contest, a chicken clucking and rooster crowing contest for the loud mouths, and a chicken dance competition for the hoofers; also hillbilly horseshoes with junk toilet lids instead of horseshoes because horseshoes were apparently hard to come by these days.

Thinking about what Veenie said about my hair, I flipped off my laptop and eyed myself in the dark refection of the computer screen. My hair, snow white, looked like a halo around my head. My ragged bangs hung like drapery across the top of my glasses. I was sixty-seven and looked pretty darn normal to me. "What's wrong with my hair?"

"Same darn thing that's been wrong since high school. It's flat. Except when it rains. Then you look like a dandelion that got caught in a lawn mower. Plus, looks like you've been whacking at your bangs again. They're square. You use Scotch tape and the sewing scissors to trim 'em up again?"

I had, but I wasn't about to admit it. "Not a good look on me?"

"You look like one of them *Three Stooges*, and not the attractive one either."

I ran a hand over the crown of my hair. "It's flat today?"

"It's drizzling, so it's bristled out a bit. Puts me in mind of them razorback hogs the Weeselplecks keep out on the Devil's Backbone."

The Devil's Backbone was a narrow limestone ridge shaped like a long spine that dropped down into a dead end area known as Daulton Holler, over close to Tunnelton. Nothing much could survive down there but feral pigs. All the Daultons had moved out and over to Washington County long ago. Potato farming on a rock ridge did them all in, I reckoned.

I mashed at my hair. "You think Tinky Sue could fix me up?"

"Probably. Maybe she can slap some gel on that head of hair. Slick your topknot up."

"Like yours?" Veenie didn't have all that much hair, but it was nice and white, and she kept it neat, slicked up on top like a Kewpie doll. She kept it professionally trimmed because at four foot seven and a hundred fifty pounds, if her hair got too long, she started looking like a troll. She'd always been better at fashion than me. My idea of a beauty ritual was a morning rake-through with a plastic comb. If I was feeling really frisky, I might pat my lips with a cherry Chapstick.

I grabbed my messenger bag and the file on Gertie. Tinky Sue's beauty parlor was only three blocks south. She had it set up in an enclosed glass room that used to be her back porch.

It was a nice spring day. The drizzle looked to be passing. We could walk, get some sunshine. Since our boss, Harry, was out somewhere trying to drum up business, I scrawled a note about our new case and our whereabouts and stuck it to the front door. I stuck Tater's retainer check under a coffee cup on Harry's desk. He'd bellyache if he came back into the office before us and found us not chained to our desks. I figured the check would soften him up a bit.

Veenie slipped on her hooded poncho. It was electric blue with yellow daisies and green pom-pom fringe. A two dollar Goodwill steal. It matched—sort of—her electric blue, zig-zag yellow leggings. One thing was for sure, Veenie wasn't going missing. That get-up could be seen from deep space.

She pulled clip-on sunglasses out of her top desk drawer. The lenses were a reflective swirling mess of blues and greens and yellows, kind of like the surface of a mood ring. She clipped the sunglasses to her regular red-framed glasses and flipped them down. "How do I look?" She smiled and clicked her dentures.

There was something Elton John about the whole outfit. "Hip," I said. "Very hip. No one would ever guess you were a day over seventy." Veenie was, in fact, seventy-one, four years my senior.

"These here shades are vintage," she said. "The kids are heavy into this kind of thing." She bounced out the door ahead of me, eager, as always, to start snooping into the private lives of the poor and not so famous of Pawpaw County.

END BOOK 3 EXCERPT

Don't miss any of Ruby Jane and Veenie's crime-cracking capers.

Order your copy of the *Chickenlandia Mystery, The Shady Hoosier Detective Series: Book 3*, today at Daisy's website: https://www.daisypettles.com

If you missed Book 1: *Ghost Busting Mystery*, download it wherever ebooks are sold, or order it as a print paperback. All Daisy's print books are available in a larger trade paperback size (5.5 x 8.5 inches) because itty-bitty paperbacks aren't oldster friendly.

Daisy's print books are available at your favorite retail outlet. Visit your local library to request copies in print or through the Overdrive ebook system.

JOIN DAISY ONLINE!

Blog: https://www.daisypettles.com

Twitter: @DaisyPettles

Facebook: https://www.facebook.com/daisy.pettles.author

Email: daisy@daisypettles.com

If you liked this book encourage Daisy to pen more stories. Review this book online wherever you download books and media.

Every review is a vote to keep this series going.

And remember, if you're feeling down and blue, stop and eat a pie or two!

ACKNOWLEDGMENTS

First, a big thank you to the residents of Jackson, Lawrence, and Washington Counties in the hilly—"knobby," as we Hoosiers say—part of southern Indiana. Medora, Indiana, is my hometown, and I can assure you that no better folk exist anywhere. Go Hornets!

Many people helped me bring to life the quirky residents of Knobby Waters and Pawpaw County. Linda Beal—an honorary Hoosier, hailing from Kentucky—peppered me with sayings and character notes until I created this series. My amazing companion and forever friend Cindy Yager applied her proofreading and plotting skills to polish these tall tales. Her unflagging encouragement and love is a gift that can never be paid. Jonna Yager, blessed with a big heart and a sharp red pen, read a lot of bad drafts and gifted me with feedback that helped refine the plot and flush out the action. My storytelling—indeed the entire world—is much better for her kind-hearted efforts.

Every day my big sister Ginger East and her friend Melissa Horton post something online that tickles me, causing me to create new characters and impossible predicaments worthy of the supreme nosiness of RJ and Veenie. Book 3, *The Chickenlandia Mystery*, now in progress, is entirely their fault.

Finally, growing up in a small town is a gift. Everybody in town becomes your friend, forever. Little did I know that fifty years after grade school I'd be borrowing bits and pieces of all our lives to create a quirky town populated by love and laughter. Thank you Ramona Guthrie Owens, April England-Haggerty,

Pat Hume, and Jean Ellen Hansome for being my first and most loyal Hoosier fans.